Marah Ellis Ryan

A Flower of France

A Story of old Louisiana

Marah Ellis Ryan

A Flower of France
A Story of old Louisiana

ISBN/EAN: 9783743305229

Manufactured in Europe, USA, Canada, Australia, Japa

Cover: Foto ©Andreas Hilbeck / pixelio.de

Manufactured and distributed by brebook publishing software (www.brebook.com)

Marah Ellis Ryan

A Flower of France

A Story of Old Louisiana.

BY

MARAH ELLIS RYAN,

AUTHOR OF

"TOLD IN THE HILLS," "SQUAW ÉLOUISE," "A PAGAN OF THE
ALLEGHANIES," "IN LOVE'S DOMAINS,"
"MERZE," ETC.

THIS,

A STORY OF OUR SOUTH LANDS,

TO

𝔄𝔫𝔫𝔞 𝔒𝔩𝔡𝔣𝔦𝔢𝔩𝔡 𝔚𝔦𝔤𝔤𝔰

WITH THE EARNEST FRIENDSHIP OF

THE AUTHOR.

CONTENTS.

A FLOWER OF FRANCE.

PROLOGUE.

THE INSURRECTION.

THE golden light of morning crept through the pale curtains of vapor that were spread over the bayous north of Orleans Island. The awakening beams gilded the gray-green festoons of moss-draped, century-old cypresses, and touched caressingly the white-winged herons that rose softly from shadowy wood-depths and took silent flight outward and upward in the October air. A flock of vultures, many as a gathering of crows in autumn, sailed low over the swamps and with outstretched necks reached eagerly toward the west, where the mighty river of the New World dragged its way to the sea through many channels. Occult sounds drifted along the brown waters of the bayous—smothered, misty sounds of forest creatures. Now and then the shrill scream of a bird would cut sharply across the humming song of the insects and the soft rustle of the reeds, and again the muffled howls of animals would come across the vast levels and warn one of dangers lurking in the savage gloom of the forests.

Small wonder if the slave of the Afric coast and

the courtier from the French court alike dreaded
the jungles of that vast unsurveyed portion of New
France stretching north and east from the little settlement of Acadians, and west past the domains of
the weak and friendly Alibamon race, and into the
hunting-grounds of the fierce nations.

Demons of Indian superstition and the avenging
gods from Afric land were known to lurk just outside the cultivated plantations and hurl strange ills
on the colonist who dared to tempt fate by sleeping
in the perfumed shadows of those mysterious depths.
But past the myrtle and orange orchards (mementos
of the banished Jesuits) a pirogue drove through the
clear brown water of Bayou Petite and headed
toward the places of dread, slipping through the
willows where each sinuous belt of water entered
seemed just like the one left behind.

No other canoe was seen on the waters that morning. Never a boatman of France or of Spain called
greeting across the levels. Of all the colonists, no
others were without the gates of the town that
morning, where, in the Place d'Armes, an excited,
gesticulating mass thronged. Cheers for the
King of France sounded under the windows of the
Spanish governor, while the tricolor was run aloft
and floated gracefully, dreamily over the insurrectionists, who consisted of the French creoles, the Acadians who had sought rest in the warm delta lands
of the Mississippi, Alsatians cajoled to the New
World by that most clever of Scotchmen, John Law,
and the few "Americains" who had drifted down-
ward on the water from Kentucky and entered into

trade and barter between the colonists and Indians. Coming thus within the lists of merchants restricted by the hated laws of Spain, laws suited so ill to the struggling life of the new country, dissatisfied, the seed of revolution had been sown, and they had arisen as one man to drive out the representatives of Spanish dominion, to whom their beloved France had faithlessly sold them six years before.

They were as children; those warm-blooded, impetuous, but not persevering creoles; children cast off by the mother-land, to whom their loving hearts turned pathetically; children made reckless and quick to suspicion by the knowledge that their homes and their hearts were the playthings of those two kings across the ocean, and that they were sold to a new master as completely as were the girls and boys from Africa whom they themselves bought from the slavers of the Mexican sea. Yet, inconsistent as children or as mobs, it was the buyer against whom their wrath had arisen, while voices, French, Acadian, creole, called under the tricolor the huzzas for fair France, blessings on the good Louis (Louis XV.!), the selfish, unscrupulous figurehead of a nation.

Such was the picture lit by the sunrise that October morning of 1768. The first blow against foreign dominion in the American colonies was being aimed there by the American creoles of Louisiana, who, having no flag of their own, waved the beloved tricolor and fancied it a symbol of freedom.

And back of the master race thronged the blacks, three to one of the colonists, and heard their mas-

ters demand freedom, and looked at each other with
memories of Guinea showing in their soft, black,
velvet-like eyes, and wondered if the change of the
flags would lighten the chains they felt the weight
of so often — a weight they bent under, they and their
children, for a hundred years longer.

"The town is ours, yet not a life has been lost to
gain it," said the youngest of those revolutionary
leaders, the ardent Bienville, as he smiled at the
array of arms carried by their men, an equipment
of old muskets, staves, clubs, knives — anything and
everything — gathered to emphasize their demands
for the exodus of Charles III. of Spain in the
person of his governor. But Foucault, the crafty,
who stood near, heard the young enthusiast's words,
and lifted his head in quick remembrance of one
unseen.

"De Bayarde, where is he?" he asked; and the
faces near turned to each other.

"Who has seen him since the dawn?" asked some
one else. "He was then beside me near Tchoupi-
toulas gate, he and the boy. Did he not enter with
us, he so delighted?"

Foucault's face grew dark. The delighted ones
— the enthusiasts he could not afford to lose — they
make excellent tools for the plotter they trust.

"Find Hector de Bayarde," he said; and a little
later some one brought word he was not within the
town — more, that a young Acadian volunteer had
seen him fall near the gate, struck by some missile,
but that he had arisen, said it was nothing, and
leaned on the banquette as the others marched

through. Then all else had been forgotten in the rush of the insurgents. Where the missile came from no one could tell, but the missile itself was found, a broken bowlder the size of a man's clenched hand, and along its sharp edge was the stain of blood scarce dried. The mark of a bloody hand was left on the gate, as though one had staggered there in passing out; but that was the last trace left.

And the missing one?

He lay in the pirogue threading Bayou Petite as the sun arose. But he saw none of its glories. He did not see even the falling tears of the boy who paddled with all his strength through the still brown water, nor noted the smothered sobs that must have reached his ears.

He lay with closed eyes, the lids quivering at every rough motion of the boat. Blood-stained was the rough-hewn sides of the tiny vessel, blood-stained the yellow ruffle at his neck, the brown cloth of his coat, and death seemed to have touched his pale forehead.

"Basil," he whispered, "my little one, have we not yet arrived?"

And the "little one," who was perhaps ten years of age, shook back the fair curls from his face, and controlled his voice to reply.

"Not quite, papa, but soon."

Each spoke in the tongue of France, the polished intonations of the man suggesting the usages of a different life than that found in the cabins of the colonists. But the boy's speech was not so pure; he seemed a pretty Acadian peasant doing the will of some grand marquis; yet their tones held love as they spoke to each other.

"But it must be soon, very soon, Basil," he murmured, "else it will be too late. Do not weep. You are . . . my brave one; you will . . . in other years, perhaps, carry a sword for the France·. . . I love . . . and your mother loved. You will remember? Our love will watch over you, and you must work for France."

The halting whispered words were so low — so low! but the boy's ears were keen.

"Yes, I will remember," he said. "Rest now, and maybe when we return the good physician—"

"No, it will not be. You, . . . my boy, will be my physician; . . . you will help me to die . . . in peace. Ah! the way is long."

"We have arrived." And the boy guided the pirogue gently to the slight beach of sand, where thickets of willow threw shadows of pale leaves in the water, and a little up from the wet shore a rock, huge, upright, and solitary, arose like a sentinel over the jungles.

"We have arrived," he repeated; and his tears fell on the hand stained that deathly red. "Papa — tell me, what is it I must do?"

"Take the shovel, dig deep close to the white side of the rock; deep, so no waters will wash it away."

It — the boy did not know what that meant. In his heart he thought his father was made mad by that murderous blow in the dusk at the gate of the town. He had seen one who was mad in the sum-

mer just past — a slave brought from over the sea —
and he had been shot just as a dog had been that
went mad once there in the town. Basil knew, he had
heard, and his fright had been great when his father
also spoke as though in madness and asked for a
pirogue, while the blood unheeded blinded him.
Surely he was mad, but were the silent bayous not
preferable to that crowded town where the people
shouted, where they might shoot him if they knew
it, as they had shot the slave and the dog?

Basil thought so, and with his little heart filled with
fear, and with the foreshadowing of a great grief
over him, he did as he was told, manfully striving to
hasten the lifting away of the heavy sand, fashion-
ing a hole there deep as his father wished.

And then he saw what it was to contain, a decan-
ter of glass, a thing he had delighted to play with
when he was quite little ; but now it was filled with
paper instead of sweet syrups, and the sparkling
stopper was tied down with strands of hemp black
with tar. It did not look pretty as of old, but the
man touched it lovingly.

" Wrap it in the tar-painted cloth you found with
the boat," he whispered. "So! Now set it there —
deep — by the great rock; cover all; then I will tell
you ; but — hasten."

The little hands smoothed effectually all signs of
disturbance of the soil. His father could not see ;
he was simply trusting that all was done as he
asked; and the boy was faithful.

" It is done. What more?" he asked, and Hector
de Bayarde's hand raised as though blessing him.

"My brave one," he said, "we will go back now. Once more I may see the tricolor waving alone in our new land. Go gently. . . . I will tell you, . . . and we will go back. Do you listen?"

And as the pirogue crept gently back through the willows the boy heard without being conscious of the significance weighting his father's words.

He had heard them so often — so often — those words of the two kings across the water; of the two flags fluttering as neighbors over the colony, French at heart and Spanish in form. There was another ruler over the sea whom he always got sadly confused with those two; it was the British sovereign who had driven the Acadians from their fair homes into heartless exile. His mother had been of those wanderers. So long as he could remember those tales of the gorgeous oppressors and the pitiful oppressed had been told him, as the stories of saints and of fairies were told to other children; and it seemed but the same thing over again as his father said:

"It will always be so; never forget, my little one. Many nations may assault . . . may control the life of our little city of the great river; but her heart will never change. It is the French heart that will beat through her body while the river runs. Some day you may carry a sword for France, as I have done. She may want help when . . . you are a man. When that time comes — you are twenty-five — not before, come then to the great rock; take help from the papers there. They have power; I was exiled; . . . a plot; . . . the papers they never got. They have power. When I am dead put your hand on mine; . . . promise to forget where

. . . they are hidden . . . until you are so old; . . . to utter no word ; . . . no living thing must know ; . . . no one."

" I will promise now ; and, oh, you will live — you will live ! "

But the man knew it could not be. The warm, growing sun was burning mingled fancies into his brain. He seemed striving to keep his thoughts on but one path.

" La Belle France, . . . mon brav Basil ! It is a good sword. . . . Ah, my wife Suzette ! Basil, through the willows . . ."

So he murmured, with long pauses between the sentences ; so they moved on through the water toward the warehouse of the king, toward the Place d'Armes, where the people shouted for freedom.

" Back to the flag," he whispered, coaxingly. " I see it no more — Basil ! "

And thus it was that the pirogue was seen close to the willows by the tower gate as the sun rose high, and within it a dying man and the weeping boy, who could satisfy their curiosity so little.

" He loved the boats and the water, so I took him where he wished to go — in and out under the willows — and now he speaks no more, and I — ah! be kind with him. He is so good — and he can not speak ! "

His fears were allayed, and Hector de Bayarde was borne unconscious past the groups of sanguine patriots whom he had striven to serve. Every heart beat less gladly as they learned his fate. Ill would it have been for the thrower of that murderous stone

2

had his name been known, for this the first life sacrificed for their cause had been one much loved, much trusted.

As the sunset light touched the flag native to his heart, he spoke for the last time:

"Basil — *mon brav* — La Belle France!"

One year later, when the fleet of Spanish ships rested before the town and the hundreds of Spanish grenadiers landed to enforce, if need be, Spanish laws, those insurrectionists of '68, who had called themselves patriots, were treated as traitors.

It is a dark page that holds the record of Spain's vengeance on the colony: the hearts pierced by the bullets of her soldiery, the imprisonment of patriots in the Castle of Morro, the lives banished forever from the lands of Louisiana, the confiscation of all properties belonging to the leaders; the power landed with so much pomp and ceremony on their shores was most relentless.

All of those horrors had been mercifully spared de Bayarde by his death on their first day of triumph. In the records of the Spanish custodians his name occurs as a most earnest rebel — a traitor who escaped justice through death. To outraged Spain naught was left but the land owned by him, and the slaves who had called him master. These were accordingly confiscated.

But in those records no mention is made of the boy who bore his name — a name that was all the inheritance allowed him by the new power, the power absolute. And even the name of an insurrection leader was made a thing of burden to the bearer in those days.

CHAPTER I.

GREAT changes and grand manners of living followed in time in the wake of those grenadiers of Spain. The languorous life of creole repose was cramped in the straight-jacket of pomp and form and distracting ceremony. The civil offices of the town were of no more consequence than of old, yet the titles bestowed on the holders of them sounded so grand and fine in the Spanish words that they diffused a sort of awe over the colonists, for back of those many-syllabled titles was the Spanish council, or cabildo, that conferred them, and back of the cabildo ranged the vessels with the soldiers and the ruthless governor-general, and back of them the throne of Spain.

And La Belle France, and free commerce, self-government, and the many utopian ideas and shadowy wraiths of hope chased by the Louisiana creoles?

Alas! they were spoken of with tears and sadness in those days, but under compulsion the dreamers of those dreams wrote their names in the great book of the cabildo and subscribed themselves subjects of Spain, and were quite as well off after it as before had their prejudice allowed them to believe it.

But enough of the old customs remained, though

rechristened, to gradually win them to content. Their religion was left them ; in the ruling of their slaves little was changed; each owner was still invested with full powers of police over his black toilers, and for lack of a newer mark the *fleur-de-lis*, the flower of France, was still branded as of old on the body of refractory slaves.

Ah, yes, the new rule had its good points, after all. To be sure the heart of the life there was French ; so at length the creole lips learned to smile again, to murmur condolences to each other with languorous acceptance of their lot, and as their possessions and privileges grew with each blooming of the myrtles, they looked with more kindly eyes on the exiles from Spain. In time their sons and daughters helped to close the breach with lovers' promises, and society grew into a tranquil institution, with more of leisure for the little refinements of their old lives in the countries of courts.

And the hunters and traders from the north countries and the lands of the Illinois beheld with wonder the changes each journey witnessed in the palisaded town on Orleans Island. Ships full of stores glided into her harbors, and bore away in exchange the products semi-tropical of the soil and wealth of skins from the creatures of the forests. Not alone Spanish ships, for after a season of ostracism the ever watchful British crept again into the toleration of the people and moored their trading vessels along the shores.

One by one the Spanish merchants, bidding for fortune, varied the architectural features of the town by building in the midst of their gardens the picturesque dwellings of old Spain. They were all but one story high, those quaint mansions, with their inner courts where oleanders and orange-bloom shaded the restful galleries from the tropic suns.

There were Moorish arches under which one walked into those gardens circled by the dwellings, and the latticed windows, long and narrow, were banded by metals from across the ocean, while within the shadowy living-rooms were spread great skins from the bear and the tiger, and bright weavings of rugs from the Indian hands of the East. Soft carpets of feathers were formed by slave fingers from the smooth breast of the wild duck, and couches of mahogany were draped in silk and linens; tables of finest woods were inlaid with the pearl shell of the shores, while vessels of precious metals filled with Spanish wines were borne to the white rulers by half-naked slaves. Surely, of all colonies on our coasts, none bore with it such atmosphere of beauty and gracious oriental fancy as circled the life there shut in from the gaze of the world by the vast wilderness draped with the curtains of gray moss.

And so it was that fabulous tales of luxury were told of the Louisianians in many a log cabin of the East, where the hunters wandered — tales that raised many conjectures among the simpler pioneers who tilled the earth with plows of wood and ate their dinner of corn and beans from bowls made of gourds and spoons cut from white ash.

Of a certainty there must be kings dwelling at the

gate of the great river, they decided — only kings
drank from jeweled cups and dressed a favorite
slave in cloth of silk and silver arm-bands.   In the
book of books such things were told of, and the God-
fearing knew they were the temptations of Satan,
and warned those wide-ranging traders to beware
of his nets that were surely held in those barbaric
hands at that port of the South.

But in the more ardent adventurous minds those
abominations had an aspect most enticing, and earnestly did they ply the chance traveler with questions
of the grandeur down there; of the old governor
who had gone away after many years; of the new
governor who had taken his place; of the jewels,
many as the sands, rare gems from the rich mines
of Mexico.

And the wearers of those jewels; fair they must
be, of course, said report, though in truth few of the
traders from the inland could testify to that, for caste
was a high barrier in those days, and the wives and
maids of the rulers were not to be gazed at as freely
as were the shy, half-naked *sauvage* girls who drove
their canoes through the lagoons in search of fish.

But had any of the curious ones been allowed the
privileges of the gray parrot that swung so demurely
in the garden of Mons. Gaston le Noyens, that one
would have found proof positive of the beauty shut
in by the high hedges of green.

For two girls talked under the parrot's perch,
and were screened from house and garden by the
latticed, vine-covered bower; two as widely different
as light and darkness, yet each surely beautiful.

They were very close together; their speech was disjointed and broken at times, as by smothered sobs. The jeweled, lily-like hand of one rested on the silver-banded, bronze arm of the other, who crouched at her feet. One was of the ruling race and color, the other a stray from Africa; one was mistress, the other slave.

And on the slave's shoulder, where the snowy chemise was pushed back, was the mark of a cruel deed, the cause of those despairing murmurs; for crisp and gray on the brown skin was branded the sign of a rebellious slave — the deep-burnt *fleur-de-lis*.

"But you, Zizi, are not of the insurrection blacks," pleaded the soft French tones of the mistress: "then why—?"

She stopped speaking and waited for the girl at her feet to answer the muttered question. But the eyes, red from weeping, looked shrinkingly into the tender blue eyes above her.

"No; I never go where other black people go — to whisper in crowds. No: some one lied, maybe; some one jealous"— and she moaned a little, repeating the words —"some one jealous, that I never sent to the rice plantation; that's why, maybe. And now — oh!"

"But, Zizi —"

The slave-girl raised her head and hand; she had oddly commanding gestures for her race.

"No; please, ma'm'selle — good Ma'm'selle Felice, give me a new name. I'm new nigger now; that's all. Zizi carried no shame burnt with iron on the shoulder; Zizi sung songs all day; Zizi was happy; Zizi now dead — dead and gone to hell — white master's hell. Oam-me!"

"Zizi!" scolded Mademoiselle Felice, half frightened at the wildness of speech, "never more say such words — you hear? I will not love you, I can not, if you grow wicked. What if the *regidors* (rulers) or *alcaldes* (judges) should hear words like that? Could I keep you from the rice fields then? No; not even your master could do that."

"Master not care!" burst out the slave. "Master hope I drop dead, I know. I say few little words, that's all, and he look — ooh! how his eyes look at me! then he go way. By-in-by cabildo men come, put chains — so! pull me to calabozo — send me back with this!"

Her agitation was so great that her speech — French, and very imperfect — was disjointed. Mademoiselle Felice watched the expressive face for the meaning instead of trusting to the words with their decided coloring of the African coast — so many words of France, or of English, are impossible to the native of West Africa; and the girl, though wearing a silken sash above her buff linen skirt, and though bands of white metal decked her shapely arms, was yet without doubt a native of the black lands.

"No; your master has been a good master to you," contradicted Mademoiselle Felice. "Did he ever make Zizi work on the plantation? ever make her wear 'nigger cloth,' like the others? ever make her do work but wait on me? ever make her sleep but at

my door? No, no, child; he never want you to die.
Some one told him false of you, maybe — yes, surely;
but your Master Gaston loved you kind, Zizi."

A queer little sound, like a scornful moan, came
from the child, who was perhaps nineteen, and older
by a couple of years than Mademoiselle Felice.
"Bouf! kind love — white man's love — oam-me!"
and she rocked her body in a sort of derisive misery.
"Zizi know — I know — white man's love. Look on
my shoulder! White man's love made that."

Mademoiselle Felice covered her eyes with her
hands. "Oh, you poor unfortunate! My good Zizi, I
loved the very name of France! but now I can not,
when I see its emblem burnt in your flesh; no, never
again. The chains and whips of Spain can be no
more cruel. But I love you, Zizi. I will buy you if
Uncle Gaston can be coaxed, and you will never see
the branding-iron again. Ah, how it must burn
you!"

Zizi's swaying body ceased, and she looked up
with a strange expression on her face.

"I'm all black, and you, Ma'm'selle Felice, are
white, like the magnolia blossoms, but maybe we
can feel the same; and if Master Basil, when he
slips under the trees to speak with you, would
strike you with a whip instead of to kiss your
hands, would the pain be more where the whip fell
than the ache in the heart?"

"Zizi, how dare you!"

"Ah, ma'm'selle, sweet ma'm'selle, be not
angered; for see" — and she laid her clinched hand
on her half-bared bosom — "the hurt is so bad here
that I forgot I was only the slave — I forget."

" Yes, you forget," agreed ma'm'selle, sadly; "that is why the cabildo men made you suffer, that is why I must speak unkindly. Why do you forget? The others do not."

" Heh! the others"—and Zizi threw back her head as a young mare of the desert might when touched first by the whip—"the others know why. They were slaves always, the many who come in the white master's ship; two, three work now in your rice lands that I did buy, that I did sell on my own shore. The others— were the others born, as I was born, of the king's wife? Were the others told by the old men of the traps in the king's laws, and the way to rule and make a nation strong? Were the others carried on woven mats and shaded from the sky by the broadest leaves? The others! I, the Zizi of Master Gaston, am not as the others."

Surely these were the words of the insurrection blacks who were dreaded; troubled Mademoiselle Felice shook her head sadly. The brand of the *fleur-de-lis* was not so difficult to explain now.

" Zizi, if they hear you speak like that they will take you away to the plantations, and the chains, and the brands, and the whips will kill you, maybe. Is it not better to be still, and to live where I live? Yes, I think so. The rulers will not say you are different; they will say the gold did buy you as the rest, and that your master may not keep you in the town."

" Buy me — me — never believe; they may kill me, but never believe." And the strange creature clasped her hands pleadingly. "Ah, good Mademoiselle

Felice, white ladies never hear how the white masters trap slaves with kind eyes and softest words. So Zizi was bought; so she slipped her boat in the night to follow where the big kingdom was, to sit by the kind master and be woman king in a land so big her own could be swallowed by it. Such thoughts had Zizi in her heart. Oam-me! oam-me!"

"*Merci!* Zizi, you speak like the fairy stories of the foreign prince and the charmed princess," and Mademoiselle Felice tried to laugh lightly, but was embarrassed by the outspoken fantastic desires of the favored slave. They were so droll, these black people! But Felice had never seen any of them droll after this fashion of Zizi's. She was very certain her Uncle Gaston would find grave cause for reproof in the fact that she listened to and showed sympathy with a slave who was under the ban of that flower of France. Yet Mademoiselle Felice Henriette St. Malo had all a woman's interest in puzzling things, and surely these aspirations of Zizi were the most unheard-of, ridiculous things; from whence had they come?

"Well, continue, Zizi; finish the story."

"This has finished the story," and the girl pointed to the brand and arose to her feet. One could see then the wondrous symmetry of the statuesque figure. Not the limbs of the rice-worker those. Mademoiselle Felice, in her dainty blue and white gown, looked like a pure-lipped lily beside the tawny oriental beauty of the slave. And the bronze feet, with their jingling anklets, looked strangely slim for the feet of an African. But are there not legends of the Moors ranging far down that western coast? Might not those feet be a record of their raids?

Not that Zizi's mistress speculated on these questions. Zizi was handsomer than all the other slaves; that was why she was kept like a bright picture in the house. It is pleasant to be waited on by beauty; and the spirit of voluptuous France was abroad through the land in the eighteenth century.

"But tell me, Zizi—"

"Mistress"—and the girl's voice had lost its passionate coloring, the tones were low and even— "Mistress Felice, niggers dream wide-awake sometimes—that's all. Zizi dream like that. Zizi say fool things, for reason her fine little mistress is so kind. She be good now; say fool things not any more—only find new name. Please, Ma'm'selle Felice, I hear you some days sing little song like bird; that song it say so, '*Vendaient! vendaient!*' Now what that mean, mistress?"

Ma'm'selle Felice smiled and blushed over all her witchy, softly curved face.

"Oh, that's a love-ballad, in which the cavalier laments that Monsieur Cupid has betrayed him for a glance from a lady, and sold him for one whisper through a lattice."

"And *vendaient*, mistress?"

"That is but—betrayed—sold—you know; you learn the words so swiftly."

The slave-girl nodded. "Zizi thought like that —venda'—vendaient—that pretty, fine name. Mistress, give me that name. Zizi ugly in my ears

now — Venda sound good — the song sound good.
Venda better, anyway. Jocko, who catches fish, has
a monkey devil he call Zizi; so please, mistress,
give me a name to myself."

" Well, if it please you, and if you are good," con-
sented Mademoiselle Felice, and wondered at the
childish petulance about sharing a name with a pet
animal — she who had been startling in her pain
and her passion over weightier matters not an hour
ago; and now she was smiling her thanks, though
signs of tears were yet on her cheeks.

" Um! I'll be good now — Venda will — the name
is good — Venda!" Then she stooped and kissed
the white wrist before her. " I'll be good to you,
little mistress; I'd die for you," she muttered, and
turned away. Not another word of that burning
brand. Had the gift of the new name driven away
the pain?

"It is as the planters say — they are only children, after all, Zizi too," thought her mistress.

The home of Mademoiselle Felice was by no
means of her own choosing, else it would not have
been in that suburban corner of the town, where the
streets were yet to be, and where the thick green of
the leaves shut one off as effectually from sight of
more social New Orleans as if the dwelling-house
had been without the banquette among the indigo
fields where the slaves worked.

But Gaston le Noyens, like many another volupt-
uary, enjoyed all the more the excesses of his
barrack associates and the carousals of the warm
nights because he went to them from the cloister-

like shadows where the remnant of his family exhaled a certain atmosphere of innocence about the pomegranate-walled retreat.

A man universally liked for his handsome face, his gracious smile, and the fascination which won for him friendship of men and women, though few could have told of any good deeds done by him.

Indeed, it had been whispered that it was the troublesome fascination of his manner which exiled him from the light of the king's countenance twelve years before. The king who would be paramount in chosen feminine hearts is wise when he banishes courtiers who look voiceless adoration. A suppliant at beauty's feet is much more dangerous as a rival than one who stoops to confer favors, and Louis XV. of France was doubtless aware of the fact.

But exile seemed to trouble Monsieur le Noyens but little. He had plunged carelessly, recklessly into different schemes and enterprises of the New World. He had crossed the dread lands into Mexico, and came back with strange jewels; he had spent a year about the northern settlement of Vincennes, and floated down the great river with costly stores of furs; he had crossed the Mexican sea many times to the slave markets of Barbadoes, and had ranged once — that once of which Zizi moaned — the west coast of Africa, and on his return had found his widowed sister, lately arrived, dying, of either disease or homesickness, and a blue-eyed demoiselle who called him *mon oncle*, and whose presence suggested the forming of a home against the day when he should grow too old to roam.

Such was the man, but a type of many in the adventurous life of that new colony owned by the Spanish king. And if he failed in many ways as a guardian, or in his new rôle of a domestic bachelor, well, it was only a jest to laugh at, and, after all, he thought he did well, since no lady, of whatever rank, was draped as finely as his protégée, and in all the colony none was more delicately cared for. In all the colony there lived no demoiselle so high of birth, so altogether desirable, and at the same time unwedded; but all the flattering ceremonies of their caste did not prevent the languid days from dragging wearily to her. Youth loves gay youth, and not the conventionalities of a court; and the honeyed phrases tendered her by her uncle's friends had never yet done aught but amuse her or make her weary of their sameness.

In fact, to the wonder of all, it was generally supposed Mademoiselle Felice meant to take the veil of conventual life instead of a husband, if one could judge by her indifference to the latter, and her close affection for the nuns, in whose society she passed much of her time; and in the charity hospital down there by the grasping, treacherous river the girl was not a stranger.

But never a cavalier strode by the side of Mademoiselle Felice. Zizi was there when she went abroad in the streets, and Ponto, a stalwart black of the Congo; sometimes a Ursuline nun, whose eyes were ever on the ground, but never a social friend, except it be Father Dagobert, of beloved memory and easy penances.

But ghostly associations stole never a charm of
life and youth from the flower face of Felice, and
dimmed never the bloom of the velvet mouth adorable — the mouth so sweetly tremulous, as from the
consciousness of kisses.

Did a thought like that ever cross the brain of
Monsieur le Noyens? If so, he had but to run over
the list of eligibles — among them his good comrade,
Don Diego Zanalta — on whom she had smiled a
"no," yet retained their devotion. And outside
those cavaliers and ecclesiastics the child had no
knowledge of man or boy in all the colony, unless,
indeed, it be a certain half-caste youth named Basil,
who had the trick of picking music from a mandolin
and from whom Felice had begged to learn after
hearing the notes on the river one night.

But Monsieur le Noyens counted the music-master
not at all among the receivers of his protégée's smiles.
A woman of the Le Noyens to stoop to one beneath
her! Her guardian would as soon have thought
black Ponto among her lucky suitors. And she had
not even seemed to regret those lessons of harmony
when they ceased so suddenly months ago, and did
not even know the fellow's audacity in asking Monsieur Gaston for her hand, if in five years he could
present himself with wealth and name acceptable in
the eyes of her family.

Monsieur Gaston was touched with merriment
whenever he remembered that scene. It was, no
doubt, the outgrowth of the free air in this new
land, that swept over barriers of caste and raised
hopes of boatman or merchant to the level of the

ruling blood. But it was ridiculous, entirely. Perhaps it had been amusement tempering his anger that day; anyway, he had dismissed the Pan of the river reeds with no greater hurt than a few sardonic speeches and the suggestion that he at once betake himself from the colony and return to the *demi-sauvages* of the Illinois, where there were no objectionable lines of caste drawn, and where he might aspire to the daughter of some chieftain and meet a surer welcome.

Monsieur Gaston never could remember aright just the words of the lad's reply; but he realized that the player of the mandolin, who was also a *voyageur* or boatman of the great river, could express much rage without words, and was sadly deficient in the suave manners of courtiers.

Yet his audacity had soared as high as the hopes of the highest-born cavalier on the new lands! Well it was that Felice never knew; her kind heart made her gentle alike to courtier, commoner, or slave, and the guardian of Felice understood that the presumption of the ranger needed harsher medicines than her sweet-voiced reproof.

CHAPTER II.

VENDA.

AND Mademoiselle Felice? Did Monsieur Gaston never for a moment guess that she might possess something of his own determination — even love of

3

adventure — under the tender mask of her fair face? And to what hearts do romances appeal most alluringly? Surely those shut in by the grays and the whites of the cloister's life. And the blood of youth, so quick to sympathy, reads many a volume from tender answering eyes, and heeds but little the conventional words of aged guides. Wisdom is good, but wayward folly has a sweetness of its own; its guidance is such an alluring thing.

The magnolia and the willow had drooped over many of the *sauvage* lovers of that semi-tropic land, and they formed many a natural bower for a wooing of courtlier phrases when the athletic young *voyageur* left the paddle to his comrades and touched the mandolin strings for the pleasure of mademoiselle.

And the finale? That day of Zizi's disgrace Zizi's mistress again sat in the arbor of the far gate, but instead of the sobbing slave-girl there was the form of a stalwart monk at her feet, and instead of priestly admonitions on his lips there were warm broken sentences, with which caresses mingled, and on the whiteness of her hands many kisses were pressed.

And Felice was telling him the horror of Zizi's punishment.

"And if we are to believe, it was by my uncle's commands; then think how great would be his anger if he knew all! Oh, Basil —"

But he stopped her with a smile.

"No one knows all, my little madame, not even Father Dagobert, much as he loves a love; and but to-day has Father Luis taken the way into the wilderness beyond Vincennes. Our sweetest secret is ours until we choose to speak."

"But secrets are so terrible! I grow weak when I think of his anger. Poor Zizi!"

"Dear heart, think of the boat on which we will some day sail far from these shores; think not so long on the fate of a slave, who laughs, perhaps, while you sigh for her. Be not so tender of heart, little one."

"Ah, and had I been hard of heart a certain *voyageur* we know of would now be with Father Luis in the forests instead of kissing a lady's fingers. Dare you chide me, *mon brave* Basil?"

"*Mon brave* Basil," he repeated, tenderly; "you speak for my father when you say the sweet words; they are the last of my remembrance of him. But chide you? I bless and thank you. You make me a prince when you turn from your world of courtiers and take my hand. But a brave man borrows no cloak of a priest when he goes wooing," and his face, fair with the light of youth, and softened by curls of brown, grew for a moment dark and discontented. "Had I but your consent I should claim you before all, and bear you away from their walls of caste, and their empty pride; only your will holds me back."

"And your promise — your promise to be kept one year — no more," she said, coaxingly. "Then all may know, but not yet; they would shut me away from you, perhaps, and then — then I should die, oh, love, believe it."

That his belief was willing and tender none could

doubt who heard the caressing, reassuring words.
The kisses of his lips touched her, and she flushed
as a rose under his eager eyes.

"A summer ago you would not have been so
bold," she whispered; and he laughed.

"A summer ago, and all my summers agone, I
dreamed dreams of paradise as I sped my boat
through the bayous, and the saints — you among
them — have been too good to me, Felice, for the
dreams have come true, and paradise has stooped to
me while I am yet alive."

But even in the midst of the joyous boast she
raised her hand. "To-day everything makes me
afraid," she whispered. "I do not know why, perhaps because of Zizi's grief, but every footstep
sounds like a bell in the night when the blacks arise;
and now — but now did you not hear some one
speak?"

He listened and shook his head. "It is but the
laughter of guests there at the house. But you are
right, it is not wise to linger at this hour — others
than we may fancy this shadowed corner; and so
until to-morrow —"

His arm was about her as they paced to the door
of the arbor and halted for a moment of farewell;
but ere it was spoken a scuffle of feet was heard
without, and the girl Zizi was flung from the path
by an angry hand, and a face appeared before them
at which Felice screamed faintly and strove to draw
from the detaining hand of the tall young priest.

Yet the face was in no sense a fearful one. Its
lines were rather handsome, fair, cynical lines, and
all touched just then by a smile.

"How is this?" he inquired, as if a pleasant picture had been arranged for his benefit alone. "A
scene ardent as the loves of Abelard and that other
religious harlot of old France! Do you, then, gracious father, take to your arms a daughter of Eve
for love of heaven?"

In an instant the *voyageur* heart broke through the
barrier of priestly garb; swiftly he struck, and the
enraged, mocking face of Monsieur Gaston was lev-
eled to the green grasses; blood was struck from the
mouth that had smiled so insultingly, and at sight
of it Felice screamed.

"He is dead," she cried, wildly. "Oh, good God!
Basil, you have taken the life of my uncle."

"And stolen the heart of the niece," added another
voice, and Felice saw the form of Don Diego Zanalta
standing but a few feet away. He had evidently
accompanied Monsieur Gaston and been an unseen
witness of all that passed. Zizi arose to her feet and
cast a look of hate toward him as she caught her
mistress, who drooped suddenly on the arm of the
priest, pale as a blossom beat down in a tempest.

"Take her, Zizi," said the man, who seemed a
priest to Zanalta — "take her from the speech of
these men, whose words are sacrilege to purity!"

He laid the loved form in the slave-girl's arms.
With the watchful eyes of that gay cavalier on him,
he refrained from kissing even the hand of her, but
he looked adoringly on the pale face, and raised his
hands in gesture of blessing above her head, murmuring something unheard by the others.

He watched so long as a glimpse of her could be

seen through the shrubbery; such a heavy weight seemed to fall on his heart when his eyes could rest on her no longer. So few the moments since paradise had been his, and now —

He straightened himself, remembering that other man, and the owner of the land who lay at his feet.

"Your friend is not dead," he said, as Monsieur Gaston stirred and attempted to rise. Zanalta assisted him, but his eyes were curiously on the priest-clad form and face.

"Who are you?" he demanded, and Basil de Bayarde turned away.

"Monsieur le Noyens can tell you if he chooses, and for my acts he will always find me ready to answer."

He walked away, but not until he was seen by two other gentlemen who came hurriedly from the mansion-house, where the arrival of Zizi had disturbed the smoking of gay gallants who liked well the fragrant cigars of Le Noyens. Full of wonder, they gazed at the retreating monkish form, and then at the pale, slightly scarred face of their host.

"It is but trifling, gentlemen," he reassured them; "a vagabond employé, whom I had forbidden the grounds, crept back in disguise, for the purpose of theft, no doubt, and gave a great fright to mademoiselle, my niece. We had an altercation, but it is over, and since he is gone we will do well to forget him. I will set a watch for him in future, for these rangers of the rivers are daring thieves."

His guests agreed, though quietly curious as to why the thief was allowed to walk away unarrested.

But Zanalta was not content to let his curiosity be

quiet as to the man whom Mademoiselle Felice had called " Basil" in so intimate a tone. Basil? Basil? In all their circle of the colony he knew none of that name to whom she would turn. But one thing he did know — this Basil was the man who had lured her from his arms. This cavalier of the gown should be his game, he promised himself; for all in an instant he realized that his rival was not the holy church, not the cloister of a nun, but this stalwart unknown.

" Tell me but one thing, Gaston," he asked, pressing his friend's arm with affectionate sympathy; "tell the others as little as you like, but remember you and I are more than companions of a season. Remember you have given me Felice, if I can win her; now give me also the name of the man who is my rival."

Le Noyens halted where a rustic seat was set in the shade of oleander branches.

" Ask our friends to excuse my absence for a little while," he asked, " and then come back here. If I speak to you it is best to have no walls about."

The other gentlemen had already halted at the portal, waiting for the master, but in a few smooth phrases Zanalta excused their host and placed the house at their disposal. On his return he found Gaston no longer reclining; he was erect, and walking backward and forward moodily. He turned at the step of his friend.

" That we agreed Felice should marry you, if any man, is one of the bitter things I would like to forget just now," he acknowledged. " I feel that

her guardian-angel will do well to keep her away
from me for the present, or I might be tempted to
kill her."

"Gaston!"

"You do not know what she has become!" burst
out the other; "she has disgraced her family — she,
the first woman of her name to do so. You would
not now care to remember that you ever desired
her. The women of Zanalta have been noble. You
would not want to be first to add to the house a wife
who has stooped to the canaille as Felice has
stooped. Ah, I tell you — why not? You would
learn it some day. By the cross of God, she'll pay
dearly for her gay meetings; not another day shall
she live without the walls of the nuns she pro-
fessed such liking for. That I, Gaston le Noyens,
should have been blinded so long by this praying
dame whose eyes dare not rise to meet a man's!
Oh, fool — fool!"

Diego Zanalta only watched his friend, waiting
for the wordy rage to die away.

"I ask but the name of the man," he said again,
quietly; "you have not told me."

"Then I shall." And Gaston's smile was one of self
pity. "Why spare ourselves any of the humiliation
she has bought so dearly? Months ago I told you
of a boor — a *voyageur* — floating down from the
villages of the *sauvages;* he could pick airs from the
mandolin. Well, it seems Mademoiselle Felice found
her mate in that ignorant, low-bred oarsman, for
to-day I surprised them with clasped arms, his kisses
on her lips. This meeting was not their first, be sure

of that, Diego. Could I give to my friend a wife who was the leavings of such cattle?"

"I desire mademoiselle, and hold you to your promise," Zanalta answered; "but the fellow's name?"

"Basil de Bayarde."

"De Bayarde! that is not the name of a plebeian."

"Bouf! A name is as easy to borrow or steal as the gown of a priest."

"De Bayarde — the name has a sound familiar, though I know none who answers to it. De Bayarde — that name must be for the present written on the clearest page of my memory. De Bayarde?"

"Yet you seem to care little enough," remarked his friend, looking at him sharply; "you whom I have seen rage because a little *négresse* divided her favors and gave you but half; you who have left a man dead on the sands of Spain because of a woman whose vows were as false as the jewels she wore, and as cheaply bought. Do I know you even yet, Diego?"

"Who else if not you? Bend not your eyes on me in such disturbed wonder because I am forgetting the season of the passion flowers for the sake of one fair lily I would have grow in my garden."

"Fair, perhaps; foul by the proof."

"Heed your words!" retorted Zanalta. "I have adored her through a century of waiting, and your croakings shall not mar the visions of my paradise."

"To which his excellency De Bayarde will raise a locked gate of iron," sneered his friend, whose brooding rage yet pictured itself in glance and tone.

But Zanalta tapped with white, strong fingers his jeweled snuff-box and gazed sagaciously toward the gate where the priest's gown had disappeared.

"Have no fear that Basil de Bayarde will be forgotten. Saint Satan will aid me in that, for you know how dearly he hates a monk's hood."

"Go within, Diego; you are light as the bubbles on new wine. You, better than myself, can act the host to-night. Look to our friends. I must think."

But he could not even think in repose; rage made him restless, and again his feet were turned toward the far gate where he had surprised the lovers. Forward and back he walked with bent head, not seeing the lithe form of the slave-girl who entered the gate from without, panting as one who has run far; yet her absence had been but short, and she slipped behind the myrtles, stealthily, that he might not think she had been abroad in the roads of Orleans: it would be so easy for him to fancy the truth — that she had followed the lover with word from the mistress.

Quite near her, as she stood in hiding, there gleamed something bright, as of silver, among the green of the grasses. Bending forward she saw more clearly. It was a slim, curved blade, with a handle of buckhorn; a knife such as the white hunters and the men of the river carry in their belts. It had, no doubt, fallen from under the priestly gown in the altercation so lately passed, and quick-witted Zizi knew that, if found, it would be an added cause of offense against the *voyageur*.

"When the morning comes again they will be far

in the wild woods," she told herself. "But Master Gaston walks like that for madness, and the night is long enough for him — for devil Zanalta — to do bad deeds in, and the knife must not be found by him."

But as she reached for it and stepped back again the anklets of silver she wore clinked one against the other, and at the sound her master turned quickly.

She was standing erect, there in the green, watching him with somber eyes, and gave him the impression of having stood there a long time watching him.

"Sulking still, you brown devil?" he growled, as if glad to find some object to vent his wrath upon. "Well, you'll have cause; doubt it not. When the sun comes up to-morrow, if it finds you absent from the indigo fields, fifty lashes will be added to that fine mark on your shoulder."

Her face grew ashen at his words. The indigo fields! There among the black cattle who called her "the proud" and "the favorite." No, death was best; and she held more closely that knife.

"Master, have I not been hurt enough? I will be good once more, if only you will be a little kind to Zizi — a little kind, as you were in my own land. See, I tremble; I am afraid, as little children; listen to me; be kind."

She approached him, pleadingly, her eyes moist with tears of entreaty, but his face never softened.

"Be kind to a slave who dictates terms to me? You have been mad for many months. The whip of the overseer will prove a most excellent cure for that malady."

Mad? Yes, she must of a certainty have been that, for the supremacy of the master was forgotten by her, and she laughed, though her lips seemed stiff.

"The whip of the driver! Was the Zizi you knew among the palms ever touched by the whip? Did the slaves who stooped before her ever feel the weight of hot irons? You are wise and strong, O my master; but slave Zizi that you did steal is stronger now. Before a whip touches her she will be free from your land."

"Hah! You voudou devil, do you mean you will raise the blacks? By the saints, I'll have your bones broken for that threat. To the quarters!"

"No!"

She seemed to him like a pythoness with the head and shoulders of a woman, and her form grew more majestic as if swelling with some dread import not to be worded, and her eyes had yellow lights in them and were terrible.

"Listen!" she said, and the words were a half whisper in her earnestness. "I beg to you for the last time. If I die by the whips, you will die too, my master, die in the dark when no one sees. It is the life of you I beg for; you were ever dearest to Zizi. See! I plead, I kneel by your feet. I ask that you take again to your heart the thought of our days on my own lands; the days were sweet; think of them! Touch my hand once more — once!"

Her other hand was hidden under the loose draperies of her bosom, and the point of the knife was touching the spot over her heart.

But he never dreamed that death was the freedom she meant.

"You fool!" he sneered, and struck her with his foot. "Cattle of the jungles, begone!"

It was his last word, except "Holy God!" as he fell, and the knife meant for her own heart was sunk deep into his.

He never moved, and a great sickness swept over her as she looked at him. The sneer was gone from his lips. He lay as if asleep — asleep as he had slept with his head in her lap through the hours of one sweet moon.

But no knife-hilt rose above his heart then; and with a moan she turned blindly from the path, not heeding her direction. But the spirits of her Afric land must have led her from discovery, for just then the monk's gown entered again stealthily the outer gate. He was coming in answer to the message she had left with him so lately, but she sank down under the broad leaves of a strange plant there. Earth and sky seemed meeting above her; she did not see him.

But other eyes did — the eyes of Zanalta. Impatient of Gaston's absence, he had left the gay party in the house and was moving along the path, when he heard those angry, hurried voices, and an instant later saw his friend stretched across the path.

He was about to rush forward, when he saw the lover of Felice coming straight in his direction. He watched with a smile in his eyes that presumptuous ranger of the wilds walking to fate.

Assuredly Saint Satan was good to him, and to

perfect his wishes he heard close behind him gay cavaliers, who were calling to him merrily that the wine was so good and that his desertion was not to be pardoned.

De Bayarde heard them too, and turned to retreat, when his eyes fell on the dead form there — dead on the spot where they had quarreled so short a time before — dead, with a knife sticking in his heart — that knife!

He ran forward, dropping on his knees beside the body. It was incredible; the hand he touched was yet warm — not a minute had passed since he had been struck down; but the assassin?

He saw that other man coming toward him; he heard the gay laughter of the guests change into low prayers and words of horror. Questions were poured on the supposed priest, who could answer nothing; and as he rose from beside the dead form he met the eyes of Zanalta fastened on him with a gaze so peculiar that he instinctively shrank from the meaning of it.

" But the assassin?" demanded one of the gentlemen. "His heart has scarce ceased to beat; the wretch who did the deed can not have gone far; we must search."

" Search not beyond the walls of the garden," answered Zanalta; "why even beyond the man whom we found over the corpse?"

" The priest?"

" No, not a priest; strip that gown from off the assassin's shoulders, and you will find under it an adventurer, a ranger of the rivers called —"

" De Bayarde!" answered the *voyageur*, himself
flinging aside the disguise no longer needed. " Basil
de Bayarde, gentlemen; but no assassin."

"Say you so?" asked Zanalta; "then it is your
word against mine, fellow, for I heard your voices
in anger in the garden. I hurried here, and found
you about to flee from the crime at your feet; and
see, gentlemen, notice the hilt of the knife, a knife
such as river men wear."

" And on it letters — the saints guard us! — they
spell ' Bayarde.' "

The young ranger gazed on the dark faces in
wonder. He seemed stunned by the weight of accusation brought against him. And then from the
house ran Felice to the spot where they told her the
master was hurt. But once there she gave scarce a
glance at the body of her uncle, but with a face full
of horror she turned to her lover.

" You have killed him this time," she whispered.
" Oh, Basil!"

" Felice, do you accuse —"

" Accuse you? Never that, never. You hear, gentlemen? you listen? It is my uncle who lies there,
yet I accuse — accuse no one."

And for the second time that day she swayed
deathlike, toward him. But he read, as the others
read, her real suspicion under that loyal protest
and something like a groan arose at sight of her.

" You too, Felice?" he murmured, and then turned
to the others. " You wish to arrest me, I see, and
for a murder. I have never committed one; but
there stands a man who has lied to accuse me.

and as your good laws, gentlemen, will doubtless ask
my life to-morrow, my debts to this world must be
paid quickly, and to him I owe death."

And then he leaped over the body of Le Noyens,
and full at Zanalta's throat. But a dozen forms
were hurled against him, and he was dragged backward, leaving Zanalta unharmed but a little breathless; and as the slave-girl came forward through the
shrubbery, as if fascinated by the horror there, the
eyes of the Spaniard met hers, with a wealth of
meaning in them.

"Assist your mistress, Zizi. And for this assault
upon myself, and for the murder I was witness to,
this fellow shall have a sentence heavier than death
itself — transportation for life to the mines of
Mexico."

The gentlemen looked at each other in horror.
The mines were a hell, even to the black giants of
their land; and this bright-haired youth —

"Gentlemen, if I am condemned for this crime —
if there is councilor or judge among you all, I ask
of you death — for death. I have fought for this colony against the reds of the north. I ask the death
of a soldier."

At the word 'death' the slave-girl stepped forward, but Zanalta checked her with a glance.

"I am of the council," he retorted, "so I promise
you an assassin shall not have the death of a soldier
under our laws. Die you shall — but in the mines,
where devils of your own kind congregate, and the
death will not be swift."

The accused raised his hand as if in prophecy.

"Beware, then, the day of my return, for the dead
come back, they say, and on the day when God's
hand frees me, *I shall remember you.*"

Zanalta tried to laugh, but failed; and as two of
the gentlemen touched Bayarde's arms to lead him
away, the slave-girl again motioned appealingly to
the Spaniard, but his eyes were bent on her so
threateningly that she slowly bowed her head, and
avoided the eyes of the prisoner, who turned toward
her with a mute farewell for Felice.

And the old gray parrot in the arbor chattered
over and over a name it had heard so lately -- a new
name, and strange as new music on the ear —
"venda — venda -- vendaient!"

CHAPTER III.

TWO STRANGERS FROM FRANCE.

SLOWLY as time loiters in the South lands, and
drowsily as the days pass under the myrtles, yet the
seasons are driven onward, each in its turn, and
many had passed ere the record of life on the island
by the many-mouthed river is resumed.

And it is a finer life than of old, despite hurri-
canes that had swept it, and disease that had often
weakened it. Names and families had grown
stronger, commerce had widened, plantations had
driven the jungles farther back from the gulf---
only the waters remained the same, and the green-
fenced bayous still held many a mystery.

4

And of the names known widely in the growing town, none held more power than that of Zanalta. Youth was no longer his, nor yet age; but the man of forty had developed all the promise of Diego eighteen years earlier — a good comrade, a courteous cavalier, a thorough politician. Not an office held by a servant of Spain was beyond the range of his ambitious hopes, and many prophesied that he would yet be ruler in the new land.

Was it for such ambitions that he was yet a bachelor — that, despite his gallantries to the many, he had not yet devoted his life to the happiness of any one lady?

There were those who remembered that he was once the suitor of beautiful dead Felice St. Malo, and whispered that as the cause of his celibacy. He smiled a little when these whispers reached him, and reaped the benefit of sympathy bent on him through soft eyes. It is so much easier for women to forgive constancy to a dead rival than to a living one.

But the faces of women were seldom lacking in his establishment. His house was a hospitable one; a sister-in-law from old Spain, and a half-sister, widowed, yet childish, were of his household, and beauty of high degree gathered often in his garden and under the arches of his dwelling-place, while slaves by the score called him master.

And in the spring-time of '92, when a ship of France arrived in the harbor with the exciting intelligence of revolt that was openly talked of in the streets of Paris, and when among other strangers to disembark came two cavaliers, young, engaging, and utter strangers, it was to the hospitable roof of Diego Zanalta they were recommended by the captain of the vessel. Had they letters of introduction to people who could not be found? Then most assuredly Don Diego would be the one to advise them; and the gracious commander, who scented reflected glory from those bejeweled courtiers, even took it upon himself to be their messenger, and found the family about to leave for a fête to be celebrated at the house of one of the high dignitaries of the town — one Monsieur Victor Lamort, an exile from the shores of France, but one who had brought so much of wealth into exile with him that he lived like a prince in the city of jungles, and was even called by the people "Le Grande Marquis."

Don Diego had already gone, but to the dazzled eyes of Le Commandant there appeared instead the vision of a petite dame vested in the bewildering garb of a court lady, and from nodding plume to silvered slipper there floated tissues of rose, and her voice was the voice of a child who laughs.

"In truth I am sorry my brother is not to be seen, but learning you are commander of the foreign vessel just landed, I have ventured to present my insignificant self in his august stead. Now pray tell me if your business is of weight. If so I may chance to further it."

Business! The ruler of a ship and many men was confused and dismayed by so fair an ambassadress. She prompted a man to make such declarations of love with his eyes that, abashed by his own willingness, his glances sought the tiled floor while he strove to recall the reason for his presence there.

Ah, yes; those annoying cavaliers from France who waited his return. Was he then to open the gate for them to so much of beauty? How hard it is at times to keep envy out of the heart!

And the little lady was interested so greatly. Nobles from France — fresh from the court life of Versailles, perhaps — of a certainty their society was to be desired.

"I will myself be their message-bearer to my brother," she conceded, graciously. "Tell me again their names and where they are to be found."

"Mademoiselle — "

"Madame," she corrected ; "Madame Ninon Villette."

"A thousand pardons, madame."

"One is enough, and it is granted. The names of the gentlemen?"

"First, Chevalier Maurice Delogne, late of the king's household, Versailles."

"Oh-h! this is indeed news of import; and the other?"

"Monsieur Constante Raynel, a friend of the chevalier."

"And their wishes?"

"They carry letters of introduction to some whose names have been unknown in the town for many years. Don Zanalta having much knowledge of men, I thought would be able to advise them as to where it were best to seek those people."

"I am convinced you are a most sensible and kind-hearted gentleman, and you did right to seek our house in the case of the strangers. I go at once to the fête, and am assured my brother will send immediately an invitation for the chevalier and his friend to wait upon him. Where are they to be found?"

"By my faith, that is a question not so easy to answer, madame. I can only tell where I left them, and that was near the banquette, and the chevalier was bribing little *demi-sauvages* and black children to stand still, or lie down, or dance, according to the mood of Monsieur Raynel, who did catch all their strange postures and fix them upon paper by the aid of a charcoal-stick, and the two were laughing like children, and may have wandered far in adventure ere this."

The childish eyes of madame grew more round, and she smiled in sympathy with those two whom she had not yet seen.

"Then I am to think they are not old, those two gentlemen who seek for adventure on our shores?"

"I venture to say they will never feel old when they look at you, madame." And having thus turned aside her curiosity by a compliment, Monsieur le Commandant withdrew himself from the presence of Ninon — Madame Villette — and madame, when alone, sighed distressfully, and pouted those fine lips of hers most becomingly.

"In truth I am sadly weary of these gallants of our Orleans town, and did hope this chevalier and this Constante of the charcoal-stick would at least have youth, and make it worth one's time to fashion new gowns for their eyes. Alas! this island is a cage, and I am weary of pluming myself when young eyes never look through the bars. 'They will never feel old when they look at you, madame,' and she bowed mockingly to her own reflection in the mirror; which means, in short, that they are gray-bearded ancients; Jupiters, who would make love as they forge thunderbolts, ponderously. I prefer an Adonis."

And those gray-bearded ancients?

Down where the water whimpered along the banquette as though afraid of the night coming on strolled the two strangers, finding the strange outdoor life much more to their liking than the café where they had agreed to live for the present.

The sun was sending arrows of yellow glinting across the great slow-moving river, and gave so fine a background for the human pictures ever and anon arranging themselves unconsciously for an artist eye.

"*Sacré!* I never before dreamed that a *négresse* could be good to look at," said he of the charcoal-stick, as he stretched himself along a wooden bench and gazed through eyes half-closed at a little black girl whose arm circled a basket of oranges. "Think, Maurice, how disastrous it would be if I should have crossed the seas only to lose my heart to one of these bare-legged bits of bronze flesh, or perchance a feather-trimmed savage of that rich red color such as we saw pass in the log boat. I tremble, my friend; I warn you I am afraid."

"Lose your heart, pouf! Your head, you mean;
for I'll venture an oath it would not be less than the
hundredth heart-break you have lived through since
we left our school-books. I wonder much whether
it is your art which tempts you to beauty, and love,
or love that has rendered you an artist?"

"The latter, I do believe. I always fall in love with
my model, else the work has no interest for me; hence
my rule to paint only that which is beautiful. It is
so horrible to fall in love with ugliness, and it is
dangerous, too. For once allow an ugly woman to
fascinate you, and her chain is of iron; that of
beauty is of flowers, and when faded will fall to
pieces of its own weight."

"You speak wisely as a past-master in the art of
love," smiled his friend; "but however entrancing
the subject of the sentiments, I deplore the fact that
you so frequently succumb to its allurements."

"Enough; do not resume on these shores the lect-
ures on reason which caused me so many weary
hours in the land we left; and, after all, the heart has
reasons which reason can not comprehend."

"You are a hopeless affair, Constante. We arrive
here to begin life anew, do work, I know not what
yet. Surely our prospects are most serious; yet we
have scarce touched the shore of the strangers when
you see a red maiden paddling in a boat, a black one
vending fruit on the street, and at once dream of a
rendezvous. Ah! alas for myself that I am fond of
you, else my patience would surely break. You demand everything of life, yet are willing to work for
so little. A man's life should hold action as well as

dreams. And your ambitions — your hopes for the future?"

"Simple, my friend, most simple, I assure you; only to live in this semi-tropical land as in the Garden of Eden our Father Adam lived —"

"Ah!"

"After the fall!"

"By my faith, now, but I would like to see some maiden of this savage land bring you to your senses with a love that would burn your light fancies into forgetfulness. You see in love only a pretty comedy, to be played by two, and with a laughing world for an audience, while love, the real, is more often a tragedy. All devotion, passion, is a lonely, serious thing. It is the great teacher, but its eyes do not laugh."

His friend laughed silently, and made the sign of the cross in the air with which to exorcise so formidable a spirit as serious, tragical devotion.

"Could I find Monsieur Cupid I would send him to you for lessons, Maurice. You would teach him to make every gallant a poet. I wonder now what fair instructress has influenced your ideas to such serious reflections, you that kiss a lady's fingers; but — oh, well, am I to believe, then, the gossip of the guard-room, and think for a truth that the interest of Madame la Princess de H—— was that of a butterfly ready to be caught, rather than that of an illustrious patroness of deserving soldiery, or rather one handsome soldier. That finale deserves your best bow, my chevalier."

"You need a sound caning, Monsieur Imperti-

nence," retorted the other, as a slow blush covered
his face. " If Madame la Princess needs consolation
it will not be to courtiers she will turn, but to God.
Her illustrious but unhappy life may make of her a
saint, but never a Messalina."

" You think so because she resisted the temptation
of her heart, and sent you so far she could not recall
you, eh? Oh, I see! I observed several things
there at Versailles, my friend, though you give me
no credit for seeing things seriously. But I am
proud of you, just the same, for doing the thing I
fear — oh, my tender heart! — I fear I should not have
found resolution to do. Your blush and your silence
do you honor, Maurice, and they honor that lady
across the seas who was so cruel as to banish you."

" The lady across the seas, whose influence directed
me here, was my aunt, Le Marquise de Lescuré.
Please bear that in mind, Constante. The princess
belongs to the life we have left, and is not a subject
for jests. It was my aunt who urged my coming
here to look after some properties bought here long
since by some friend. I have scarce looked at the
letters of instructions yet. She asked me not to do so
until after my arrival. Even the letters of introduction have not been examined by me, though I am
convinced they are all right. Since my birth she has
been like a mother to me ; and while I am puzzled at
her earnest desire that I should leave France for five
years, and build up interests here, yet I have refused
her nothing all my life, and did not withhold the
promise. I only want you to understand, once for
all, Constante, that it was for family reasons and my
aunt's desire that I am here."

"Um! yes. I understand, also, that the lovely old marquise is the closest friend, the confidante of Madame la Princess. Ah, Maurice, you would never make a politician, for you would be in the midst of plots, yet never unbend to ferret them out. If they grew too thick, or hedged you around, you would cut your way through with the help of your sword. But when women plot, swords are worthless as the rushes there by the river. And whether you know it or not, my comrade, not one woman, but two, drew up your plan of exile."

"And how many your own, you romancer?"

"My own? Happy am I to answer — none. You see I have not had the misfortune to be loved seriously by a saint ; and the consequence is, I had not to take a discreet farewell by touching a lady's fingers with my mustache. I assure you, no! I kissed three maids of honor most beautifully, and was about to complete a quartette when the husband of number four was so inconsiderate as to enter the audience-chamber. Ah, these husbands! By the time I become one, I hope to have learned the lesson of making my wife happy occasionally by effacing myself."

"When you are a husband? Who do you fancy will live to see that day?"

"Both of us, believe it. I am not the Chevalier Maurice Delogne, with an ancient name and prospective worldly comforts. I am only 'that droll rascal Raynel,' who has a curious talent with colors, but who lacks the application to make himself great. Well, it is so. I am content to drift with you and trust to fortune while I may. But I warn you that if a female Crœsus should cross our path, I speak for her. She is mine — do you comprehend? — for I need her, while you do not. And if I should want help in my wooing, or if other suitors intervene and have to be — well — removed, I bespeak your aid in the cause of true love."

"Love of the lady's purse, but not her heart. And what if the Lady Crœsus should be ugly, and old, and unpleasing, then what would our devotee of beauty do?"

"Win her, beyond a doubt; for I would commence my wooing by painting her a mask with so much of youth and charm in it that she would grant me the rest of her life as a reward for my devotion."

"Constante, do you never grow weary of your own fanciful dreams? Here have we talked of trifles until the sun has gone. You must wait until another day to continue your finding of pictures." And the chevalier arose to continue the walk to the café, when Constante gripped his arm and made a low whistling sound with his lips — an expression of surprise.

"By all the tints of angel faces — no!" he whispered; "turn not too quickly lest she vanish again to paradise, but note that crippled one-armed sailor and the being who bends over him! Sacre! I myself would lose an arm for such a glance of pity from those eyes. Aye, even my head."

"You have lost the latter already," returned his friend, irritably; "and as a cause I see only a slight figure in a nun's dress of gray, but with white sleeves. I can see no face, because of that gray nun's hood, so fail to discover your reason for raving. She looks, however, as though she might be the very spirit of charity from the way in which that unfortunate is gazing upward to her — but you, my friend, do not need alms, so come."

They were but a short distance from the object of their conversation, who was in the way of their walk. It seemed a very poor quarter of the town into which they had wandered — a sort of open-air hospital for unfortunates — and as the gray-garbed nun turned from the crippled man to a woman who held a sickly, complaining child, she came face to face with the two strangers, and the chevalier was so directly in her path that for one awkward instant they essayed to pass each other, yet remained to gaze with mutual wondering attraction into each other's eyes.

And then he was not surprised at the enthusiasm of his friend, for the face was so wonderful, with all its childishness subdued by the nun-like dress, and the bronze-gold hair framed in the gray hood, and those eyes with their serious directness, in color the blue-gray of the Mexican sea at twilight.

All this he saw in that moment, and had time to be glad that the waved hair about her face forbade the idea that she was entirely given to the church. And then he found himself with head bared before her, and murmured words for pardon as he stepped from her path. She made no reply, but the grace of her glance was evidence she thought him no culprit, and the faint flush creeping over her face made his breath come quickly.

He had forgotten Constante, but that gentleman had neither forgotten nor missed anything of the wordless drama before him. He touched his friend's arm with a comical expression of despair, as though to lead him from temptation, while a ponderous sigh was evidence that he noted his friend's backward glance.

"And she never looked at me," he complained. "To be sure I am not so largely built as you, but I am quite as handsome. The only thing that consoles me, Maurice, is that she is, by her garb, not my Lady Crœsus, so I can relinquish her to you with one heartache the less."

"A truce, Constante. It is provoking enough to remember I have stared at that child until her face changed color with vexation; remind me not of it. But, as gentlemen, is it not a duty for us to remain near until we see her depart from this region in safety? We heard strange, rough oaths down there by those fisher-huts, and that way is her face turned. She may be some innocent who has strayed thus far in work of charity, and suspects not the dangerous surroundings. Is that your idea?"

"I have not an idea in my head—the last one vanished when I saw her face; but it may chance I can borrow one from the man she spoke to."

And before Maurice could remonstrate, the impetuous youth had crossed the walk and was speaking to the one-armed sailor.

"Who? Oh, that is our Denise, St. Denise, so the sailors call her; and many a saint is pictured in foreign churches who had never so kind a hand for the poor and miserable, and by my oath was never so beautiful."

"Ah, that is just it; we are strangers, and feared that so much of beauty may have cause for fear among those rough comrades over there. Has she friends or guardian near?"

"Your question proves you a stranger"— and the man looked at him with sharp scrutiny —"and I would tell you, my fine gallant, that you had best dance elsewhere for a partner. A guardian? Why, boy, there is not along all this shore a man so low that he would not jump at the honor of fighting for Denise. Guardians? I could call a score of them from where I sit; so go your ways and save your time."

"Come, Constante, you will only be misjudged for your pains; we will learn of others concerning the lady. But I am glad enough to hear she is so safe."

"I'll get myself a wooden leg to-morrow," decided the artist. But his friend halted him with a rather close grip on the arm.

"I will take care that you do nothing of the kind," he answered, decidedly, "and I assure you that the Lady Denise shall not be added to your list of models. I have borne with your whims, you must bear with mine in this; do you comprehend?"

Constante only looked at him a little wickedly from out the corner of his eye, but uttered no word beyond a low muttering, which continued as they walked onward, and Maurice noticed that his hands were clasped devoutly.

"What new mischief are you brewing?" he demanded.

"Mischief? Ah, you wrong me, monsieur. I but say a prayer for the memory of Madame la Princess, a memory buried at sunset on the shores of Orleans, and under curls of deepest bronze."

CHAPTER IV.

"MASTER, BUY ME!"

ADVENTURE seemed to be abroad in their path that first evening, for they had but reached again the main thoroughfare, and were passing a *café chantant*, where the sons of planters and the younger gallants of the town were often seen, when the door burst open and a struggling couple staggered out, flanked on either side by friends, remonstrating, urging, and cursing.

The crowd gathering so quickly was of all tints and character, but it seemed impossible for any in authority to penetrate to the doorway where those two struggled for possession and use of a knife held high in the hand of the tallest.

A gentleman halted near Maurice and Constante, hesitated a moment, and then flung himself against the crowd as if to crush them aside with his weight.

But quick as light a woman sped before him.

"Hist! master," she said, shrilly, and threw up

her hand to check him; "for a slave it does not matter — wait!"

She had dropped a great basket at the feet of the two strangers, and having succeeded in turning aside the gentleman, she seemed to drop among the feet of the swaying crowd, and an instant later reappeared farther in the circle.

Room was made for her with astonishing readiness — men shrank from her touch; and when she reached those two, and leaped upward like an animal at that hand holding the knife, there was a smothered cry went up from the watching people. Would it mean death?

But the very suddenness of her grasp secured it without a struggle, and in an instant it was flung from her high in the air, and the people scattered, with cries of fear lest it fall on their heads, but they never saw it come down. Oaths came from some mouths, others crossed themselves in fear.

"The black witch!"

"Think you she swallowed it?"

"Ah! that devil-marked voudou!"

And in the excitement the wrangler who had held the knife slipped away, leaving the youth who was his partner in the quarrel standing alone, looking ashamed and puzzled, while the woman walked quietly back and picked up her basket.

"Thank you, masters," she said, softly, noting that the strangers had guarded it for her; "you are kind."

Before they could speak, the man whom she had checked crossed to her and touched her arm.

"You sought to favor me, girl, and you did a brave thing there. Tell me your name."

She dropped her eyes, perhaps in embarrassment, and arranged a kerchief over her hair — hair strangely white above the dark-imaged face — hair for which they called her "devil-marked."

" My name — Venda."

" Venda — and your master's name?"

"Master Diego Zanalta."

"Ah, I know him well, and recall now that I have seen your face in his house. Well, Venda, I shall take heed that your master knows how careful you are of his friends, and if there is aught beyond a gold-piece I can do for you, speak."

She hesitated, glancing at the two strangers, and the chevalier bowed to her questioner.

"Pardon us, monsieur; we have forgotten we were eavesdroppers in our admiration of the work just performed by this woman, whom you do well to praise. We will withdraw."

"I beg you, no, young gentlemen; our interest is mutual, since the case seems strange to us both. Speak, Venda, without fear — your wish?"

"Master Lamort?"

"Yes — well?"

"Master — buy me!"

"Buy you? Well, on my word, this is a strange request. I shall ask your reasons for it. You are valuable, no doubt; but why should I deprive Don Zanalta of a treasure?"

"You are Alcalde; you are kind to slaves, to the red Indians, even. You know many masters take

5

slaves because they live on land new-bought; so Master Zanalta took me and land for debt. He has many others."

"And so have I, Venda, and life in my house is not joyous as there in that of Zanalta where ladies laugh. I have no beauty for you to serve."

"Master, I know what you have, many hands to bear burdens, many feet to run swiftly; but I know what you need, one heart to be faithful, one whose eyes see in the dark, one whose ears are ever awake if danger hides near, one whose hand is ever ready to grasp a knife for your cause, as — as Venda did but now, master."

She dropped her gaze under his sharp scrutiny; and her eyes filled with tears when he smiled carelessly.

"To grasp a knife for me in the cause of peace? Well, Venda, you do me honor to make choice of me for master; but I am growing old and slow of thought; I must have time before making decision. Above all, I must speak to your master. So meanwhile —"

He yet held in his jeweled fingers the piece of gold drawn from his purse, more than the slave had ever owned, perhaps, but she shook her head.

"Not your gold, master; so, master, good-night."

"A most strange one, truly," commented the gentleman, pocketing again the money. "I venture to say her twin has never been born. Pray you, did either of you see the stiletto fall? I have seen such feats among conjurers of the Far East, but it is strange to see it in this new land and through an untaught slave."

"She seems less ignorant than many," declared the chevalier, "and her courage makes her a bit wonderful, so it seems to us, at least; but we are new to your shores, and have much to grow accustomed to."

"You are, then, strangers? I judged as much; and from France? If so, we are like to meet again, as the passports of strangers often need me for approval. From France, you say? I am Victor Lamort; all the towns-people know me. If I can serve you, command me."

He did not wait their reply, or names, but bowed like a courtier and walked away, touching his walking-stick daintily as he went, and moving in haste, as though too long delayed.

"There is a man I feel it would be well to meet often, despite his name of gloom," said the chevalier. "He walks like a soldier; and did you note that scar on the cheek? A battle-wound, I doubt not."

"Soldiers wear not golden buckles on their street-boots," returned Constante; "and he must be a most valiant warrior to earn with his sword such jewels as gleam among his laces. If one can creep from the ranks up to that in this country, I'll enlist. But I fancy I would grow more pride with my achievements than this grandly careless Monsieur Lamort." And the fun-loving fellow strutted and minced along as though he already bore jeweled decorations, and his cane was flourished as though it were a symbol of sovereignty.

"Modest? Yes, he is that: but it seems in him a stamp of true greatness. There is a wondrous fascination for me in this gray-bearded dignitary. Did you note his musical voice?"

"There, there, Maurice—to fall in love once in an evening is enough for even me; but you lose your heart on one corner to a gray nun, and a few paces farther yield to the fascinations of a scarred veteran. For my part, I was both bewitched and frightened by the brown dame who uses knives as playthings, and can scatter a mob as though she were a breath of pestilence. The black witch, I heard some call her. Faith! I will be sworn she is one; and she'd go begging for a master many a day ere I'd consent to make purchase of her."

And the one called the "voudou" and the "black witch" moved on through the gloaming and the soft breath which falls over the earth when the new moon shines. She was not yet old, but her step dragged heavily; no one looking on the white hair could have pictured her as ever having been that passionate bright-haired creature who had lived for a season as royal favorite in the days of Gaston le Noyens.

A judgment had come upon her in the silence of her own heart. Untrained savage though she was, the memory of poor dead Mistress Felice, and more, the lover of Felice—those two ghosts of the past days arose before her in the shadows or in the sunshine and held her very soul in their grasp, filling her life with a remorse unexpressed and unexpressible.

Thus it was that she walked ever alone in the midst of the other blacks, who sang and who danced, choosing mates, and laughing at times through their toil; but she toiled unsmiling.

Once only had she been heard to laugh aloud in the home of her new master, where she and many others of the Le Noyens plantation had been taken in payment of a debt to Zanalta.

And that one day of laughter had been one to remember in the household; for scornful Pepito, who was half white, had jeered tauntingly at fine high Lady Felice, who, it was whispered, had mated to her shame with the river ruffian exiled to the mines as an assassin.

And then had Venda laughed — laughed as one who goes to a festival — and had leaped straight at the throat of frightened Pepito, and clung there until they cut her fingers with knives, and tore her loose only when two men lifted her bodily and bore her thus with her bleeding fingers into the presence of her new master.

"Yes, I strangled Pepito, but not dead, because they were fools and dragged me away. She-devil, Pepito; say my little mistress bad, wicked; she say Master Basil bad, assassin — that is why."

And Diego Zanalta looked strangely on those bleeding fingers, so the men who guarded her said, and looked strangely in her dark, desperate face, but uttered no word of chiding.

"Did you think I would kill you if you killed Pepito?" he asked. "No, Venda; I would have you whipped many times, but I would not let them kill you. Remember that, girl."

Then he turned to the men.

" Tell Pepito she will go to the rice fields if I ever again hear her say ill words of a white lady. Go now, but leave Venda here."

And they did so, but watched curiously for her appearance. Diego Zanalta with his cool words was feared more by the blacks than any master who would storm and threaten, and many had prophesied that the new woman who had tried to kill poor Pepito would surely fare ill at his hands. They never thought to see her again in the rooms of the house.

But she walked through them all in insolent silence. They could read neither defeat nor triumph in her slumbrous eyes, but the silver anklets still made music when she walked, her bodice and petticoat were of linen, the scarf she wore was yet a thing of silk and scarlet; so no outward sign of glory had departed from her.

" She is a devil voudou, she has put a charm on the master," whispered the others, though they dared not say aught of their fancies in her presence. Others there were of the slaves who would be proud to be spoken of as favorite, but she was different; she never smiled, and she made them afraid.

Sometimes they fancied she made the master afraid too, for as the days went by they noted that he never asked of her personal service; that she served his guests but never the master himself at table; that she never knowingly entered a room where he was alone, and if by chance she did, one or the other would immediately depart. Once when he was ill for a space, the physician sent cordials and

instructions by her to him. His oaths were emphatic
as he bade his serving-man never to open the door
to her, and all through one delirious night he muttered, "Venda, Venda," and begged that she would
not be allowed to look at him so.

Yet he kept her, and thus began the whispers of
witchcraft; and she kept their fancies alive by many
strange cures performed by her. If any living
thing was likely to bleed to death, Venda, instead of
a priest or physician, was called, and with the touch
of her hands and a few muttered words the blood
would cease to flow. Let the friends say what they
would, both the white and the black people went to
her for charms, and bought from her the little vials
of serpent's-oil with which to cure strange aches in
the bones after the fever had been with them.
Even the Indian slaves, taken of old from the
Natchez tribe, would nod approval of her cures, and
call her the silent medicine-woman.

But for all the help she gave, there were many
who feared to pass her in the road when the dusk
fell, and as her silk-turbaned hair turned so swiftly
to the color of age they called her devil-marked.
And that evening when she had begged to be
bought by a new master, she walked as usual, silent,
through the streets, and never noted the awesome
glances cast at her as the natives muttered of the
stiletto yet in the air above their heads — "a good
stiletto," said friends of the owner; "and who was
to pay for it?"

But heavier thoughts than that of the stiletto
weighed her brain. She scarce heeded when her

steps brought her to the grounds of Zanalta, and would have passed the gate but for black Gourfi, who hailed her.

"Do you walk under a charm that you pass the master's door and not know?" he demanded. "Here have they waited, the Mistress Ninon and old Mistress Mercedes, for you to finish their decking for the fête, and you strolling the streets just to hear your ankle-bands tinkle — though you will never take a mate to dance to their music." And he looked at her meaningly, for Gourfi, who could speak well the language of the whites, was in much a steward to his master, and he found Venda good to look upon, seeing no reason why she should be proud with him though she scorned the others.

But she seemed not to note who spoke, only asked, " Have they departed?"

"That they have, with Sandro and Bula to carry the train of old mistress, and she scolding every step to the chair and vowing master must sell you. Si! but she was in a fine rage! She'll speak to master, be sure of it. Do you never care, Venda?"

"No, I never care." And she walked into the house and left him there watching her sullenly.

"If I was white — if I had gold, Gourfi should be her master. There is none like her among our people. She looks from her eyes like the red Indian slaves, whose race they say did once own these lands; just like them when they are angry, and silent — always silent. Voudou! I care not for the devil charms if she would but look on me."

CHAPTER V.

AN EVENING WITH MONSIEUR LAMORT.

BLACK GOURFI was entirely correct in his statement that Señora Mercedes Sofie Zanalta was in a fine rage, for so she was, truly. Even the magnificence of the new sedan-chair, in which she was borne, did nothing to temper her chagrin, and against the "black faces," singly and in a body, did she exclaim.

"Oh, aunt, be patient!" entreated Ninon, wearily. "Since you look so magnificent, what matters it whose hands laced your bodice, or clasped the plumes in your hair? I know they'll be much admired, even by the ladies. And as for Monsieur Lamort—well, he is a bachelor, but I dare hope no longer than his eyes rest on you. Come, now; think no longer of a careless slave, but please your mind with prospects of the fête we are about to enjoy. Few will gather there wearing so fine a gown, I promise you."

"Si! the costume is good enough; the catching of the folds with roses is a trick of Madrid days — the saints be blest for the memory of them! — and the veil I decided to wear was a fancy of my illustrious husband — St. Jago care for his soul! He ever liked me to revive our day of wedding by dressing as a bride — the good soul has seen but the brides of paradise these thirty years — but that devil, Venda! Think you Anite arranged the wig with the cleverness of that cursed voudou? A pretty pass, a very pretty pass, when slaves come and go as they like, and the word of a mistress weighs for nothing!"

"But aunt —"

"Seek not to dissuade me from my righteous wrath. I tell you the girl shall be sold or sent to the fields ere another blessed day of God calls us to the chapel. There are other lands than this Louisiana, and if Diego Zanalta were ten times the brother of my husband, I take charge of his house no longer unless that insolent one is banished to the fields."

"Insolent, Venda insolent! Has she ever given saucy speech to you?"

"Can one only be insolent by words?" demanded the irate lady; "her very silence is an insolence. Ah, the quiet devil!"

They had by this time reached the residence of Lamort, and the blaze of many-colored lights and the low-toned swing of the music made it a place easily marked for enjoyment; and from the arches of the portico several gentlemen, among them their host, came forward to give welcome to the fairest dame, and the most exacting, that the town held.

Don Diego approached at the same moment from another direction, but, wise man that he was, discerned the frown on the brow of his brother's respected relict, and held aloof until the compliments of gallants had softened her thoughts toward mankind in general.

And compliments were seldom lacking for Señora Mercedes, for was she not the outer gate to be captured ere a courtier gained the inner tower where Madame Ninon dwelt?

She even forgot for a space that provoking wench
Venda, as she was led into the mansion by that most
engaging Monsieur Lamort, and noticed with a
hearty satisfaction that all female eyes within range
were turned wonderingly on the rose-draped robe,
and on the girlish tissue of white falling from the
bewigged head.

But the name of Zanalta was powerful enough to
make amends for any eccentricity by its bearers;
and if one could not do as he liked in this new land,
why come? The scene was a thing semi-oriental in
its character; the dress — French or Spanish — of
the ladies, a few in the latest court robes, such as were
worn by Marie Antoinette and her maids at Versailles, but more, many more, of an older date; but
the unerring taste of the Frenchwomen made those
gowns things of grace, and buckles of diamonds fastened many a shoe over hosiery repaired so often
one could scarce find enough of the original material
to catch a needle-point in. Then there were half-
Moorish dresses of old Spain in rustling brocades
and flounced laces. The gentlemen in the gorgeous
dress of Louis XV. or the military dress of Spain;
and back of those gracious ladies and gay gallants
glided the slaves in gala-dress, bare-armed, bare-
throated, wearing sandals lashed to their feet with
crimson bands, and necklets of bone and bright copper above their vestments of crimson and pale yellow. Assuredly Monsieur Lamort understood how
to make even those black toilers picturesque.
He had brought fanciful ideas of such things from
abroad, learnt somewhere in those south seas of which

he spoke at times, and from which he had brought
great white pearls and glimmering jewels, toward
which ladies looked languishingly.

And to-night he had surpassed even himself in
his effort to entertain the families of Orleans called
noble; and Señora Mercedes was not the only one
who had gathered up her dearest bravery for his
eye — a good clear eye, that gleamed with rare
pleasure that night, and swept over the proud assem-
blage with a glance which seemed to divine every
needed attention for a guest.

"I confess. Monsieur Lamort," said Diego Zanalta, as the wine of Oporto was served by deft-
handed slaves —"I confess I tremble at the thought
of the desert we would yet be existing in here if
that lucky fight in the Floridas had not recommended us to your knowledge three years ago. We
colonists were fast selling ourselves as slaves to
commerce and financial advancement, forgetting in
our rush that the fine air of salons, after all, does
more to enliven the mind and brighten our faculties
than the weighing of gold in the market-places.
Ah, monsieur, your spirit of fine France has reminded us that our homes may be made palaces
here, and cure us of our grieving for courts across
the water. Ladies, gentlemen, I salute you. To
the health of our host!"

The eyes of their host twinkled with a humor sardonic as he glanced over the gracious company
drinking to his health there in that Orleans, where
the laws of caste were strong as. in any court of
Europe. His bow and smiles confessed himself

flattered by their distinguished homage, but his veiled eyes held sentiments unuttered by his lips.

"By my faith, sirs," he returned, "you are reminding me, by your mention of Florida, that we should repeat many an *Ave Maria* on this day, in token that we are so much better off than those in the swamps, where the Seminole warriors did battle most wickedly. Even now I can scarce see the black mud of this delta without seeming also to hear the singing of arrows and the wild yells of those savage men. Yes, indeed, my friends, we are better here than we were there."

"Yet you seemed equally at home in their warfare," remarked a Monsieur Villeneuve, whose youthful admiration for the scarred veteran was apparent in his eyes. "That, my first battle, is a memorable thing to me, especially as I shall always carry with me the vision of your face as I saw it first. It seems to me yet that you were really laughing as you came to our relief across the sands, and gave us and the savages an idea that you had an army at your heels; few of us would have seen Orleans Island again but for you and your crew."

"And I might never have become one of your citizens but for the chance that sent my little vessel to the shore there that day. So you see it was I to whom the saints were kind. I was a stranger to your land, but you did not long allow me to remain so; and now — well, the building up of a grand commercial center here has become a pet fancy of mine, and I am proud to count myself as one of you. But I ask pardon of the ladies for speaking of commerce; we well know they dislike the term, and love only the things it brings to us. Even you, Madame Villette, you own a great warehouse; but have you not made us all wretched by stating that you will never give your hand to a man who buys or sells in the market-places?"

"Then am I likely to walk alone forever on this island," laughed Ninon, "for the gallants of Orleans are all awake to the advantages of bargains." And the latter part of her speech was discreetly murmured, and only Monsieur Lamort caught its meaning or understood the quizzical glance she gave him; and more than one of those ambitious gallants would have given their youth for the smile of comprehension she exchanged with the scarred veteran. Assuredly, Madame Villette and Monsieur Lamort appeared as good comrades.

"Oh, but I have a message to deliver here to-night," she cried, suddenly; "I had well-nigh forgotten it, but it has concern with other strangers from France who arrived to-day, on the anniversary of your meeting with Orleans men, monsieur. And, Brother Diego, I did entertain the commandant of the French ship since I saw you. He came to ask leave of you to present two strangers who sought names, or a name, no longer found in our town. The commandant seems a good soul, and was anxious to serve the strangers, whom he terms illustrious."

"And their names, Ninon?"

"Ah! forgotten already by me, except that one is a Chevalier something or other, and the second has Constante for a part of the name. Beyond that I have forgotten."

"You might as well have forgotten in the beginning," laughed her half-brother, "for we are little the wiser. 'Chevalier,' of course, tells us somewhat. Captain Nirosse? Yes, his word is a good pledge. I shall be glad to serve his passengers."

"Can you remember, madame, if the men were young?" queried their host; and Madame Ninon raised her hands in pretty dismay.

"Oh, monsieur! when I have not even seen their faces. The one thing I did hear of them — their names — I have forgotten. So why ask of so simple a person the impossible?"

"Be not distressed, madame; I am only your host this evening, not alcalde, so your evidence is not an imperative necessity to the assembly. But my question was not quite idle, either. This evening at sunset I met on the street Condé two strangers from France, most amiable in appearance, and the thought came to me that they may be the ones of whom you speak. Would I had known earlier they were recommended to your interest, Don Diego; it would have been pleasure to have asked them here this evening. One's first day in a strange land is so often a lonely one."

"It is like you to remember that on this anniversary," said one fair woman of France whose eyes looked kindly on him, eyes aged through tears instead of years — a woman of an exiled family, and whose two sons slept under myrtles there in the sands of Orleans. The suns and the breath of the swamps are often so hard on the new-comers. And those two strangers?

Monsieur Lamort looked across at her, and, coming nearer, kissed her hand.

" Madame Vraumont, you help me to remember something more, merely that it may not yet be too late to ask the presence of those gentlemen. What say you, Don Zanalta? Would it please you, or think you a messenger could find them — the ' chevalier' and 'Constante ' — address, nowhere?"

"To be sure, and the thought is a kind one. Through Captain Nirosse they can be found in less than the half of an hour; and, if they are disposed, we can make their first evening a merry one — if indeed they prove not to be gray-heads who have forsworn merriment."

" For my part, I fear much that is just what you will find," sighed Madame Villette.

" Well, whether gray or golden, we will send the message. Don Zanalta, will you word it?" And Monsieur Lamort signaled a slave, who stepped forward.

"Sebastian, you know where the sailor captains are to be found when ashore?"

"Yes, master, where many are; and one can always tell where another may be."

"Good! Go there; ask for Captain Nirosse of the French ship Celestine, just arrived in the harbor. Give to him the letter, and conduct here the gentlemen he may command you to. Take carriage, and be swift."

"Yes, master."

Don Zanalta came forward with the note he had written and passed it to his host for approval.

"Very good. Surely, if they are disposed to be on good terms with Orleans, they can not resist the courtesy of your words; and as there is yet room for another name, I shall add that of Victor Lamort."

"Oh, thank you, monsieur. You are very gracious."

"Not at all. Your guests are welcome under my roof, and as this is the anniversary of my own meeting with the gentlemen here, why not celebrate it more fully by gathering in other new-comers to your shores? And, by the way, Zanalta, speaking of the gentlemen whom we hope Sebastian will bring back; if they are the ones I met this evening I have special cause to remember the occasion, because of some one who was there, and who belongs to you."

"Ah! an adventure; pray tell us!"

"Only a quarrel for a knife at the door of a wine-shop. Two men struggled, yet their comrades were so close no peacemaker could approach. I was about to make an attempt to push through and separate them — one looked a mere boy — when a slave of yours bade me wait, stepped before me, reached them as though she had been a spirit, and flung the knife they fought for high in the air before the combatants realized who had secured it. A most strange woman for a black, but she tried to do me a service there. I even feel tempted to offer you fair returns for her if at any time you should choose to part with her. I asked her name. She said Venda."

"Ah! that black witch!" broke in Señora Mercedes, who drew near and heard the last of his

6

words; "well might she serve you, who art a soldier, and a brave commander of your own sea-vessel, but to a lady she is very wearing with her silence and her tricks of witchery with which she affrights the other slaves. Diego, I tell you plainly none other will ever bid for her, and since you yourself love her but little — though you never will chide her — I say, take Monsieur Lamort at his word."

Don Zanalta sent one angered glance at her, but his smile came quickly again.

"Your suggestion has at least one earnest advocate in my own household," he said, carelessly, to Monsieur Lamort, "but I fancy the recommendation my sister-in-law gives with it will not strengthen your intent to purchase."

"On the contrary, those voudous, as they are called, are an interesting study to me; and is she one? I would find it easy to believe, for the knife she threw in the air was not to be seen again."

"Oh, we have heard many tales of her," agreed one of the ladies. "She is a strange creature, but she does no ill."

"Except to my aunt's nerves," smiled Madame Villette. "She is a most capable woman, but silent and dreamy while the other blacks sing songs and dance dances. I have no dislike for her, though I certainly would be glad if she was taken away, simply because of the antipathy my aunt feels for her."

Zanalta heard the words, and while the others chattered of Venda and her strange ways, he was thinking quickly:

"Well, why not? The money would come handy.

Those games with that infernal Rochelle have made
a difference with me. And, after all — eighteen
years — eighteen years I have kept her and feared
her; yes, curse her! that's the word, feared her.
And all for what? She dare not speak; reason tells
me that. Then why hesitate? By the saints! my
mind is settled on it; she shall go."

It seemed as though Monsieur Lamort as well as
Venda was gifted with occult powers, for just at the
finish of Zanalta's reasoning he came forward smiling, as though he knew the result.

"Well, Don Zanalta, is the voudou to weave her
spells in my house instead of yours?" he asked,
nonchalantly. "If so, name the amount, and I'll
free Señora Zanalta from her *bête noire*."

"Yes"— and Don Diego spoke with haste of one
who was afraid he might repent — "yes; it is a
strange sale and conducted quickly. I never meant
to sell her, though I have had many a war in the
house because of her. But she may amuse you. She
is strange — some say mad — so I give you warning;
but she will work well. Yes, she can be very useful,
if she chooses, and she is yours at your word."

Victor Lamort bowed to the agreement. "I will
have an article drawn up at any time, to-night as
well as another. I fancy her looks. She will make
a strange picture in the house. I never saw so
young a negress with white hair."

"It is because of that the other slaves call her
devil-marked. But, pardon me, is that not the return
of your carriage?"

For wheels had just rolled over the shell-lined

drive, and Zanalta had scarcely spoken when Sebas-
tien announced, " Master Chevalier Delogne, Master
Constante Raynel," and Victor Lamort went forward
to greet the strangers.

"It is as I fancied — you do not come to my house
as strangers, gentlemen, for have we not met earlier
this evening? And here is Don Zanalta. It is a
pleasure to me that you meet under my roof."
And Maurice Delogne found himself looking again
into the eyes of the man who had attracted him so
strongly but a short time before, and Constante
drew a long breath of pure delight at the semi-
barbaric surroundings.

"Ah, messieurs, for a year and a day am I your
bond-slave in payment for this evening's glimpse of
paradise. See! I bend my neck for the yoke — a
year and a day!"

Don Zanalta liked more thoroughly the light chatter of the artist than the more level-eyed youth, who
spoke graciously but with less extravagance.

"He is but a day in your land," smiled Delogne,
warningly; "and lest you, not knowing, take him at
his word, let me confess that he is vassal to so
many things of impulse that I should fear to vouch
for his faithfulness to one."

"Is not my name Constante?"

"Would it have been had they waited a few years
for your christening? But aside from this badinage,
gentlemen, pray believe that we feel deeply the
kindness you have been pleased to show us. To
strangers in a strange land, a hand that welcomes
means so much."

"We have all learned that lesson on these shores, Monsieur Chevalier," assented Lamort. "So few of us were born here that we have all been strangers in the land on some day of our lives. We but give to you from Orleans that which Orleans has granted to us, and that which no doubt you yourself will give in the future to a later comer. But come, I would like to have you meet others of my guests, and you see they have followed the music and left my palm-room."

Constante was at the same moment exchanging bows with Villeneuve, and a little later, when these two were left alone for a space, they proceeded, after the fashion of youth, to become at once well acquainted.

"My faith, monsieur, do you all live like princes in this romantic land of exile? Is our host the reigning sovereign?"

"Oh, no; though perhaps an heir apparent — who knows? He is, they say, a power beside the throne here, if not behind it; at least one thought well of, and deserving of it all. There was a time in this colony when people of France were not in high favor; but it is said that Victor Lamort has swept away every lingering prejudice in the space of three years. To be of the mother church and of sufficient age and intelligence are all the requisites to position here now. French and Spanish alike control the town and guard against their common enemy, the English."

"Ah! then the spirit of war is abroad here as well as on the shores of Europe?"

"Well — yes — but whispers, whispers only. The English smugglers are causing much trouble slip, ping into our ports on every thin-veiled excuse. You see our civilized neighbors cause us more trouble than the savage people."

Constante's eyes were busy noting the strange feathery foliage of palms, and catching now and then glimpses' of women's dresses through the green.

"By my own vision of things you seem to have few troubles here beyond finding the days long enough for your pleasures, and you certainly have nymphs of the tropics to assist you. There goes a face that is enchanting. See — the one looking this way, moving there beside the lady with the — hum! ahem! — the bridal-veil over her tresses."

Villeneuve smiled at the enthusiasm of the stranger, a little pleased to see that Orleans had beauty remarkable even compared with beauty of the French court.

"Ah, there is golden treasure as well as bright eyes in that group, Monsieur Raynel. It is Madame Villette, the wealthiest widow in the province — slaves of her own by the hundred, and vessels of her own on the waters. The other is her relative, Señora Mercedes Zanalta. A good old Spanish name is hers; but, alas! she has no gold to gild it."

"Alas!" echoed Constante, unconsciously; for in his own mind he knew at once it was the uncomely old woman who was the wealthy widow, and it was the childish-faced sylph who had only the ancient lineage — did not the fates always divide favors in

just that miserable way? And yet how charming
was that bearer of the ungilded lineage!

And at the first opportunity he did a thing very
remarkable for Constante. He did not seek presen-
tation, but slipped alone where the palms were thick,
and where he could see all the room, and couples
saluting each other in stateliest fashion, with many
a gracious curve of body and many an arch erecting
of proud head. And his eyes would wander ever to
the dainty grace of that figure in the rose-color
and silver tissue, and from her white unjeweled
throat he would glance toward the more matured
charms of Donna Mercedes, and note the gemmed
buckles glinting as she moved.

And then he would sigh like a furnace, and assure
himself for the hundredth time that he had met
fate; and that it was very hard, in the face of his late
decision to wed wealth, that he should meet on
the first threshold he crossed a being to tempt him
from every wise decision he had ever made. The
temptation of St. Anthony — bah! it was trifling, he
knew, compared with his own.

So he assured himself. He was in his imagination striving to renounce the one and offer his
hand to the other, yet had never spoken to either of
them in his life!

Oh, love! love! that spirit binding us with a
chain of glances from bright eyes, and bringing to
us instincts of knowledge deeper than all the philos-
ophies. A wild folly when it is another man the
madness touches, but a soul's tragedy when it
touches ourselves.

How many a heart lives more fully in visions of what might be than in the life men call the real!

So if jovial Constante chose for a space to let his thoughts wander in the strange paths of imagination — well, he was not the first beggar to claim riches from such a source. To be sure, he would marry the widow, despite his sighs for that lovely kinswoman, for Monsieur Raynel was a gentleman of thrifty instincts. Yet, just for the present, ere he had addressed either, how comforting to fancy that the beauty in rose-color owned the slaves and the ships, and that he, Constante, was commander of all!

And a sigh, earnest as any Romeo's, touched the palms because of the sweetness within vision, but toward which he must never reach.

And he courageously turned his eyes to the more matured dame of the golden buckles. There, he knew, was the path for him. Had not he asked for that? Well, when the saints are kind is it not wise to accept what they send? Assuredly.

Constante had devoted this five minutes of his life to a bit of serious contemplation, and arose from it with the grim design of being presented to that widow within the earliest time possible, and then — well, trust to Dame Fortune and youth's audacity.

Maurice, who met him a few moments later, looked at him wonderingly. It was a strange thing for Constante to creep thus modestly from sight, especially if there were ladies to pay court to.

"What! you, Constante Raynel, alone there in the garden when all this feast of beauty is spread before your eyes? Why, sir; does it mean that

you have closed your book of French folly, and commence here to peruse the leaves of the New World's
wisdom?   You are certainly courageous to commence a reform in the midst of such temptations.
Did you note the ladies I spoke to just now?   They
are most gracious, and Madame Villette has commissioned me to present you."

"Madame Villette?"   And Raynel arose with a
resigned air and went to meet his fate.

He met first the entrancing eyes of Ninon.
Heavens! she was looking at him — at him out of
all the room, and looking at him exactly as if there
was not another man within a mile.

"She is adorable," he muttered to himself, and
immediately added, "Don't be a fool, Raynel."

Then he heard the names Señora Zanalta, Madame
Villette, and he was bowing to two ladies, and trying, for his own soul's sake, to avoid the glances
of the prettiest, and offered his arm to the veil-
bedecked lady while he tried vainly to comfort his
heart by gazing on those diamond buckles.

But if you are young, need I tell how lightly diamonds weigh when one longs instead for the touch
of a loved hand.   And if you are old — well, the old
have memories.

So Constante, on his newly adopted path of wisdom, walked on thorns, and never came so near to
hating Maurice as when that gallant led the one
adorable into the place of the feast and sat himself
at her side, wickedly thoughtless as to his comrade
and the dowager.

But Ninon was not so careless.   Her eyes were

big with wonder as she noted the devout attentions
won by her kinswoman from that handsome young
stranger — for that he was handsome was a thing
quickly decided by her. She even felt that her eyes
must have betrayed to him her opinion when their
glances met, and her face grew warm at the thought,
for had he not turned deliberately from her and
given his attention to Donna Mercedes? Did he
mean, then, to ignore the beauties of Orleans, and
show his indifference by paying court to one of the
most antique?

Ninon's silvered slipper tapped the floor to emphasize her own thoughts. Ah! how she would
like to teach that Monsieur Indifference one lesson!
Just to bring that handsome head to her feet for
once — one little minute. Of course she would
laugh at him then, and dismiss him. Yes, she would
teach him not to slight a lady who had so kindly
suggested that he be presented. Ah, the ingrate!
But how handsome he was, and what bright things
he was saying to Señora Mercedes and Monsieur
Villeneuve.

And Madame Ninon Villette forgot the Chevalier
Delogne who was beside her, and strained her ears
to hear the words of the ingrate who would not look
at her.

Alas! Ninon; all sweethearts pray for her!

But Maurice did not feel especially neglected, even
though the lovely widow did note Constante's words
more than his own, for Monsieur Lamort was near
enough for speech, and the younger man listened to
his words with great interest.

Some one was speaking of a ghostly craft seen by
black sailors on the river but a short time before — a
phantom of the starlight, over which the masters
were laughing.

"Those are bad subjects to humor the blacks in,"
decided Monsieur Lamort; "they are so credulous,
and one will frighten another, so that in a short
space a whole plantation will be panic-stricken. I
strive to reason with them in such matters, and if
that fails I try ridicule. I find they do not like to
be laughed at."

"Then you think, of course, the return of the dead
is a thing ridiculous?" asked Don Zanalta, with a
degree of earnestness noticeable after the careless
chatter.

"I?" queried Monsieur Lamort. "Well, there is
much to consider in that question. And did not the
Son of Mary come back to be seen of man after the
tomb was sealed? Yet the blacks in their ignorance
should not be given that knowledge; their minds
are too childish to grasp the reasons for it."

"But I mean men of to-day, not of the past,"
persisted Zanalta. "Suppose a man vows to himself that he will return, and bends all his thoughts
to that end, think you he could win the power?"

"To make such a vow a person must have an all-
absorbing purpose, at least so it seems to me; and
whether or not he could gain that power would, I
think, depend on whether or not that purpose was a
thing just in the eyes of God."

Zanalta looked at him a moment, and then said,

carelessly, " Well, I have heard sailors and soldiers tell strange stories of those who return."

"And I too," asserted his host; "but I fancy the ghost most men see is conscience. And if a shadow in the moonlight takes the form of a person who once lived, it is sure not to be a stranger, but one whom we have sometime wronged."

The wine-glass slipped from the fingers of Zanalta and broke on the white floor. The wine splashed and lay like a thin rivulet of blood at his feet.

" I am growing clumsy in my old age," he said, and laughed ; but in the same breath he added, " The glass scratched my hand. It is a trifle, but wounds are not pleasant things to keep at table. Will you pardon me ? "

His host bowed assent, but watched him curiously as he arose. Monsieur Lamort had very sharp eyes, yet could detect no wound on the wrist, where the handkerchief was pressed quickly, and his gaze followed his guest, who disappeared amid the palms.

"A prick of a pin is as annoying in time of peace as a sword-thrust in the heat of battle," he remarked.

But Colonel Durande, who sat near, looked across knowingly, and spoke more lowly.

" Poor Diego encourages conversation on that theme, though I fancy he is never the happier for it. You see, Monsieur Lamort, there is a story, known to the older people here, a tragical story, in which he had a slight part — nothing to his discredit, you understand, only he was threatened with after-life

vengeance by a murderer of this town whom his
evidence sent to the galleys, or rather the mines;
and I really fancy he thinks of it at times and grows
morbid."

"Indeed, one can imagine Don Zanalta in any
rôle rather than the tragical. He seems so generally in tune with everything that is bright and
joyous."

" You are right.   But his memory plays him tricks,
no doubt, as it does with us all at times.   And it was
really a very sad story.   A lady of high degree who
stooped to be loved by one of the *canaille*, a shame-
ful love affair, and the lady's guardian was murdered by the lover one day in this very garden.
Does not that interest you, Monsieur Lamort?   You
are living on the stage of a former tragedy."

" But what part did Don Zanalta play in it, if I
may ask?"

"He was the friend of the murdered guardian,
and saw the crime committed.   More, the lady was
intended by their families to be his wife; so it was
said, at least.   But she died a recluse soon after the
man was sentenced.   Some say she went mad.   Anyway, an aged relative removed her to a plantation
near the Acadians, and she ended her life there.   A
sad story; and a girl so beautiful one can but wonder
that evil would lurk in her mind."

" Yes; I heard a crime had been done here.   The
blacks speak of it, and shun one path when the dusk
falls.   But Don Zanalta said naught of it to me.   You
know I made purchase of the place from him."

"Yes, I remember.   I was one of the judges on

that trial, and remember also the settlement of the estates. You see, as I said before, Diego and Le Noyens, the murdered man, were close comrades. But Le Noyens lived wild and fast, and many purses of gold had Diego filled for him — some over the gaming-table, for Zanalta dearly loves the excitement of play. At any rate, when the end came it became known that Gaston had given mortgage to Diego for many acres and many slaves; and thus it was that Zanalta held this property until you took him at his word and made purchase of it."

In other parts of the room gay words and soft laughter sounded. Villeneuve was beside Ninon, and they were chatting with much spirit, and both laughing a little when they would look at Señora Mercedes, who was rapidly growing as girlish as her attire under the attentions of the bronze-haired stranger whose tones were so caressing.

And Maurice, freed from attendance on any of the fair ones, was pleased to listen to the story thus strangely started — a romance of these rooms where gay companions laughed. He had not expected to find romances in the new homes of Orleans.

"And you were one of those who sentenced the criminal?" he asked, speaking to Colonel Durande. "I always felt — pardon me if I give offense — but I feel that, honorable as that position is, I would never wish to fill it. Suppose one should condemn innocent people — sentence them to death, perhaps, and learn long after it was unjust. I have read of such things."

"So have I," smiled the colonel; "we see such

things in romances, but I have not yet met them in
life. Yes, I helped to convict Basil de Bayarde,
and all the town thought he was lucky not to be
executed instead of exiled. In fact, it was to the
clemency of Diego Zanalta that he owed his life,
for Zanalta opposed execution. Some of the people
claimed he should be whipped, as a warning to
other aspiring rangers who might fancy a lady's
love instead of seeking mates where they belong —
among the *canaille;* but that favor was not paid to
popular opinion, so he was not whipped, but only
sent to the mines for life."

"De Bayarde?" repeated Maurice, who seemed to
have heard only the name — "De Bayarde? Pardon
me, but in France that name is of the nobles, not of
the people. Who was the man?"

"A ranger of the river, a player of the mandolin,
an Indian-fighter, and a conjurer in the game of
love, since he bewitched the fairest lady of this
province," answered Colonel Durande, lightly; in
fact, the sort of adventurer whose stories read so
prettily when set to rhyme, but whom prosaic,
respectable people ever avoid."

Maurice laughed, and glanced from the colonel to
his host.

"I very much fear, then, that I am entering your
Orleans under a cloud," he said; "for, gentlemen, I
must confess that the only letter of introduction I
have with me is from my aunt, the Marquise de
Lescuré, and is to an old friend of hers called De
Bayarde."

Both gentlemen showed their surprise, and the

colonel looked frankly uncomfortable. Assuredly Chevalier Delogne was lacking in the tact of a politician.

"Our theme was unfortunate, Chevalier; I am distressed that I may have made music unpleasant for you. I beg your pardon."

"Nay, nay, Monsieur le Colonel," returned the other, quickly; "the coincidence of name is but a jest to laugh at, after all, for the man I seek is not named Basil, and if living he must be quite an old man now. His name is Hector—Hector de Bayarde."

"Was Hector," said the colonel; "but that was many years ago, Chevalier—before you were born, no doubt, for he died during the insurrection of '68.

"Little wonder, then, that you failed to find his address," remarked Monsieur Lamort. "And was he also an adventurer?"

"On the contrary," answered the colonel, with decision, "he was a soldier and a patriot. It was a name the Frenchmen here liked to remember. Old men still like to speak of him as a martyr to a lost cause. The saints were good to him that he was not allowed to live for exile and imprisonment such as the others of that revolution lived through. Only of late I was searching old records of the French occupancy, and noticed his name and the list of properties confiscated by the Spanish ruler, for you know all lands and slaves of the revolution leaders were added to the properties of the crown, and used at the pleasure of the governor-general."

"No, I was not aware of it; neither, I am sure, was my aunt the marquise. I have not yet examined

the papers intrusted to me, but know from her word
that Monsieur de Bayarde was one whom she knew
well in her youth; more, that in some way she
blamed herself for his exile, and even sent to him a
sum of money through a friend, hoping that she
would not be suspected as the giver. The money
was given with the suggestion that he live as
beseemed his station; but his senses must have
been keen, for he detected the plot, and wrote her he
had purchased the estate, but for her, not for himself
— or rather had taken it in his own name, and would
forward the papers of transfer as soon as they could
be executed. Well, the papers never reached the
marquise; nevertheless she is confident they were
sent, for his word was given. But ships were few in
those days — some were lost, and much that was valuable went down, including, perhaps, De Bayarde's
message. And then there was a marquis at that
time, and rumor has it that he was most watchful of
his fair bride, or any message that came near her;
so who knows? I am here to please my aunt, and
whether I find him or no, I am to remain a space
and study the new land and my fitness for it. I confess I feel that I am simply searching for the sequel
to an old lady's romance, but so charming an old lady
that I am quite willing to swear myself her knight.
And, in truth, had I been in De Bayarde's shoes, I
should have stolen her in her youth, and not crossed
the seas alone; for she was only a betrothed at that
time, and not a wife."

" I feel like an audience of one, for whom you and
Colonel Durande are reading romances of the past

7

this evening," said their host, who seemed closely
interested in Maurice and his mission. " But is it
not strange that through all these years the marquise should never have learned of his death?"

" Scarcely ; her life has been that of a nun ever
since I remember. Only this past year, and at my
entreaty, did she return to court. But, monsieur, I
beg many pardons for thus filling your evening
with my family history. I scarce know how it
began, but I am sure it will end with your other
guests crying out against my selfishness."

" From only Madame Villette must we crave
grace," answered Monsieur Lamort. " All the rest
are too far away to be affected by our withdrawal
from their gaiety. Madame, will you pardon us for
daring to spend five minutes talking of a lady across
the seas when you yourself were within hearing?
We are very humble, and willing to drink any number of glasses to your health, if you will but take us
into favor once more."

Ninon nodded, and smiled her assent, inwardly
thinking, " A toast — then of course he must look
this way for an instant, and I will seem not to know
he is in the room."

And Monsieur Lamort arose and asked his guests
to drink with him to the health and happiness of
Ninon — Madame Villette; and the readiness of all
was shown by the smiles directed to charming
Ninon.

There was only one exception. The exception
was Monsieur Raynel, who, to be sure, met his host's
proposition with a smile, but, strangely enough,

looked into the eyes of Señora Mercedes when he lifted his glass, and drained it as though it were a love-potion longed for eagerly.

And in truth poor Constante was having a glorious hour of it, and dared not let his glances wander lest they should never come back to linger on the owner of those uncounted acres.

" And you are an artist ? " she asked, with the most flattering surprise. " Ah, monsieur, you know not to what a desert you have come ! Art ? — the word is forgotten here by any who ever knew its meaning. But I, well, I am from Madrid, and what need to tell to you, an art lover, of the masterpieces there on which I was used to gaze ? I have missed them sadly here, and can promise you the sympathy of one soul in this town, where — alas that it should be so ! — few people care for aught but a rush for wealth."

" Sad indeed is it to see humanity waste its energies in the pursuit of dross," agreed Constante, with the most *spirituelle* expression his face was capable of. " It is much to be lamented."

" Well may you say that, my dear Monsieur Raynel. Indeed your whole manner of conversation betrays you as a gentleman of most exemplary thought. Believe me, I am indeed gratified to have made your acquaintance, and trust we may continue it in my own house, where you will be welcomed most heartily."

" Ah, madame, you dazzle me with your kindness. What return can a poor artist make for the exquisite pleasure you have given me ? To be met with sympathy for my work on the very threshold of my life here — sympathy from a lady — such a lady! Madame, pardon me if I express poorly my thanks; but be sure your kind invitation will be most gratefully accepted."

"I shall look forward, then, to many interesting discussions on your chosen art. We possess some examples of portrait-work that are not bad, but nothing late, nothing of my own, in fact, since my marriage, though I have several times contemplated having one made.

"Ah, madame!" and Constante looked at her, but his voice, or his conscience, could take him no farther — his meaning was interpreted by a sigh.

"Well, well, we will see," remarked Donna Mercedes, coquettishly, and showed by the half-promise that the language of sighs was not forgotten by her. "And our church here needs sadly the hand of an artist. In fact, we have spoken more than once of sending to Spain for one. So it may be of substantial interest to you to call when your leisure will permit. My brother-in-law, Don Zanalta, whom you have met, has much power in such decisions here, and I will see that he is interested."

"Dear lady," and Monsieur Raynel's tones were infinitely caressing, "it has been said that 'out of the fullness of the heart the mouth speaketh.' I turn infidel to that from this night, for to my lips will come no words fit to thank you in."

And then the rascal gave silent thanks to the saints because the guests were dispersing from the table, and he could betake himself from the widow's

side for a few blessed minutes — a liberty he took
quick advantage of, and found himself a little later
beside Maurice, attempting a cigarette, and feeling
as tired as a man who has run a long race.

"Well?" queried his friend, looking at him smilingly and speaking in the tone that asks, "How is
the world treating you?"

In fact, he himself had met so many things of
interest that he had well-nigh lost sight of Constante. But that worthy was not disposed to be confidential. He scowled slightly at his questioner, and
gripped the cigarette until it was twisted past repair.
In fact, the mercenary path he had chosen seemed
filled with every conceivable annoyance ; and this
was only the beginning — one short hour borrowed
from the paradise he assured himself he would ask
ere long of the gracious widow. For had she not
shown by her very flattering attention that no
advance of his would be thought presuming? He
sighed even while he congratulated himself.

"You are a fool, a hopeless fool, Constante," he
growled to himself. "Is it not what you have
asked for — money, wealth to last you all your life,
leisure with which to enjoy every gift of glorious
existence? And the owner of it ready to drop at
your touch like a ripe peach — ugh! — overripe!
That maddening girl with the eyes! — what is it her
concern? Why must I feel her looking at me, even
though I do not see her? And to look at me, too,
with that pretty curl of the lip — the insolence of it!
— but the charm of it! Suppose I should build a
little cabin, such as I could afford, and ask that por-

tionless mademoiselle to enter it with me? Constante, my boy, you are mad, quite mad. Heretofore, however wild your plans may have been, the vision of marriage has never entered into them. It is the free air of this land getting into your brain like wine, but it won't do, it won't do. The commonsense thing for you, Constante, is to ask the widow to go into church some fine morning, and thus settle yourself for life. That will not fulfill your vision of marriage, perhaps, but it will be a very sensible arrangement. And those eyes? Ah, well, they will· serve for a Madonna in the church I am to adorn."

And a few moments later Delogne missed him again, and found time, in the midst of his pleasures, to wonder what contrary wind had struck Constante? To be sure, he was always a fellow of whims, but not whims that left him silent and thoughtful where others were gay.

But Maurice had pleasant things of his own interest to consider, and it was small wonder if he soon forgot his friend's unusual manner, for· Monsieur Lamort had said, when they found themselves alone:

"Come to me to-morrow, my dear Chevalier, and it may be I can help you to unravel this tangled maze to which you are trying to find the clue. At any rate, if you will so far honor me as to trust me with the letters, I will advise you to the best of my ability. In fact, I confess I feel an interest in your welfare, and as it may be in my power to serve you, I beg that you will at any time come to me freely. No, do not thank me. You are of French blood; so

am I. That alone is a bond on a strange shore; and
you will no doubt often hear my house spoken of as
"the place of exiles." So you will be here to-morrow? That is well."

And Maurice congratulated himself that he had
landed in America under a lucky star, for his meetings had been most successful. And that one meeting down there by the hospital near the river, and
the brave yet childish eyes of that girl? He had
but to close his own eyes to see them yet. They had
drifted between himself and many another face that
evening.

But in the midst of his selfish reverie he heard
the faint cry of a woman near by. The musicians
were playing. No one else seemed to note it, and
he turned quickly toward the palms from which the
sound came.

But swift as he was, another was more swift, and
that other was Constante. Where he came from so
quickly was a mystery, but he was there; in his
arms was a slight rose-draped figure and at his feet
a sputtering candle smoldered in its frills of paper,
now ashes. A smell of burnt silk was in the air,
and one wing-like sleeve was gone from Madame
Ninon's gown.

And the closeness of that embrace was explained
by the lady's danger, for without doubt the uncere-
monious grasp had smothered the blazing sleeve,
and perhaps averted a very serious accident.

But at the voice of Maurice the two chief actors in
the little drama drew apart like a couple of culprits,
Constante white as a sheet, but Madame Villette
pink as the gown she wore.

"I — I was frightened, monsieur. I — am so sorry to have troubled you," she at last succeeded in saying, but with her eyes on the floor.

"I beg pardon, mademoiselle, for approaching you so roughly," murmured Constante, meekly, his usually audacious gaze averted. He was so angry with himself because his voice trembled, and he could feel that his face was pale; and there was Maurice, too — Maurice looking at him in wonder. Did it not seem as though the very devils were in league against him? And his tongue seemed tied fast.

But as Maurice was the only one whose wits were under control, it was he who offered his arm to Madame Ninon.

" It is most natural you should be frightened," he assured her. " Permit me to conduct you to a seat. Were you at all burned? Can I do any service for you ? "

"No, no. I am recovered — quite. The wind but blew the gauze of my sleeve across the chandelier. Then it was quick flame, so quick it did not scorch me, and then your friend did arrive; and I am distressed, monsieur — I am indeed. Were his hands not burned? Pray go and see — do not trouble any one about me. I am heartily glad the others did not hear my cry. I will await you here, if you will but learn if he is hurt."

" Hurt? " repeated Constante when Maurice questioned him. Then he opened his hands, looked at them as if for the first time, picked from his sleeve a shred of silk tissue and retained it in his fingers.

"Hurt? No; a bit scorched, but that is all. What concern had she with the candles that she must festoon them with her draperies? *Sacre!* There must be an especial saint in these parts to look after the simple."

"Fie! That is by no means a gallant speech, my friend. Come you, and let her see you are not injured."

"I? Not a step will I budge. She will find plenty to give sympathy without me making longer the list. I am going to the gardens."

And out into the lawn he did go, and no words from his friend could prevent him or gain a reason for his whims; but after a space of loneliness there, and more quiet thought than Constante generally gave any question, the finale of his self-argument was reached, by words not loud, but evidently earnest.

And the words were, "To the devil may go the diamond buckles!"

And having confided that statement to himself, he drew a long breath, as of a man who lets fall a heavy load by the roadside, and walks on without it, free.

When he saw her again she was seated demurely between Maurice and Colonel Durande. Over her shoulders lay a shawl of lace, and the burnt sleeve was never missed, and the serenity of the evening had not been disturbed by the others hearing of her danger.

And farther away across the room sat the lady of the diamond buckles. He was delighted to observe that she was circled by dowagers, and that no one could be expected to approach.

He again felt Ninon's eyes on him. Ah, if she knew he had meant to have those diamond buckles! How grotesque everything was!

He approached Monsieur Lamort and Don Zanalta; the latter was laughing, and held a paper in his hand.

"Yes, it is all satisfactory, and a good business for us both, I suspect," he was saying. "Monsieur Raynel, we may ask you to be witness to a swift bargain we have made this night — a droll thing to do at a feast, but why not?"

"And you say she can dance, this very peculiar slave?" asked Monsieur Lamort; but the other shrugged his shoulders.

"Ninon says so — I have never seen her; but it is no doubt simply extravagant postures such as the Africans use before their idols in their own land. Yet if she were here she should show you. It would be an amusing thing, at least, to see her, and a novelty for the ladies."

"Indeed, yes; we should have thought of it sooner. There are so few diverisons or amusements in this town. Would she were here."

And Constante nearly fell over a great vase of blossoms when close to him a voice said:

"Do you want me, master?"

She came through the curtains of the low window and stood before them — Venda. Her dress was different than that of the day. It was all white; of the coarse linen, it is true, but very white. Her anklets and necklets glinted against the brown skin ; her feet bore sandals bound with white, and about her waist was a girdle of snake-skin.

She stood there impassive as a statue, not looking at Zanalta; but he moved a step farther from her, and clinched his fingers nervously. She was always a ghost to him.

"Your Mistress Ninon says you dance well, Venda," said Monsieur Lamort, kindly. "Your master has offered to sell you to me ; will you dance for my guests in my house?"

"If Venda may speak to the music-players — yes, master."

"As you please. Tell them what you want, and then commence."

She did so. Two of them, a violin player and a guitar player, came forward with her down the room to a sing-song cadence that was no tune, yet the motion to it was rhythmical. And those blacks who swayed down the room in advance of her until they reached the center separated that she might go first. Had they all learned together that same chorus of motion in some strange pagan ceremony? Had they been of those whom she had boasted of buying and selling in her own land? For their eyes looked proud as they touched the strings to the weird cadence and glanced at each other.

And the dance? Well, it was not such as the blacks dance together on the threshing-floors or in the yards of their cabins when the moon comes up. There was the semi-oriental obeisance to things unseen, but on which her eyes appeared to rest.

There was a crooning sound from her lips as she swayed backward and forward, with eyes half-closed, as one who charms and draws to her a thing unwilling. There was a call triumphant as she leaped forward with hand outstretched to claim a victory; and then, as though holding an imaginary hand, she danced — a dance with the writhing grace of a serpent through every movement; the quick dart to right, to left, and then the quick curl of the body; the quick motion of the head thrown back as if for kisses; and ever that one hand poised as though held by one who danced unseen beside her. Then the touch on the guitar grew swifter, stronger; on the strings of the violin more fierce and fast; the waving arms and lithe body whirled with the abandonment of madness before the astonished guests. Then there was a final cry of the music — a "honc!" — from the players, and Venda stood one instant straight as a cypress-tree before them, and then bent low to the master of the house.

"Did I not tell you?" asked Señora Mercedes of her neighbor. "She dances with the devil for a mate, for what human thing could move alone like that? Is it wonder that I dread her in the house?"

And, indeed, the lady found many another to sympathize with her in that notion, for one sorely repented that medicine for rheumatism had been gotten from that same slave to cure a cousin of hers. To be sure, the cousin grew well and sound from it, but who was to tell that the evil one had not a claim on his soul for that cure?

And each asked the other if she had seen any

feature of that shadow dancing beside the witch; and one was found who fancied she saw the hand Venda clasped; another was sure there was the shade of two bodies at Venda's feet; and all shivered a little, and were glad when the more rational music called the white dancers, who one by one drifted away from the corner where the slave stood.

But Monsieur Lamort looked at her curiously, though kindly.

"Well, you have done well, though strangely," he said, and then turned to Don Zanalta, whose face showed wonder, uncertainty, and some complex feeling that made his hands clinch. "So, Don Zanalta, now that she is here, and has danced so bravely for my guests, is she to remain in my house? The bargain, as you said, is a quick one, so why not conclude it? The paper is ready; shall we sign?"

Zanalta threw back his head as though to shake away some unpleasant thought.

"Why not?" he asked. "Monsieur Raynel, will you witness this?"

"My purse, Sebastian," said Monsieur Lamort; and directly it was placed, heavy and clinking, on the table. A sum was counted, that stood in little gold columns side by side, and on which Venda's eyes rested, while her hand crept to her throat as if to choke back a sound that arose there.

Don Zanalta looked at the gold, and stepping forward took the pen Sebastian held ready. Writing his name, he gave the pen to Constante, who signed as a witness, but kept respectfully distant from the creature purchased. As a product of civilization, he did not quite feel comfortable near this thing from the jungles, who danced, but without mirth, like a prisoner loosed from the inferno.

And as he moved away the creature crept nearer Monsieur Lamort. As the gold-pieces clinked one against the other she dropped to her knees, and her lips touched his hand. He had not noticed her, and the touch startled him. He looked down quickly, she must have thought angrily, for she raised her hand as though in pleading.

"Master! it is only that I hear for the first time the sound of gold paid for me. Venda was never before bought with money; but she kneels to say it is music in her ears, because now for all her life she may call you master."

Monsieur Lamort glanced at the strange, whimsical creature with a smile, and he looked across at Zanalta, expecting to see him amused also at the demonstrative speech, but there was no amusement on the Spaniard's face.

He was glaring at his lately sold slave as though to compel her to look up and see the threatening, unspoken *something* in his eyes. Monsieur Lamort did not understand in the least what that something was, though he instinctively felt the savageness of it, and dropping his hand on the woman's white hair he looked questioningly at Zanalta.

But the don quickly recovered himself, swept the last gold-piece into his pocket, and bowing as one who ends a discussion, he followed Constante, who was nearing the dancers. A certain lace-draped form there drew that young man's attention in a manner most distracting. And in the stately music of the minuet all seemed to forget the wild, dark dancer, who knelt near the palms, speechless, at the feet of her new master.

CHAPTER VI.

THE NEXT MORNING.

THE day was yet young when Maurice and Constante bade each other good-morning after their first sleep in the new land. Up from the slow-moving river came a breath of the sea, and beyond its silvered land-line quivered the green of the willows.

"How little we fancied that this exile would lead us amid scenes so oriental as that of last night," remarked Maurice, lazily arousing himself from visions of palms and beauty. "But, Constante, I would give a ring off my finger to know what changed your nature in Monsieur Lamort's house. Why, sir, I had to tax my ingenuity more than once to excuse your lack of appreciation of the beauty about you. I never imagined you could be so indifferent."

Indifferent! Constante looked at him with eyes that had not slept for one moment of the dying night or the growing dawn. What a meager gain sleep would be if in exchange he gave up those waking dreams conjured by two appealing brown eyes and one quick, smothering embrace there in the garden of palms!

So Constante had kept that which was sweetest to him, and made no reply to the badinage of his friend. His thoughts were concentrated on the fact that in six hours he might possibly risk the consternation of the Zanalta household and call, as the dowager had made request. To be sure they would all wonder at his haste, but in the cause of art — ah! that thought was a veritable inspiration. In the service of art one dare be as eccentric as pleases oneself.

Therefore, in exactly six hours by the clock he would venture across the threshold where the beautiful one of the ancient name resided. To be sure he would have to see the lady of the diamonds first, and to be sure he would have to tell many curious tales to excuse a call at breakfast-time; but what mattered all that if in recompense he could see one white hand through a lattice, or meet again those mutinous, wondering brown eyes?

The chevalier glanced at him covertly several times during their preparations for the street. For the first time he found Constante a closed book to him, a surly, frowning person one moment and a dreamy, smiling one the next, but never a word.

"Well," said his friend at last, "if you will not speak, are you able to listen? I have been looking over the letter of my aunt the marquise — heaven be good to her!— but, much as I love her, the letter does not make me happy. Oh, these plots and damnable intrigues of the court!"

"Hist!" and Constante turned with uplifted hand. "Be wary, and less loud with your free speech. Walls may have ears in this land as in the old; and if you should care to return to France, it is as well not to have treason to answer for."

"Treason! Never to France, but to the shifting, vacillating principles of ministration. Who can swear fealty to that which can not assure itself of its right or its stanchness? The ministers are changed as one changes his coat, and each new one has his own little personal ends to secure, let who will suffer. But that I — that my name — ah!"

"What do you mean?"

"Read that. It is infamous."

Constante took the letter, a very long one, and read the sheet pointed to:

"'My dear one — my son — for you are as a son to my heart — I ask your pardon for thus sending you from me in ignorance of my reason. I fear you will blame me for making you seem like a coward in the eyes of others; but be sure I would never have sent you from a battle where the contest was fair. Listen, and forgive me because of my love; and I hold you to your promise to remain where you are until I ask your return, or until the five years have passed.

"'Maurice, none knows more clearly than I that you have nothing to blush for in the friendship of Madame la Princess; but it is none the less true that jealous eyes are on her. She is not one to be influenced by either husband or courtiers from her ideas

8

of right; but—how shall I say it?—there are those
high in power who have striven to draw her into
plans where she could be of use to them. Her husband is one of them. His anger has led him to be
jealous of some one—any one whom he fancies frus-
trates his plans by rendering her impassive to his
influence. Maurice, because of her interest in you,
he has chosen to mark you as chief enemy to his content. And the reason why I have been so strangely
urgent in this matter of your departure; why I send
this letter to you only when I see from the shore that
the sails are set—the reason for all this is that I fear
hourly the gates of the Bastille will be closed on
you; and through the princess I know enough to
be sure it would be useless to contend against the
evidence they have arranged. It has been disclosed
to her as a threat of what will be done if she still
combats them. She has asked time to consider; and
closely watched as she is, has yet managed to tell
me of the plot. Do not think of returning to help
her; it would mean, perhaps, death to you both.
She will always have help from me, and mine will
not injure her in the eyes of her world, as yours
would. Bear that in memory, my son. Any help
you could offer would only strengthen their conspir-
acy against you. She knows you to be innocent, and
sends her prayers to you; heed them, and be content.'"

"Whew!" whistled Constante as he held the paper
at arm's-length; "that suggestion of the Bastille is
quite near enough with the ocean between us. It is

as I thought. Well, my friend, I congratulate you
on getting away from it so easily."

"Congratulate—pouf! You do not then consider
that I will be accused of flight—flight before that
figurehead of a princely house. Ah! it is all ridiculous."

"No"—and Constante spoke with a gravity unusual—"there is nothing ridiculous in the risks
taken by those two ladies to warn you. The mean-
nesses of his royal highness are most extreme;
but his wife comes of too powerful a family for him
to vent his rage openly on her. She will be relieved
to know how entirely you have eluded them—and
more, that you are content to abide by your aunt's
judgment and remain. I advise you to write by
the first ship that sails, and let the marquise see
that you do not rebel against her wishes."

"Well spoken, Constante!—and—I accept your
advice and hers—but—"

"Nay, nay; not a regret, Maurice. Our life-lines
are here; let us make the best of them."

"What has made you a philosopher?" smiled the
other. "Was it the sparkle of those diamonds you
spent last evening so close to? But you are right.
I will seal the good resolution by calling early on
Monsieur Lamort and presenting those papers to
his notice; so for an hour or two you will have to
seek your own amusement after breakfast. Be wise
as you can, and lose no more of your heart to those
Indian boat-paddlers."

And the wily Constante bowed to the advice in
silence, and with never a twinge of conscience let

his friend pass out in ignorance of the heart. weighted dreams flitting through his own head — dreams for the future, a future made luminous by the memory of soft black eyes and a mouth tender in its curves as the mouth of a child. To be sure she might refuse to speak to him, beyond a "thank you" for that episode of the blaze. Well, even so — that spell of love's first illusion was yet with him — he was sure he could adore her forever at a distance.

But once in the ruthless sunshine of the streets, face to face with the lazy yet curious eyes of the natives, he felt the courage of his solitude oozing away at the prospect of meeting also the dame of the diamonds — perhaps having to even woo her to win the other.

Don Zanalta was not at home, by black Gourfi's statement — a fact for which Monsieur Raynel was grateful. It is so much more difficult to explain one's enthusiasm to a man — women are more sympathetic, especially if the enthusiast be handsome.

But Madame Villette — the ladies? Oh, yes — the ladies were home; and even Gourfi's face expressed the thought that it was a strange hour to be anywhere else — breakfast was so lately over.

"Ask Madame Villette if she can grant me an interview so early, or if not, to let me know at what hour I may return and see her."

"And the name, master?"

"Constante Raynel."

Madame Villette gave a little gasp when the message was brought. He — so early, and so — so determined to be seen! Ah, this was delicious and

unusual — all the more delicious because Donna
Zanalta had not yet been seen without the walls of
her chamber that day ; so it would be a tête-à-tête —
it even seemed an adventure in her too prosy life.

And you may be sure Madame Ninon did not
leave her chamber without very critical glances at
her image in the mirror. Her prettiest slippers
were donned, her most delicate-tinted scarf, and, as
a crowning charm, she wore on the open-throated
white gown a cluster of yellow roses.

And Constante — the hypocrite - had discovered on the wall that long-since-painted portrait of
the Spanish lady, before which he was posed when
he heard that little tap, tap of dainty heels on the
waxed floor.

He turned with his most impressive bow, with
eyes drooped in diffidence most charming.

"Madame Villette !" murmured the rascal, as
though he had waited ages longing for her face.
Then his eyes traveled up from her slipper-tips
along the childish figure to the adorable face, and
suddenly he stood erect and confused. "Mademoiselle !" he stammered, " I — pardon me —"

She smiled, and reached out her hand as a friend
might. He touched but the tips of her fingers, and
looked at her.

"Pardon you that you served me last night, and
that you so kindly come to ask after me to-day, monsieur?" she said, teasingly. "Do you think, then,
that you committed a fault when you smothered
those flames? But pray be seated ; and though you
have answered neither of my other questions, I am

going to ask another. Why do you call me both Madame Villette and mademoiselle?"

"Because, mademoiselle —"

" Nay — madame."

"Madame ?"

Was the handsome stranger mad? She was really startled at his wild eyes and sharp tones.

" Madame — yes, certainly," she answered, with a certain soothing intonation. "Had you forgotten? It is so easy for a stranger to forget titles where he meets many new faces; and then, again, there are those who think they compliment by calling a lady mademoiselle. Perhaps when my hair grows gray I too will want to hear it; but just yet I am madame."

Madame! Constante looked at her stupidly. He wondered if he had been drunk or crazy last night that he had muddled things so, or interpreted them wrongly. Madame! Then she was a wife — some man's wife! For one instant he felt that the floor was slipping from under his chair. Then with an effort he spoke, and kept his voice steady:

" It is unpardonable of me to have forgotten anything concerning you, madame, but your good heart has divined the cause of my mistake. I fancied you were mademoiselle, and your relative madame."

"You are correct only in her case. She is also madame, or señora, and a widow. I see you pay attention to that painting of her. As an artist, you of course are critical, and we can show you few treasures except some pieces, curious only because of their age; but my aunt tells me we may hope now to have some worthy work for our church since you have come. The news is welcome. And do you paint portraits too?"

Paint portraits! Ah, that dreamed-of Madonna with her eyes! She madame — a man's wife? Then he bowed low and found his voice.

"You are pleased to be gracious to me, madame, that you show interest in my work. Yes, I have painted portraits, and hope to begin again on your shores. The lady — madame, your aunt — gave me permission to call to-day and hold converse with her concerning works of art. My enthusiasm must be my excuse for so early a visit."

"Your enthusiasm for art?"

Almost his eyes betrayed him, as he felt they must have betrayed him there in the room of the palms last night. And she a wife! It would not have been the first wife to whom Master Constante had uttered love-vows with as little provocation—and she was so alluring with the color and perfume of yellow roses about her; but the confusion of her revelations was yet over him, and his eyes avoided hers.

"Yes, madame; even a wandering artist must have some ideal that serves as an anchor — a mistress to whom he swears fealty; and art is gracious enough to accept all devotion."

"But art draws to herself so much that we miss in the more human world — as a mistress she is to be envied."

"Nay, nay, madame; she but soothes the discarded hearts, and recompenses them for the floutings of the world. She accepts so many who would find no welcome in a lady's bower."

She glanced at him with softly closing eyes and a mutinous *mouc*. A most eloquent glance for a wife to give, thought poor Constante. Alas for his Madonna !

"And your friend, Chevalier Delogne, is he also devoted to art, and thus self-exiled from converse with us poor ordinary mortals? I trust myself to say 'no' to that, for he was not too far in the clouds to know us all last night — and even remember our names."

"Madame, what better excuse would a man need for hearing nothing — remembering nothing — of the world about him than that he had once looked upon your face?"

"Very pretty — very pretty indeed, Monsieur Raynel. Would the fine ladies of Versailles pardon forgetfulness for a speech like that?"

"Surely; especially if their own hearts told them they had not been forgotten — that it was only the light of their eyes that had banished from one's memory all titles, or conventional bonds of the world. You are pleased to be very unforgiving to me, madame."

Ninon thought him handsome enough to be granted absolution for any crime. A winning face is a wordless voucher for merit — to most women. But she only smiled and gathered her scarf about her.

"Come, monsieur. On the subject of art or of memory, we do not seem to agree very well. Perhaps on the safer one of flowers we may comprehend each other better. The gardens of Orleans may seem novel to a stranger. Will you walk in ours?"

Would Adam walk through Eden at Eve's call on that first day of her creation? And Constante followed quite as willingly, but wishing vainly that some one would appear an instant and call her clearly by name and then take himself away again immediately; for try as he would he could not settle in his mind her station and that of her aunt. One was señora and one was madame, it appeared; one was a widow and one was a female Crœsus. But either Villeneuve or his own stupidity had confused him much, but he dare not expose himself to her raillery by further questioning; and he had not yet heard any mention made of " monsieur."

And how gay she was; seemingly care-free as the birds among the magnolia-boughs. A wife — he had seen no wives like her; so girlish, so alluring, yet with so much of provoking innocence in her eyes. Should he ever be able to paint all that?

" This side of the rose-walk is the special province of my aunt," she remarked, smilingly; "of course you will want to become acquainted with that."

" Most assuredly — some day when its chatelaine is gracious enough to conduct me; but is there never a bower of your own in all this glow of color — or am I for my sins forbidden entrance to it?"

" Have you sins?" she asked, unbelievingly; " if so, of course I shall find you a retreat for prayer. Come; it is where I used to go when I was naughty and had been told to spend an hour in thoughts of penitence."

" Is it so? Then rather let us seek a place less sanctified. You went there for prayer, but I, alas!

must confess that the sins oftenest to my charge are
those of which I can not repent, and such a soul can
hope for little grace."

" Ah, monsieur, are you then serious?   But if you
would but try to repent, if you would but say you
were sorry, surely absolution would be granted you."
And the hypocrite felt a wild temptation to cover
her hands with kisses as she looked up at him, but
he shook his head.

" Nay, madame, I fear not; for only this morning
I begged pardon for an unwilling offense — begged
with both heart and lips, but my confessor gave me
no hope of forgiveness."

Ninon looked incredulous, yet full of sympathy
for his sorrow.

" But what a hard heart to turn you away hopeless.   Was the offense then so grievous?"

" Most grievous."

" Yet if you repent —"

" So I hoped, madame ; but she —"

" She ? "

" The lady who thought me unpardonable — the
lady whose name I had forgotten."

Fairly caught, Madame Ninon laughed aloud —
laughter filled with the music of the universe to
Constante ; but the merry sound reached other ears
than his, for a window opened near them, and through
the lattice the visitor caught a glimpse of a white-
draped figure of ample proportions and heard a voice.

" Madame Villette !" it demanded, as from some
one within —" Madame Ninon Villette laughing
like that out there in the garden and entertaining

gentlemen ere people of quality have yet had coffee
or prayers! Give me my gown this moment, Pepito! What!—you can't find it? That is some of that
Venda's work. I doubt if we shall find aught for a
good seven days after her departure — the beast!
Come now — move quickly! I will see this gay
gallant who laughs under my windows, so —"

Her kinswoman did not wait for the conclusion of the sentence, but beckoning to Monsieur
Raynel she sped through the arches of shrubbery
and perfume of roses until they reached a little gate
at the side of the garden, and halted, flushed and
breathless, listening for pursuing footsteps as a
naughty child who feared punishment.

"Sometime when the day has grown older, monsieur, I beg that you will return to talk of art and its
charms to my respected aunt; but if you come
earlier than noon I warn you that for a full hour
you will have only myself (*only*, oh, Ninon!) to talk
to, and it seems we do not agree well. So I dismiss
you most abruptly, lest you have to take your share
of a scolding, and art might be the loser. Adios!
I will see you again when you come to paint the
portrait of Señora Zanalta."

Surely this was a most intimate parting for two
people who did not agree well. It was so sweetly
puzzling to Raynel that the pleasure of it brought a
pain in its wake — she was a wife!

He looked at her with curious scrutiny in his eyes.
She was so much engaged in listening that she did
not note it. It was all so delightful to her — a real
adventure; and the handsome fellow was plainly

loath to leave her. She was smiling at the certainty
of it, when he spoke:

"If I might hope to do your face as well,
madame?"

"Mine—my portrait? Well, perhaps. Yes, I
think my brother would like it; we shall see."

"I am grateful." But his voice despite his thanks
had a certain hardness and directness as he looked
at her. It was preposterous of course, but he could
not endure uncertainty any longer. "And would
monsieur also care for one? Shall I meet him? I
think I have not yet had that honor."

"Monsieur—?"

"Pardon me—your husband?"

"*Mon Dieu!*" And she made a little quick sign of
the cross. "Monsieur Villette! Yes, I truly hope
you and he will some day meet. It would be well
for you, as he was always a good man."

"Was?"

"Certainly, Monsieur Raynel; and in Paradise,
where one lives with angels instead of poor human
creatures, he is surely no less excellent."

"Paradise!"—and all the green garden swam
before Constante's eyes. "Oh, madame, pardon me!
You will think me a heartless animal."

"Not at all"—and Madame Ninon's eyes had a
twinkle in them not brought there by the memory
of that soul in the celestial regions—"only a man
who is curious—"

"Madame!"

"My aunt is coming! Adios, Monsieur Raynel."

CHAPTER VII.

DENISE OF THE CONVENT.

AFTER the noon hour many people were astir in the streets that day. It was a holiday, and the creoles, eager as children, never missed a day of leisure or of merrymaking. Gay-turbaned negresses rustled their "bettermost" petticoats for the admiration of their kind, and down by the river where the trees grew they gathered and gathered toward the sun's sinking, waiting for the cool when the music would come for their dancing under the stars — their music, in which there never was blended the sound of a drum. That instrument had for so long been the signal by which the masters warned each other of an uprising among their blacks, that it was never used in their merrymakings; the deep, thunderous tones had too often borne startling messages to the hearts in the black lands, messages of war and devastation.

Chevalier Delogne walked again on the street by the river, finding all the strange new life most interesting, but keeping a sharp lookout for Raynel, who had someway drifted into other channels — on the alert for artistic material, supposed his friend.

He heard his name spoken, and turning found Don Zanalta at his elbow, smiling most pleasantly.

"What, Chevalier, have you already smelled out the corners where the most amusing sport may be had? You make quick strides; but, after all, it is tame beside Paris."

"No doubt." And the stranger's voice took on a certain curtness. He did not like much this powdered, perfumed Spaniard with the affected strut that had in it the airs and graces of a dandy, or of a woman who is vain. But his eyes had in them no feminine gentleness. They were keen and alert as they noted the wild whirls of the colored creoles, especially the bare cream-like arms of one of the women classed among the "brown people."

"Not bad — that," he remarked, appreciatively. "Anything darker has too much of coarseness in feature; but those yellow ones ape all the fine manners of their mistresses — that is what makes them so amusing."

"To tell the truth," remarked the chevalier, "they do not appear to me in the least amusing — their eyes look to me pathetic as those of driven cattle."

"That is because some of the prettiest are looking at you sentimentally," laughed the other. "Oh, it does not take them long to spy out a face and figure like yours. I assure you, you will not have to sue for favors."

Maurice looked at him in amazement. He had dropped a mask worn the night before, perhaps thinking to fall more quickly into friendship with youth by the use of flattery and allusions that would prove alluring to many a stranger in search of adventure.

"I am not looking for favors," he returned, care-

lessly, "but for my friend Monsieur Raynel. He is
sure to be where music sounds."

"I saw him across there but a few minutes ago.
He had a pencil and paper on which he seemed to
be fixing the outlines of those three red men who
lean against the wall, but never sing and never
dance like the black slaves. In truth your friend
has strange fancies to picture those sullen slave men
instead of the bright faces of the brown girls."

"Strange fancies — yes, many a one ; but I rather
like this one of his, for those Indian men make a
peculiar picture as they stand there, watching. Does
not the taller belong to Monsieur Lamort? I think I
remember seeing his face in the grounds there this
morning."

Don Zanalta laughed shortly. "That proves
nothing," he made reply. "All our slaves in the colony flock to the door of Lamort if they have a
grievance to moan over — and it is seldom they
have not a pretense of one. But I think he owns no
Indian slaves, for he has been trying to influence
the cabildo to set free all the red men yet in bond-
age. However, it has not been done."

The two had by this time sauntered to a seat,
where they disposed themselves, and Don Zanalta
tendered his snuff-box to the young man, and used
it freely himself, in the same delicate, dandified
manner peculiar to him. Maurice had heard him
spoken of as a clever and subtle mover in the circle
of politics, but was inclined to think the reputation
very easily won as he noted his little affectations.

Yet he of course was well versed in knowledge of the new land, having lived there so many years.

"And why set the red slaves free and not the blacks?" asked the stranger. And again the townsman smiled patiently.

"The blacks — *sacré!* No one has dared mention that in the ears of the governor. It would mean revolution — no less. And as for the reds — well, there are not many of them now. Strange how they die out in captivity, instead of increasing like the Africans. Stranger still when one considers that it is they and not the Africans who are native here; so it can not be the climate that kills them. But they die nevertheless, and die as they live — silent, amid all the music. And Monsieur Lamort has unearthed a neglected declaration of O'Reilly's that said the inhabitants of Louisiana must prepare to emancipate the red slaves — the natives of the soil."

"And the declaration has never been enforced, or made into a law?"

"Oh, no; it is waiting for the final decision of the king, and his royal wisdom has not yet led him in the direction of that action."

The chevalier glanced at him quickly to see if there was cynicism in the face as well as the words, but could perceive none. The eyes of the Spaniard were roaming idly over the groups already dispersing, for the permit of the slaves seldom allowed their absence after nine o'clock — only the free people were remaining.

"But has it not been several years since the

governor, General O'Reilly, made laws for the colony?"

Don Zanalta looked surprised at the stranger's persistence.

"Yes, certainly; twenty-five years, I think it is — a lifetime to some of them. But do you too, monsieur, intend taking up the study of the slave trade? You will find it irksome, I fear."

"No; but if, as you say, Monsieur Lamort has business with such questions, I shall doubtless hear more of them. This morning we agreed that I am to be his private secretary."

"Do you tell me so? Well, well, I must congratulate you on having fallen in with so good a general. A wonderful man is Victor Lamort. You will doubtless learn much from him; but do not let him teach you to upset the slave laws. I, for one, have trouble enough with mine now. But you must come to my house, Chevalier. A member of Monsieur Lamort's household is always welcome to us; and you, believe me, my young friend, are welcome for your own sake."

Maurice had but time to murmur his thanks when Zanalta arose abruptly and stood looking across the moving people to one figure walking alone and quickly. Following his glance, the young man felt his heart leap as he saw a gray gown and caught sight of a white sleeve.

"Pardon me; I wish to speak to some one," said Zanalta, and walked swiftly across the little open space. There was more of decision and less of affectation in his gait, and he was going to speak to

9

the one whom Maurice in his thoughts called St. Denise.

She raised her eyes as he came close, and looked quickly around as if to turn aside ; but it was too late, and an instant afterward he was bending with head uncovered before her.

"Ah, mademoiselle, the saints are at last kind to me. Do you know I have watched each morning for your accustomed visits to the poor, and only to-day did I learn that you came no more in the morning? But you must not go alone at nightfall, my child. Let me carry your basket."

"Monsieur"— and the voice of the girl was tremulous—"monsieur, perhaps you mean to be kind, but I have not come out at nightfall that I might find some one to carry my basket, and in all this town there is none that will molest me, so I need no cavalier. I have the honor to bid you good-night."

"Nay, nay, child ; let me walk beside you, at least. It is not seemly that a maiden should venture in this quarter alone."

"And less so that a gentleman of rank should escort the messenger of the convent. I am safe alone, monsieur. Pardon the plainness of my words, but I am much distressed that you — that you persist in meeting me when — when —"

"When you have said 'no' to all the advantages offered you. Ah, Mademoiselle Denise —"

"I beg you, sir — no more!" And her eyes were both frightened and angry. "I shall never again walk alone on my errands if no hour of the day is to be sacred from these persecutions. By what right — "

"By the right of love," he murmured; "the strongest right — the greatest force the world knows, my charming saint — and it will yet draw you to meet my thoughts. Ah! I shall claim sweet words from you some day for the smiles you deny me to-night. Come, now — "

But the girl had caught sight of a face in the scattering groups, a black woman whom she knew, and she slipped quickly to her side.

"Here, Maum Rosy, carry my basket and walk with me to the Place des Invalides."

"Hi! ma'm'zelle; Rosy — him got go home this minute — him got — "

"Come!" And the girl's fingers closed over the dark arm with compelling force. "Adieu, monsieur!" And she swept him a courtesy with a mockery strange in one of the gray habit, and walked rapidly away with the protesting Rosy. To Don Zanalta nothing was left but to return her bow courteously, and none in passing would have guessed the small drama enacted there before them all.

Only the Chevalier Delogne stood apart and noted the brief pantomime. He envied Zanalta the acquaintance permitting him to halt and speak to her in an evidently confidential manner; but that mocking bow puzzled him.

He was still standing there when the Don sauntered back, looking serene and unruffled.

"A charming child, that," he remarked, with a gesture in the direction he had just come. "Too bad that her popularity won by charity and good works is having a frivolous influence over her. It is never well for a community to let any one creature fancy himself a necessity."

"But she seems to be really so to those poor folk by the shore."

"You know her, then, already?" asked Zanalta, slowly, and eying him with a glance that was suddenly guarded. "You know this Mademoiselle Denise?"

"I know her name and face, monsieur, and from a crippled sailor we heard last evening a hint of her virtues; but I have not the honor of being known by the lady."

"Lady! Well, she is scarcely given that title; in fact she is an unclassed sort of being — a protégée of the good nuns, and intended, I believe, for their order. Too dull a fate for so pretty a face, eh?"

"Not if the convent is one of the gates to heaven. Is not the world called to give its best to God? What fate more tranquil than the life she would live under the sisterhood of Mary."

But, quietly as he spoke, a chivalrous protest arose in his breast against the force of his words. So fair, so girlish; and the cross is so cold on young hearts.

Don Zanalta smiled and twirled his walking-stick jauntily.

"Very wise decision if made by a graybeard, my dear Chevalier, but not very human when uttered by lips of twenty-five. Nay, do not blush; you will outgrow your age, and haply also such cold-blooded disposal of beauty."

At that moment a man approached who had been standing a little way off watching those two for several minutes. He looked like a sailor as to dress, and half white, half Indian as to race. He spoke Spanish, and said :

"Pardon, Don Diego Zanalta, but I bear a message that the Sea Gull rests among the willows to-night, and her captain asks company of yourself and friends." There was the slightest sign of hesitation in his manner as he glanced at Delogne.

"Dolt!" muttered Zanalta, drawing the man a little aside. "Why speak aloud until you know who listens?"

The other shrugged his shoulders. "When the words of France are spoken by these people who pass, he opens his ears and smiles; when Spanish is spoken, he is in the dark and the trail is lost. I watched him; I know."

"When did Rochelle come back from the Alabamas?"

The shadow of a smile touched the face of the half-breed.

"This day ere the sun rose out of the sea."

"And goes when?"

"Who knows?" returned the other with indifference. "Maybe this night, maybe next year. Have you a message?"

"Yes." But he looked disturbed, and hesitated. "To-night of all nights; it is most unfortunate — this coincidence. Yet must I see Rochelle. He is as whimsical as royalty itself, and — yes, I must see him. An hour late perhaps, because of this other; but Gourfi can keep her guarded till my return. It is the best I can do." Then from these ruminations he aroused himself to look at the waiting half-breed. "Say yes. I may not be early, but I will be there. You comprehend?"

The man replied by the slightest inclination of his head and a lazy droop of lids over his watchful Indian eyes. Whoever he served had not taught him to be servile.

"One would think I held audience on the street Bienville, since even my moments of rest must be distracted here by business," Zanalta remarked in an apologetic way, turning to Delogne. "And have you not yet discovered Monsieur Raynel?"

"I think I see him now, and coming this way."

"Then I shall feel the less regret at leaving you, Chevalier, when I see you with as merry a companion as your friend, and I have some matters that need attention this evening; so, adios."

"Ah, there you are!" called Constante, and in a moment was bowing to Zanalta. "What, monsieur, do you withdraw at my approach?"

"To my regret," responded the older man. "My time is limited this evening; but there will be others with better fortune for me, no doubt, and on the earliest night at your convenience I should be pleased if you would dine at my house, gentlemen."

"You are kind," began Delogne; but Zanalta checked him with a gesture and a smile.

"Kind!—say, rather, lonely. And the ladies will also be glad of your coming, I promise you. My sister-in-law is already much interested in the art-work Monsieur Raynel is to produce here. I shall give myself the pleasure of calling on you to-morrow."

They exchanged bows, and he was about to turn away, when Constante seemed to recall another cause for delay.

"Ah, monsieur, just a moment of your time. Pray tell me who one Capitaine Rochelle of the Sea Gull is ; I am curious regarding that character."

Diego Zanalta wheeled about and gave him a look as though demanding whether the question was prompted by insolence or ignorance, then smiled in a hard way that was half-mocking.

"I regret that I am unable to satisfy your curiosity on this point, monsieur, but unfortunately my acquaintance does not embrace every smuggler and night-sailing vessel on our waters. In fact it would take a man with no other employment to keep informed on those troublesome points, and as a newcomer I should not advise you to become entangled with their mysteries. Again, *buenas noches!*"

Constante stared after him with wide eyes, and then whistled in a manner lacking dignity.

"What think you of that speech, Maurice?"

"Nothing. Why should I? You have, it appears, made inquiry of some one whom gentlemen are not supposed to know. You have, as oft before, been indiscreet, and Don Zanalta resents it. However, he will learn ere long not to lay so much stress on your words. But who is this debatable one of whom you speak?"

"Rochelle? Oh, I have been talking to some old

sailors who sprawl across the green over there. They were telling me wonderful things of sea and land about here (while I paid for their wine), and among other things, of the Sea Gull, a little vessel, seemingly English, that appears like a phantom to the superstitious; never lays in known harbors, yet is seen fitfully on the waters; is supposed to deal in wine, but none knows its customers; is said to have an Indian crew, yet its commander is a white man. Some think him the prince of evil because of his various knowledge. One man there swore to his conviction that he was Bowles, the white chief of the Creek Nation — Bowles who was also an actor, an artist, an American tory, an ex-British officer, and the commander of a piratical crew which had proven most disastrous to American and Spanish stores."

"But how could it be this many-sided Bowles when the Spanish authorities had secured him through some of his treacherous followers, and even now he is captive in the castle at Havana; and indeed did we not hear of late that he had died there — a prisoner?"

"True enough, but there are those about who seem to think that that many-sided adventurer was something supernatural; and just as he disappeared from these shores there came this other one, who is just as strange, from the description they give of him — a man who handles the cards as though the devil marked the winning ones for his hands, a man whom no one has seen in the daylight, and who makes music on a viol as though the angels taught

him. He also can speak as the red men speak ; but
the one difference between him and Bowles is that no
one can tell of actual crime he has done, therefore
he is not called for by the law. But his mysterious
coming and going can not have an innocent meaning ; and the folk here just think he is the devil —
the devil who was Bowles and is now Rochelle."

" By our fortune, now, but you seem to have been
studying very closely the history of New World
adventurers the past couple of hours ; no wonder
Don Zanalta was not flattered by your question.
And what for this evening, Constante — to the café ?
Our days together will be few now, as I am promised to Monsieur Lamort for a season, so we must
make the best of our time."

" We can not do that in the crowd of the café.
No, let us stroll — so! I am too restless for a seat
at a table. I want to move — to walk — to fly if I
could ! "

" Indeed ! Well, when you take flight you will
leave your intended address, no doubt. Could it by
any chance be the house of the gentleman who just
left us ? "

" How did you come to guess that house ? " demanded Constante ; and Delogne smiled at the half-
assent in the words.

" How ? My friend, do you forget that you passed
all the evening at her side — that she was the only
lady you noticed ? Whatever the rest of the assembly thought, I was convinced that you were at last
serious and had concluded to be no longer a mere
poacher in the field of love."

Constante stared at his friend as though mystified, and then smiled in a forced, half-hearted way.

"Oh, you thought so, did you? And the lady —tell me what you think, now, for the one who looks on sees best how the game goes, you know — think you she will approve — will —"

"Approve! Certainly, Constante, you are grow-ing modest when you doubt your own attractions. I venture to say she is ready to say yes to you in less than a fortnight. Does that not cheer you?"

"Immeasurably," groaned Constante. "Oh, but you are a helpful friend to cheer a poor devil when he is in trouble."

"Trouble! You surprise me! But of course they are heart troubles — the only kind you ever have. But if it is not that comfortable Donna Zanalta, then you will have to confess, for I have not been observing you closely for the past few hours, and am ignorant of the latest. Pray whose wife have you been swearing devotion to now?"

"Maurice, I beg you not to walk brutally over my feelings in that fashion! I was going to confide in you, but I will reconsider the subject until you are in a more sympathetic mood — and I'll repay you," he added, maliciously, "by telling you the other ninety-nine theories I heard about Monsieur Ro-chelle and the Sea Gull."

Delogne suddenly contracted his brows and made a gesture to his friend for silence. He was trying to think what other voice had uttered that name, the Sea Gull, in his hearing. Not the voice of Con-stante, but a lazy, yet melodious, voice — a voice with

certain peculiar intonations — the voice of the half-
Indian who spoke Spanish.

"Well," demanded his friend, "I beg permission to
speak when your disposition will warrant it."

"Constante, have you observed that small as this
colony is, it contains several problems to test our
wit?"

"Ah! have I not? One alone have I found that I
will joyously devote my life to solve."

The dusk had fallen — the odorous darkness of the
South-lands. The stars were out here and there in
the warm sky, but clouds scurrying up from the sea
effaced their glitterings; and the unlighted street
was very shadowy, save at times when a sedan-
chair with a lantern on its poles would be borne by
trotting negroes across the avenues, and they, few
and far between, looked liks fireflies.

Afar off, along the bank of the river, sounded the
strings of a guitar — sweet tones of the South and of
night. Slave-voices sang somewhere in the dark
where boats were moored, and the sounds blended
harmoniously with the warm wind under the stars.

The two friends halted, and smiled into each other's
eyes, and by silent mutual consent leaned against an
old live-oak and listened. The new land, with its
music and strange shadings, its adventurers and
grande seigneurs, and withal its remoteness, was as a
land of romance to each.

Standing there so, without words, they listened to
the charming sounds of the night, and noted the
approach of a small chattering black boy and the
gowned form of a priest, who passed within arm's-

reach of the two in the shadows, yet evidently did
not see them, intent no doubt on some soul near
death or in sore sickness toward whom he was
hastening.

"That monk is but a part of the picture," remarked
Constante. "How well he fits into this scheme of
starlight, and far soft music. He brings me fancies
of a possible señorita under a rose-trellis, and a possible Fra Lippo hastening to a tryst there."

"It requires but little to start your fancies in that
direction; but have you noticed where we are? I
did not until now; this is surely one side of the
grounds belonging to Monsieur Lamort's dwelling.
You see it touches three streets."

"And a very snug abode for this land of the savage people. Ah, that palm-room! No wonder my
fancies turn readily to trysts here. The very atmosphere suggests adventure."

"Hist! look at that!"

"That" was a form approaching, but not in the
frank manner of the priest. It was slipping along
in the shadows, and halting every now and then to
look backward, as though waiting for some one. As
it came nearer, yet without sound, they perceived
it was some one barefooted, therefore a negro; and
the stealthy manner of the man made the two in the
shadow fairly hold their breath that they might discover what purpose he had in view — theft, perhaps,
as he was approaching the dwelling of Monsieur
Lamort in that suspicious manner.

No other house was very near; gardens and
empty spaces lay around; the nearest building —

and that distant — was the place of the nuns, where a light glimmered at the gate ; so surely it must be the property of Monsieur Lamort on which the man had designs, and from his manner he was evidently awaiting a comrade.

They were quite sure of this fact when far down the street another form was seen approaching, walking rapidly, but wearing shoes — evidently a woman, or else a man wearing a long black cloak. At that distance in the darkness they could not be certain which it was, but one thing they could be sure of was that a third figure, resembling the first, and also barefoot, was following close behind ; and with every moment the three conspirators, if such they were, were drawing closer together. The first to arrive stood in the shadows, awaiting the others.

Three little notes like the call of a drowsy night-bird sounded through the silence from where he was, and the two strangers in the darkness by the live-oak felt it was a signal to the others that he waited.

But only the one who came last seemed to heed it, and at the sound his stealthy stride changed to a run. Because of his bare feet he made no noise, and he could almost touch the gowned figure when that waiting one stepped swiftly from the shadows.

Then there was a smothered scream, a drapery quickly flung over struggling arms, and in less than half a minute the second figure was but a shapeless bundle of dark cloth, being borne lightly in the arms of the two blacks, who fairly ran across the street and directly toward the live-oak tree.

"Get to boat, quick!" muttered the first one, who seemed the leader in the affair; "place all quiet now, but quick!"

And then he uttered a snarl of rage as he was obliged to halt in the midst of his haste. The sword of Chevalier Delogne, glittering in the dim starlight, barred the passage of the blacks and their burden.

"Lay down that person, whoever it be!" he commanded.

But the black had no notion of obeying. He caught his load on one arm and with the other whipped out a rapier, with which he lunged forward blindly, without effect, however, for his bared arm was pierced with that long glittering wand of steel, and the weapon fell from his useless hand.

At the same moment Constante, though wearing no sword, fell on the other black with his cane, to such purpose that the two rogues, seeing a second champion make his appearance, concluded they had run into an ambush, and throwing their motionless burden at the feet of the strangers fled into the shadows and disappeared in the direction of the river.

The Chevalier sheathed his sword, and Constante picked up the rapier.

"If the blacks of the country carry blades like this it must be that they have gold in their purses, or else most generous masters," he observed. "What say you now of adventure, Maurice, and what think you we will find in this wrapping of sail-cloth?"

Maurice did not reply; he was on his knees beside the swathed figure, unwrapping quickly as he could the smothering stuffs, until out of the folds a limp white hand fell upon his own.

"A lady, Constante! *Mon Dieu!*— my heart told me so. Quick! here, unwind this as I lift her. Heavens! it is she — and she is dead — they have smothered her!"

But Constante was the wiser, and shook his head as he bent over her.

"No, indeed; she will live to see her own grandchildren, be sure of it. They have frightened her into unconsciousness, and small wonder — but it is not death."

"Then come! At Moniseur Lamort's we will find help for her. Ah! the black fiends, to touch you — you!"

"May I assist?" began Constante; but the Chevalier made no reply, only arose from the ground with the unconscious form in his arms, and bore it swiftly through the grounds to the door of Monsieur Lamort — an open door, through which he strode without ceremony.

A slave — the new slave, Venda — came forward at the sound of feet on the tiled floor, and raised her hands with a gesture of wonder at the sight of the young stranger bearing a lady in his arms; but with ready comprehension she led the way to a couch.

"How can I serve, master?" she asked, as he laid his charge on the soft cushions. "Is it sickness — is it hurt?"

"A fright — that, I think, is all. Care for her quickly — tell your master — ah! do anything but let her lie there looking like death!"

Venda called for a black girl to bring water, another to bring wine; and in the midst of her work of chafing the girl's hands she looked up at Chevalier Delogne with a look of comprehension in her seldom-smiling eyes.

"You drink also of the wine," she nodded — "all your face white like lady's. Lady will live; its heart beats good now. Master comes; master knows medicine — him tell you."

And just at that moment Monsieur Lamort entered the room, drawing back at first when he saw strangers, and then recognizing Delogne he came forward, with surprise and interest at sight of the figure on the couch.

"A lady, and one in the dress of a nun!" he exclaimed. "Well may our local government be called faulty when such a one dare be abducted ere darkness is well over our streets. Venda, you know most people — who is this?"

"Master, she is the Convent Child."

"But there are many children under the care of the good nuns, and they all have names."

Venda bowed her head.

"All have names," she agreed; "this one is called Sister, and Denise, and the old people call her the Convent Child."

Monsieur Lamort's eyes were bent on the unconscious face with a strange baffled expression, as one who tries to recall some elusive memory.

"A most lovely maiden," was all he said. "Care for her well, Venda." And then he turned to speak to the gentlemen. But Chevalier Delogne was walking to and fro with noticeable anxiety, casting every now and then a look toward the privileged couch, and scarce seeming to see the host or think of conversation.

And the older man must have had a wondrous amount of comprehension of even youth's leanings, for he raised his brows in a comical way and met the glance of Constante with a smile.

"Ah, well! Jove might be pardoned, for she is a wondrous fair maid," he remarked; "and now tell me how it occurred. Have you anything by which you could identify those blacks?"

"Not I. To me every man of them is as a twin to the last one I saw, save when one is either very large or very small, very old or very young."

"And they fled — whither?"

"Across your grounds and toward the river. Now I remember me, they said 'to the boat.' Faith! I might have followed them. I did not have the lady to carry."

The lady was reviving under Venda's hands, and Monsieur Lamort drew near as she spoke.

"Ah! those wretches! have they brought me here? You are his slave — you —"

Her head dropped back weakly, and Venda gave her a little wine despite her shrinking murmurs. Monsieur Lamort saw she was still frightened, and spoke.

"Those wretches you fear have been beaten away by these gentlemen," he explained. "Chevalier, will you come forward and reassure the lady? She seems uncertain as to the hands she has fallen into."

10

Maurice did so, blushing with pleasure as her gaze rested on him, and seemed to say, "I trust you."

"Mademoiselle, be quite sure that in the house of Monsieur Lamort you are safe. This is he. He is glad to serve you, as are we all. Can you but give us a hint as to who your enemy is, that we may punish him?"

She turned her eyes to the face of Venda. "You — you," she muttered, unsteadily. That white-crowned head seemed to hold her attention closer than the others.

"This is Venda, my slave," explained Lamort. "Do not be afraid; she is kind of heart."

"I know," said Denise, more clearly; "but she is the voudou woman — she is the slave of Don Zanalta."

Her voice had a ring of accusation; but Monsieur Lamort seemed not to notice it.

"No; until yesterday it was so, but now she is of my household, and is at your service."

She breathed a little sigh of content, and closed her eyes for a moment, but the color was once more creeping into her lips.

"And I am really in the house of the powerful Lamort?" she asked at last, with a sort of childish pride. "How strange that seems!"

"Only the manner of your coming seems strange to me," answered the man she called powerful. "My house will always be honored on the days when the garb of your order enters it, mademoiselle. But you seem to know every one and his calling here."

"I know you," she assented. "They say you are pitiless to the rich in the court of law, but I only know you as one who is good to the sick, and who gives money to the convent that the poor may be cared for. Ah! monsieur, I have divided many loaves among the infirm — loaves paid for with your gold. You are in our prayers often; it is not strange that I should know you."

"Then am I more blest than I dreamed of, my child." And he bowed as to a princess, and touched her fingers with his lips, an act that sent a rosy flush over her pale face. "You give me strength to withstand all the thunderbolts of the nobles when you speak so graciously of the little I have done for your poor."

"Young mistress drink more wine — little bit?" queried Venda; but the girl shook her head, and her eyes passed over the slave and rested on the two younger men.

"I think I can rise now, and I should like to thank those gentlemen," she said, shyly; but the effort to stand was ineffectual, and Monsieur Lamort gently reseated her among the cushions.

"Not yet, mademoiselle — one does not get over a smothering so quickly; and as for these gentlemen who have been so fortunate as to serve you, they are quite ready to receive their reward — here at your feet."

With a gesture he brought them nearer, and Constante bent low as his name was uttered.

"I assure you, mademoiselle, we did not half enough in your case. I should at least have brought

you those slave-heads on a salver. I have not
earned a kind look from you. I was not allowed to
even lift you from the ground. It was my comrade
— Chevalier Delogne — whose arm and sword did
you service."

"You!" she said, and looking at Maurice, held
out her hand; but she seemed to find no other
words for him, only the shy proffer of her hand, and
her eyes thanked him, and to tell the truth he
looked as though fully recompensed despite her
scant words; but to Constante she could speak more
freely.

"Nay, monsieur, I am sure your words are less
valiant than your deeds. You are at least stanch
to your friends, and though I have known few gentlemen, I am convinced that such men are always
the bravest in time of need. You came at my need
to-night, and I thank you — both."

"If you could only give us some clue as to the
enemy who would do you harm," ventured Monsieur Lamort.

But the girl raising her eyes met the level questioning gaze of Venda. The face of that slave
seemed to disconcert her in some way, and she
answered, hurriedly:

"I? — an enemy! Sir, if you would ask of all
New Orleans who would harm Denise, the answer
would be, 'Not one of us.'"

"Then perhaps some stranger?" suggested Delogne. "Those who traffic in slaves would scarce
hesitate as to whom they would kidnap. Mademci-
selle, when it pleases you to walk again after night-

fall, pray let us know; I can promise you at least a guard of two."

"Believe me, monsieur," she replied, in evident distress at what she mistook for reproof, "to-night's delay was an unusual accident, and even now the good sisters will be much disturbed at my absence; I must go."

She arose with more determination, and despite Monsieur Lamort's entreaties declared she was strong enough for the walk, which was but short.

"I will at least send with you a woman, lest you have need of her," he declared; "and, gentlemen, which of you—"

"If mademoiselle will allow me the privilege, I will gladly be her escort," answered Delogne; "and Constante—"

"He will follow after to see that you return—that no one kidnaps you on the way home," Constante amended; "and, by the way, I've just had a fancy as to who those blacks were working for. Does Monsieur Rochelle of the Sea Gull add the kidnaping of ladies to his long list of accomplishments?"

"Nonsense! Raynel. We have made mademoiselle quite nervous enough with our conjectures," warned Delogne; "and, after all, we have little foundation to go on—how could we, being strangers? But of course you would want to draw your latest enthusiasm into the affair. You talked of him to-night until misfortune was brought to those who walked our road; so I beg of you—"

Monsieur Lamort glanced at them both, and caught the careless smile on the face of Constante.

"Is Monsieur Rochelle so privileged as to be among your friends, then?" he inquired. "If so, you surely have been making rapid strides in your knowledge of the New World and the people who live in it."

"He is a romancer," explained the chevalier, "and this Rochelle is simply the latest mystery he has stumbled on. The things one does not know about a man are always myterious to the visionary."

"I protest, monsieur, that the Capitaine Rochelle is mysterious to many besides this gentleman," smiled Denise. "I confess he is so to myself."

"Ah, mademoiselle," and Constante's hand touched his lip and breast in most profound obeisance, "I pledge myself your faithful servant for so graciously coming to my rescue. Then this picturesque character is interesting also to you?"

"I can scarcely say that, since I have never yet looked on him, monsieur; but there are strange tales told of his doings, and I have liked to listen to them."

"But not to-night, I beg you," said Monsieur Lamort, with a smile. "It is bad enough for a lady's nerves that she begin the evening with kidnapers, but to finish it with a recital of wicked old sea-kings — it would surely prove fatal to sleep; and when I call to inquire after you to-morrow I hope to hear an account of dreamless rest."

"I would that you might come," said the girl, simply, "that our good abbess might thank you with more fitting words than I can use. And now it grows late, gentlemen, and I must go. Yes, I will accept also the service of the black woman, monsieur, and I thank you — I thank you."

CHAPTER VIII.

THE MAN ROCHELLE.

THOSE drifting clouds had been wafted westward by a persistent wind of the sea, and the stars twinkled unmolested over the waters where the reeds grew, and those alluring shadows where huge alligators heaved up heavily from their favorite playground.

No moon shone, and a gloomy magnificence seemed the prevailing tone of the night. Afar off a twinkle along where the land and water met would show keen eyes where the town lay; but out there in the alleys of the marshes not a light shone. A ghostly bird drifted low over the reeds at times and buried itself in the far cypresses.

Yet a schooner lay moored there in a lane so narrow no coastman would have discovered her. The pilot who guided her over that water-path must have had help of angels — or of devils; and the latter were commonly supposed to man her, for it was the Sea Gull.

Everything was so still about her one might have fancied her a phantom vessel. But suddenly two figures appeared on deck, and the taller ordered a boat lowered.

"Do you go back to shore to-night?" asked the soft French voice of a creole. "Ah, my Capitaine, you are ever restless when so near the shore that you live on both land and water. For me I would rather see you set sail from this country once more, and let us linger in those South seas where the Spanish and Americans need never make us weary with their clashings."

"Wait, Robert; when the night of life comes closer we will have a chimney-corner somewhere, and a good bottle ever beside it — there we will doze in content, but not to-night. Does that prospect please you?"

"Aye; but the flakes of snow in my hair are already many," said the other, ruefully. "You will have us wait and wait for evening in this world to claim our rest, but ere we know it we will have reached a morning in another, and the rest will have been left with yesterday."

The other laughed, and stretched his arms as a man who is only weary of inaction. "Chut! Suppose now you were called to a battle, eh — how much repose would you halt for then? No, you only play your infirmities to remind me of my own years — years, bah! I feel like a boy again when I hear the kiss of these waters and the music of these reeds. The night always plays the devil with me; it bewitches some people, I think. When I was young, darkness on the water made me ambitious to do one of three things: fight the English, whom I hated, play grand music such as I had never heard, but loved, or —"

He ceased speaking and watched some ripples on the water made by some unseen sea-creature.

"Or make love to some fair señorita, eh?" added the other. But the communicative mood appeared to have left the commander. He straightened up and looked across the dim vista to the tiny twinkles along the shore.

"You have never been a lover, Robert, else you would know love makes itself," he answered; and then added, abruptly, "Lower the boat; Nicholas will take me across. Weigh anchor an hour before day breaks — all will be aboard by then. Make no stop until the Apalachees are reached."

"It is only *au revoir*, Capitaine; you will sail with us again?"

"It is always 'only *au revoir*,' Robert. An hour, a night, a lifetime, and we are together again! So until we meet —"

Then the boat dipped with a splash into the dark water, and the capitaine descended, spoke a few words to a wiry dark man bearing the oars, waved his hand to his mate, and dropped full length on the rug of skins spread in the stern, his face turned up toward the sky as though to read something of import in the stars.

The oarsman glanced at him from time to time, but ventured no word to disturb the thoughts of the one musing there. They were speeding over the water in a boat so light that it flashed through the resisting ripples as a thing alive, and a curl of foam spread outward like wings on which they were borne.

And the lights along the shore grew larger. Once the man in the stern noted them and raised his head.

"Rest the oars, Nic. It is early. I have no longing for those shores; it is better here wild and free on the waters. How do you feel about it?"

"I? The water is good — yes." The man had the words and the curled hair of the black, but not the features. He wore an Arab-looking scarf about his head and beads glinted on his belt.

"But what of the shore?" persisted the master, and pointed landward. "That is the land of your people, your mother's people; how do you feel when you come in sight of it — the fair domain of the Spanish king?"

The sailor threw back his head and looked at the questioner through eyes suddenly narrowed. His teeth showed in a sinister way when he spoke.

"How you know what man feel here, even if he never speak word?" he demanded. "You know how I am made to feel," and he touched his brow and breast. "You know maybe how I want all the knives the Spanish make to be put in one big knife, and I want all the strength of all the Indian and all the black blood over the sea to be put in one man's arm — my arm — that I could cut the whites who are thieves from out this country, and pile them many as the stalks of corn when the harvest is. If the priests would give me prayer like they do white man, I would ask that the rainfall of all the world for one year be given in a night to our great river, that it might sweep the Spanish and the other bad whites into the sea!"

His face was the face of a devil, and his voice had in it the hiss of a serpent. But the white man opposite watched him with unmoved scrutiny; a little smile as of sympathy touched his lips.

"Yes, you can hate, Nic," he observed. "Did your Indian mother teach you that?"

"No; I was only a little child when she was sold away again. But blood tells you things to feel though no one says words to you, heh?"

"Does it?" asked the other, watching him as though it was a curious specimen he was studying and understanding. "Let me hear what it tells you."

"Ugh!" And the fellow leaned forward on the oars that crossed his knees. "It tells me voudou things, for they were lived when I was not born; tells me of my mother, a maid of the Natchez, of snaring her in the woods, and shutting her in the ship till the Cuba was reached — the white thieves did that! They gave her on that island to a black man for a wife, and my blood tells me she wanted to kill him, just as I wanted to kill him when I grew older and saw him asleep in the sun. Some black men good — him not good. She hated like I hate — I know. Then when her master sold her, but not me, she ran quick up where the cliff rises from the sea and let herself fall where the sharks lay. Every time I see a shark I think of the white men who live along the river that was ours."

The other man made a queer little sound like a laugh in his throat.

"There are men who would deem such a possession as Nicholas a thing of danger," he soliloquized; and then aloud, "Do you know it is my people you are throwing hate at?"

"I know," assented the fellow. "You bought me out of hell, and I would make myself a carpet for your feet, but I can not kill the hate for the grand white rulers over there. I can not; I do not want to."

"Nor I either," muttered the other. He lay there quiet for a little while, master and slave alike steeped in reverie, the oars forgotten. They drifted noiselessly under the stars, and the man who was white clinched and flung out his hand, with an imprecation, as if some audible expression must be given to his feelings.

"Ah, the accursed lot with their paltry titles, their toy aristocracy with its paper walls of caste! How I long to crush it like a bit of rotted fruit under my heel!" Then he looked across at the sailor, and thought, "He hates like that because of wrongs done ere he was born — he, a slave! Then how much my hate should exceed his — I who bear in heart and brain the cursed records their jeweled hands have written — ah! Take the oars, Nicholas; we will move inland. Keep your words about the whites for my ears, my lad; no other will understand them so well. You are a good hater, and such a one is faithful — it is good."

The sailor nodded, and again the boat seemed to wake into life at his touch; and as they sped over the waters one could picture a tryst to be kept where lattices were not too closely locked, and the man in the stern a cavalier who could carry a knife for a love as well as kisses.

Not a youthful man by any means, though his full beard was black, and the hair too, hair tied back, but not netted or braided, just left in curled locks about his brow and throat, joining his beard until his eyes and upper face were simply framed in the silky darkness — a sea-king truly in appearance, and one would judge him Spanish, yet by his own words he hated the Spanish, and each man of his vessel was of part Indian blood — a very good reason for the suspicion that he also was connected with some tribe.

Nicholas avoided skillfully all craft in the river and guided his boat less swiftly and in perfect silence along the shadowy shore, passing here and there the "flatboats" of Kentucky traders, and of insidious English, who could be trusted for but one thing — their certainty to draw strength, as a vampire sucks blood, from the very heart of the French and Spanish colonies.

The place they were approaching was by no means the select corner of the town. Hostelry and café elbowed each other in house of logs and house of plaster; women's laughter came out across the water at times, and the tinkle-tang of the banjo, or the softer, deeper music of a guitar.

In one of those places a woman — the wife of the accommodating proprietor — was singing a song for the pleasure of some *Américains*, who paid for wine and ate and drank like savages — a very spirited song, full of so much revolutionary spirit

that a Spaniard in the military dress raised his
finger and shook it at her, with a smile of reproach.
But as Señor Grenadier did not look at all ferocious,
she rewarded him with a little *moue* that was like a
mute invitation to a kiss, and finished the *ballade* in
triumph.

"If ill fortune did not force me to be on guard in
an hour, I would remain, to be sure that no revolutionary seed was sown here," he said, jokingly, over
his cigar. "Do you know, Madame Manette, that
your pretty songs might not be much liked by the
señors of the Cabildo? To be sure you only mean
to be merry, but they are dull to comprehend a jest,
and if others of the guard should chance in I would
have to beg you to cease — you comprehend? I
only speak in the interest of peace, for civil war is
an ugly thing to manage, and from a song might
grow a battle."

"Oh, we thank you, Señor Soldier." And all
madame's pretty teeth shone. "It pleases the
rangers to hear those *ballades* of Paris and the
revolt, but I assure you I will not sing them for the
nobles of the Cabildo; but for your good-will I
promise to sing any Spanish song you ask for when
you come again. *Buenas noches*, señor."

After the departure of the gentleman of the
guard, all the remaining visitors were of the ranger
class. Kentuckians, with their long knives and
their flint-lock muskets, sat around enjoying Spanish
tobacco and French wine, though the older ones
invariably called for rum, and then the spirits dis-
tilled at Jamaica filled many a cup quickly emptied.

Then there were the semi-French, semi-Indian *voyageurs*, with their fur-trimmed garments, and the bright gleam of quills and beads glinting over them as they turned in the light. Many slim young faces belonging to bodies lithe and alert as deer-hounds, and in their expression a sagacity not seen in the young faces of the courts — a keen directness to see and judge — though there in the café by the river their whole attitude spoke of relaxation. They had come far through the wilderness; had reached, perhaps for the first time in a year — two years — a place where music sounded, where men were merry, and where a roof was the usual thing to sleep under instead of the high sky and the unwalled horizon.

So they paid out their bits of silver coin for the enjoyment so rare to them, and on the tables where they had eaten, the platters were pushed aside and playing-cards were produced. Pretty Madame Manette was most helpful in forming the games; and an hour after the Spanish guardsman left more than one player had little piles of silver before him and was striving for the smile of Dame Fortune.

It was then that a newcomer entered — a man in long cloak and slouch-hat, who stood inside the door and swept the room with keen eyes, as if in search of known faces, and not finding them, advanced indifferently.

"Any one been here for me, madame?" he asked, as one who is acquainted.

"No, Señor Zanalta, not yet; but the night is yet early. You see all these are strangers of the north countries, traders and trappers — no more."

"More are coming now." And Zanalta looked toward the door, where steps were heard, but he stepped back into the shadow until the newcomer was seen.

There was no concealment, however, about the stranger. He strode in and looked around, with a wave of his hand that bespoke good-fellowship. A boy at one of the tables was whistling an air, and ceased in the midst of a strain to place his money, when the stranger coolly took up the measure and whistled the finale of it himself, causing all the heads to turn toward him; and the youth grinned in a puzzled way, feeling honored by the drollery of so imposing a person directed toward himself.

"Cracky!" called one of the *Américains*. "If you can play, mister, as well as you can pipe I'll not be one to enter a game with you, though I'd cheerfully pay for your rum to hear the whistle again."

"Anon," returned the other. "And how goes your world, Madame Manette? Faith, you grow more charming with each return trip I make to your port."

"Then is it seemly I should beg you to come with more frequency," she returned, with an innate coquetry in her shrug and glance. "Though Capitaine Rochelle can not enter our door too often, because of the merry spirit he ever brings with him. But see, monsieur, there is some one besides me to greet you — Don Zanalta."

"Well met, most gracious señor!" And the hat of Rochelle was lifted with an exaggerated flourish. A spirit of bravado seemed natural to him; even his

voice, deep and somewhat husky, had ever a suggestion of buried laughter.

But the smile of Don Zanalta was not very cordial
as he returned the salute. "It is pleasant, of course,
to know that our friends are merry over meeting us,
monsieur," he said, in a tone showing chagrin; "but
why take this *canaille* into our confidence?"

"Oh ho!" laughed Rochelle; "that, *amigo mio*, is
one of the disadvantages of being one of the 'noble.'
The rulers of the land must never be seen in the
modest corners of their domains without a mask, lest
they be thought to possess modest aspirations themselves. But I thank the good God I am not proud,
in proof of which I am willing to empty a bottle
with you, even in this unaristocratic corner."

The mockery set Zanalta's teeth tight on his lip,
but he followed to a table in the corner, though evidently unwilling.

"You are, to say the least, in a devil of a mood, to
choose this place for meeting," he persisted. "Why
not the cabin of your own vessel?"

"I can see the cabin of my own vessel every day
in the year, if I choose," he returned, carelessly.
"But I fancy new faces and walls sometimes. I
fancy corners of Orleans unspoiled by the conventional shackles of aristocracy. You comprehend,
my noble friend? And then the songs of madame
have always excellence — more than is apparent in
the wine she serves us."

"It is natural you should grow fastidious," assented
Zanalta. "You yourself have choice of so many
wines in your voyages to — "

11

Rochelle laughed. " Never mind the port. You know you enjoy it all the more from the supposed fact that it belongs to lawless traffic. Of course you are a good subject — long live the king ! — but how you all love to cheat him of his perquisites."

" Be wary, Señor Capitaine ! In your choice of meeting-place who can tell what ears listen ? Who can be sure that the Spanish guard will not echo your steps as you leave here ? "

" True — true enough," assented Rochelle, with a wise smile in his eyes. " But have I not friends in Orleans who will see that no harm comes to me from the state ? I can mention at least six whose good hearts would not let me suffer — yours heading the list, *amigo mio.* But " — and his brow showed a deep wrinkle —" where is our friend Señor Ronando to-night ? Is his stomach too weak for this ? " And he nodded toward the assembly in the center of the room.

" No ; it is awkward, señor, excessively so, but the money he owes you it is impossible for him to raise at this season. His father, the old judge, holds him in bad favor for other things just now."

" Ah ! "

" Yes ; his highness has suddenly drawn the lines very tight about poor Gabriel, though to be sure it is more the fault of Monsieur Lamort than any other. He has been unearthing buried and forgotten laws, and from his own eminence he looks on all pleasant folly as a crime, and wherever he finds laws to agree with him he takes exceeding pains to enforce them."

"You have mentioned this Lamort ere this, so have others." And Rochelle looked interested. "The aristocrats give him wishes that are near curses, I hear, but the *canaille* look on him in a different light. Drink down your wine, and tell me of this priestly law-giver."

"Priestly, no; I have never seen him enter a church. But he has a scent like a fiend for a path that is crooked, and chains for a neighbor of his that walks in it. I tell you it is well for you that King Charles' men and not Victor Lamort have an interest in knowing when your cargo is unloaded — and where."

"Bah! — a French adventurer who tries to climb to high places by dragging others down."

"Not quite. He has refused the high places so far offered him ; therein lies his influence with the Cabildo — with the governor himself. When a man punishes vice through love of virtue, you must agree he becomes somewhat of a wonder, and wonders have their influence."

"And the aristocrats do not love him, though they sit at his table, I dare say. Could you not take a friend of the sea with you some fine evening when you want to sup?" And Rochelle laughed quietly at the dismay on Zanalta's face. "Never mind, I shall call alone to present my respects to him some morning ; and if debts of honor are not looked after more closely in the colony I will take a hand in the game of virtue played by Monsieur Lamort, and might give him some points for his prosecution."

"Tut! — you are not serious."

"Why not? I might turn monk or saint yet, and I count on my luck-money buying me peace with heaven."

"Then I must contribute my share." And Zanalta drew some rolls of gold from his pocket — the gold received for Venda — and stacked them beside the wine-glasses. "I should not want you left in purgatory because of my debt."

"Lest my spirit should haunt you?" said Rochelle, with that laugh in his throat; but the face of the other changed to a quick frown.

"Make your jests on some other subject, if you please," he answered, curtly. "I do not relish such things."

"I see — and I wonder why, *amigo?* Now if it were I — I am expected to know something of sending souls to paradise, and should grow nervous at turning dark corners lest some soul shut out is waiting me there; but you — why, you have been a loyal subject, a proper man, and without a record against you in the courts, so the unhappy dead will not howl at you for a chance of revenge."

"Cease! can't you?" growled Zanalta, and tossed down another goblet of wine. "By heaven, you are a worse croaker than an old voudou! I will talk to you some other night; I am going home."

"Why such haste? Better wait until the moon comes up; the night is at its darkest."

"Its darkest!" Zanalta dropped again into the chair. "Then do something," he suggested; "get the cards — sing a song — do anything but sit there and talk of gruesome things."

"Just as you say — I am ready for a game at any hour of the night; but I remind you that when we played last you insisted you would not touch cards with me again."

"True — the devil played with you that night, and I was vexed at your luck; but to-night I will not risk enough to spoil my temper."

The seaman was clearing the glasses from the table, pushing them aside, and dropping the gold in his pocket.

"You have not even looked at the amount there," remarked Zanalta; and the other smiled.

"Never fear that my Orleans friends who know me will ever try to cheat me," he returned. "You see how implicit is my faith in you?"

Zanalta said nothing. He was galled by the thinly veiled suggestion of Rochelle's speeches, and once or twice that evening the idea came to him that never before had he presumed to be quite so much given to covert threats; and looking across at the careless roysterer something of temptation to murder crossed his mind. He hated so this fellow of bravado — and knowledge.

But the fellow played with the cards, and hummed a love-song in a deep bass, and seemed to enjoy rolling out gold-pieces to make the game of interest.

"So Ronando is in disgrace — eh?" he asked, carelessly. "Is there a cause?"

Zanalta made a contemptuous motion of the lips.

"Monsieur Victor Lamort has persuaded the Alcaldes to that effect. The reason given is the breaking of the law under Article 6 of the Black Code."

"Ah! Has the persistent Lamort then discovered that pretty creole slave and her white-skinned child on the Ronando plantation to the north? That is a pity. He should have learned wisdom from his father, who was too much of a fox to let his amusements be known to his neighbors."

Zanalta, too astonished to speak at once, simply stared.

"So you know that?" he said at last. "I have no wonder that people call you a man from the devil."

"Do they call me so?" smiled Rochelle. "I take it as a compliment to be thought unusual in these straight-jacket days, when the Cabildo decides everything on Orleans island from the gate by which souls enter heaven to the fashion of a man's temper on earth. And so Monsieur Lamort is looking up those troublesome old slave laws? What an unpleasant neighbor he must be for you, *amigo*."

"I have not the honor to understand you," retorted Zanalta, with a scowl. But his opponent only laughed, and dropped his last card on the table, winning the game.

"You mean you have not the inclination," he answered. "And there may, after all, be little to understand; only I have heard of some curious dealings on this soil — dealings accepted by the local government in past days — and if this meddler should chance on some of them — well, more than Ronando might have slaves confiscated, and acres too."

"Ugh! Can't you speak of less somber things? Tell me any word you have for Ronando."

"Only this, that within thirty days I must have my money."

"Monstrous! — that is — well, he simply can not make settlement."

The smile in the eyes of Rochelle changed to a fierceness — a cruelty, and his fingers clinched. One could tell by a glance at him then what a tyrant the man might be when a passion of his was touched.

"I am not accustomed to the words 'can not,' Señor Zanalta," he answered, with a cold sneer. "Debts owed to me must be paid to me — else —"

"Well — what?"

The seaman recovered himself at the question, and the smile, like a dropped mask, was recovered.

"Oh"— and he sent a shower of cards in the air and caught them by some slight of the hand — "I might think it my duty to kill him if he refused; and then I might simply lay the case before his august father, the judge."

"Yes; and be called on to stand a trial for smuggling."

"Ah! — perhaps; but, after all, who knows that I smuggle, if I do? The gossips along the streets, who repeat my name, and fancy me pirate, and Indian, and devil — which of them has ever seen me dispose of a sou's worth of merchandise? Not one. And, on the other hand, the aristocrats like yourself, who have a fancy for wine such as is drank in my cabin — well, if a boat touches the shore with kegs of that wine for you, are you going to give in evidence that you have cause to think I smuggled, for you received the goods? Ah, *amigo mio*, think not to trap a wolf with cobwebs."

"But think of Ronando's necessities at present," insisted Zanalta, as if not noting the argument advanced. "He has but just been married, and —"

Rochelle laughed heartlessly, and arose, slipping the gold-bits into his pocket as though he loved the sound of them, letting them fall one on the other with slow deliberation.

"Married, is he? That is good. A marriage no doubt arranged with all proper ceremony by the families, as the marriage of an aristocrat always is — a marriage to make glad the heart of the old judge — eh? I like to think of that. Wedding-bells! Well, we can't have them down in this corner, but we can have other jingles. Madame Manette, wine for the house! And how is it you have no music and dancing to-night? Do you assume mourning for the dead in Paris?"

"No, monsieur; but to tell you truly, that beast — that monster, Pierre, has been swilling some vile stuff elsewhere, and he's now stupid under the table of the kitchen. The violin is there — yes, but not one to play it; and these strange men from the Kentucky do ask me to sing and sing, and I can sing no more. That beast Pierre!"

"Do not grieve your gentle heart, madame. Ho! lads, are there any of you would shake a foot if the music was made? Good! Then listen. A bottle of wine to the one who changes his steps oftenest,

and another to the one who can dance longest.
Now dance, you devils, dance!"

And they did. Madame Manette had brought to
Rochelle the fiddle, and with one long draw of the
bow, like a wail, he played.

Zanalta, standing back near the wall, watched him
— the hat thrown off, the foot keeping time gaily to
the music; his laugh and his jests flung out to any
who challenged him.

"Fiddle? Oh, yes; and dance too, Madame Manette, if you would be my partner."

"You play pretty airs, monsieur," she commented,
beating time with one graceful upraised hand.

"Why not? Have I not your eyes for inspiration?
You drive away prose, and I am young again to-night.
Encore, my lad — that was good! Come now, thou
hardy ranger, does the dance tire you so much
sooner than the chase? Split the boards, my lad,
and another bottle is yours! Dance now, dance all,
and the devil keep time!"

So he played there, played, and jested, and laughed
— a lusty Pan scattering gems of music on those
uncritical dancers. And the one cultured taste in
the café stood astounded at the revelation given of
musical talent — something more than mere talent,
a wild sort of genius that spoke through his fingers
and set the blood tingling, the spirits leaping.

"A fiend, I truly believe; and yet all the people
to whom he speaks wish him to speak again," muttered Zanalta. "By the saints, it was an ill day
when our paths crossed. Yet — who knows — even a
savage has, I suppose, some friend of whom he

grows fond, and of all the men with whom Rochelle has played he seems most kindly to me. Yes, even Ronando noticed that, and thought my influence — but bah! who can influence that bravo there if he once sets his mind to be displeased? I wish with all my heart he would play himself into a fit of apoplexy."

And with this unchristian thought the Spanish gentleman approached the fiddler.

"Well, Rochelle, since you are wed to music to-night, I will take myself away. May I not hope to take kinder words to Ronando?"

"Assuredly, señor; take to him what kindly word pleases you — all the love of your heart — but from me give him the thirty days."

And the musician smiled, and nodded to the music, and to emphasize his words, and then added, "A moment, señor. I may like your island well enough to be within sight of it for a space. You may need a friend, and I may let you know where I am to be found; but, *amigo*, do not come again with the hat and cloak of a disguised brigand. I assure you there are no assassins in these corners waiting in the shadows with hidden knives."

Zanalta bowed, and walked out into the darkness.

"Perhaps not, Monsieur Rochelle," he said to himself; "we shall see."

The wild beat of the music rang through the room and out into the night. One by one the dancers left the floor until only two danced, encouraged by the laughter of their companions — until one suddenly stood still.

"What a fool I am to hop like this when no matter which of us wins the wine both will help to drink it," he decided, with late-come wisdom. Whereon the wine was ordered, and all drank thanks to the music that had been like a bit of witchery to their feet.

But the musician only smiled and nodded his black head, not ceasing his playing, only drifting into different themes — music to sing with or pray with, wild airs with storms of the seas rushing through, and sweet calls as of birds after the rain is over and the sun slips through the clouds.

He appeared oblivious or indifferent to the people about him, though they had all grown less hilarious. Their tones were lowered ; one youth even whispered when he asked, "Who is that?" And Madame Manette crossed herself and shook her head. To say for a surety that this was the laughing Rochelle — she did not know what to tell herself ; but she well knew music like that had never been played before under their roof.

And when he ceased all drew a longer breath. They began to chatter aloud once more. When madame came forward he handed her the violin and some coin.

"That for the reckoning ; and there is Pierre's fiddle — I may borrow it again. *Buenas noches*, señora. My lads, *adios*."

Not a laugh, not even a smile, as a finale for the evening he had made so hilarious for them. He pulled his hat over his eyes as one does when the sun sets the sands or the water all a-glitter, and without further words walked straight through the room and out.

"Begad, but that furrener is a curious mate to cross trails with," said an old hunter. "I was a-thinking he'd be a prime one to have on a trip if provender was short. He'd make ye forget all eating and drinking if he had but a fiddle."

"Aye, but I'll go bail he has his sullen fits too," observed another; "and I'd choose to be far away when they touch him."

The semi-French *voyageurs* from the Illinois chattered of him in their soft *patois*, and gesticulated to emphasize the spirit conveyed to them by the music; and one old north countryman puffed at his pipe and frowned into the smoke as one does who tries to collect scattered memories.

"Once did I know of one like to this — this gentleman of the museec," he remarked at last. "It was of many years gone I have the memory — of up the big river to the place where the black gowns built the crosses and taught to the *sauvage* men the true religion. Yes; I was young man then. He was young man too — a boy who loved the boat on the water and the jungles, and who could sing the songs of the birds, and traded all the skins he got for new things of museec to play on. Ah! the good priest did make lament over that sometimes; but the boy was close to his heart after all."

"Pouf! Is that all the tale you will tell of him? Where did he range to with his songs and his music?"

"We never did know. Once — as it had often

happen — he did enter a boat with the good Father
Luis to drift down where we are now. The good
father did return when the time was ready, but the
youth of the songs we never did see — not any
more ; and I did not think to live to the day when I
would hear again sounds like he would make on the
fiddle, but it has been. I did hear it to-night when
the Spanish-spoken man made the museec."

But the finale of the old *voyageur's* story did not
interest the younger members. It was unsatisfactory
to hear but a fragment of a life-story, and the old
man was questioned no more ; he was left to enjoy
in silence his pipe and his memories.

And the Spanish-spoken man ?

He was out alone under the stars and the pale late
moon, sitting on the side of an old boat left because
useless along the shore. The little lapping waves
came almost to his feet, and reflected broken fragments of those lights in the heavens. He had
walked up and down there in the loneliness of the
night for some time, as if in deep thought. The
boat from which he had alighted was not to be
seen ; but he did not seem to be looking for it, only
wanting a place alone in which to mutter either
curses or prayers, for each seemed to be finding
vent through his speech, as though he were bor-
rowing an hour from life in which to let loose
some wild mood that even the music would not
serve to quell.

Yet, were not all the seas wide enough for any
discontent of his, that he sought this lonely bit of
one small island?

Far off some guard on duty called the hour, and a bell sounded across the water. It was midnight.

He arose at the reminder, and flung out his arms as a man who is weary or slothful.

"An empty night after all," he muttered. "Well, progress is a question of moods, and my mood was wrong to-night; and then, well, even the devil must grow tired — tired at times, though he has his own way in hell."

He looked around in the moonlight dimmed by the fog. No moving thing was visible but the little waves and their wreckage, though if his eyes had been sharp enough to see through the darkness to the heavy timbers a few paces away he would have discovered a black form flat on the ground along the shadow of the piled-up logs, passive as though asleep.

But at the first step of Monsieur Rochelle the head was raised ever so slightly — listening — listening!

And as he walked slowly past, with bent head and hands clasped behind him, the figure arose to its feet and ran in a half-stooping, stealthy way, ready to drop flat on the ground if the man ahead of him should turn around.

But he did not. Once he halted and listened to a sound that seemed to come from an open boat-house just ahead of him and a little to the left; but it was not repeated, and he walked on close in the shadow.

But just as he reached it there was a sudden rush of bare feet behind his back, a warning cry from the boat-shed, a crushing stroke of a stick that cracked and broke, a howl and a curse as some one staggered hurriedly away. It was all done so quickly that Monsieur Rochelle could but spring aside and turn, with his hands on his pistols, when it was all over; and before him there stood only a slave-woman with white hair and the splintered stick in her hand.

"He is gone—but see!" And she pointed near his feet, where a sinister-looking bag of sand lay. "Black man creep, creép where you not see—but I see, so I wait; I do so." And she made pantomime of striking with the stick. "He feel me, see me—think me voudou. He run—hch!"

"And this was for me?" he asked, pointing to the sand-bag, though his eyes never left the woman's face.

"For you. He run; he fling it back so, to let it strike on your head. Then this fell heavy across his eyes, and he make tracks quick across there."

She looked across there, but the river-fog had blotted him out. She pointed, but the white man's gaze did not turn from her.

"And you are —"

"Venda, master," answered the woman, with one beseeching look upward to him; and then, as he looked at her with only curious interest, she dropped her head and crossed her hands on her breast.

"Venda; it is a good name, girl. Are you free?"

"No, master. Venda not want freedom; Venda in happy home."

"Ah!" And he gazed at her as though weighing all her words, and the honesty in them. Might this assault be only a trick? Might the woman be a spy who helped her work by doing him a service? " If your home is happy why do you walk abroad when all home-loving people are sleeping in their beds?"

She hesitated, and then touched her brow with her finger in mute token of submission, and looked up at him.

"Master, last night I slept in my bed — my first sleep in a bed that was new to me. In that sleep I saw a man whose heart was angry walk on these shores with a danger hanging from above. All day has Venda kept the dream in her breast, and when the night crept along and was old she comes here alone to see. So it is, master."

" You are voudou?"

" So the people say to each other." And for the first time something like a smile came about her lips.

" Venda, and a voudou," he persisted; " and what else?"

" Faithful," she said; and the words were low but earnest, and her hands clasped each other tightly. " Faithful if you ever come to a day when you want one you can trust."

" And all this because of a dream, Venda?"

" Yes"— and her eyes met his with a sad, curious look in them —" all this because of a dream, master —a dream."

" Well "—and he shrugged his shoulders and thrust a hand in his pocket —"if you wanted freedom I would try and give it to you because of the good turn your dream has done me to-night; but since you are not to be bought, you will take a few coins in memory of the stranger?"

She set her teeth close, and shook her head.

"Venda needs no gold — not from you, master."

"Then what do you want?" he persisted. "People don't lose their sleep for half a night, and all for naught, and for a stranger too."

"Maybe — maybe not," she answered, vaguely; "but if you ask of Venda you will hear that her head thinks strange things — maybe witch things. So she thinks to-night. She has spoken to you, master, and she thinks it will bring good luck. The good luck is better than gold-pieces."

"H'm! — perhaps." And he kept watch on her from under those black brows. "Do you choose to tell me any more of yourself?"

"No, master. I dreamed, and I came here; that is all."

"If you ever see me again, will you, if you need help, remind me of this night, that I may repay you?"

She raised her head quickly at that, and her eyes looked glad.

"Yes, Master—Venda promise that; and she will take one coin if you will put a mark on it, and on the day when Venda shows it to you and asks a favor you will say, ' It shall be.'"

"Agreed! This sounds like compacts the devil binds souls with. Was it one of your imps you flung into the fog just now? But I'll trust you if you

12

will tell me one thing. Do you know who sent that man with the sand-bag?"

She hesitated, and then said, "Venda have to say 'yes' and 'no' to that, master. She can't tell who said the words, but she know that black man lives on Master Ronando's plantation."

He nodded, and laughed silently. "You're honest voudou, Venda. Here is your piece of gold; it is already marked with a hole through the king's head — some one trying to send him to paradise by witchcraft, I've no doubt. Now where will you go?"

"Where you will, master."

"Then I will that you go to that house of yours that you like better than freedom. Go! There is no danger for me in the night now; I have been warned. Go, and the saints be good to you, Venda."

"No — no!" she muttered, and held up her hand. "Venda know that church meaning; don't say that to her. She don't ask you to say saints' words to her — no, no!"

He caught her by the arm and turned her face with a certain roughness toward the pale moon.

"You are a black woman, ain't you?" he demanded, and then let her go, with an embarrassed laugh. "By heaven, you are such a cursedly strange creature that you start wild fancies in a man's head — you with your white hair and your fear of blessings! If any one doubts that you are voudou send them to me, girl; I am sure of it. Now *adios!*"

"You will not forget the promise, and the hole through the king's head?"

" Never fear that I will forget the hole through
the king's head."

She drew a long breath of content, and bowing
her head passed across the little circle of light and
into the fog-land. On the verge of it she cast one
glance backward. He was standing there in the
same place as if watching her ; then the veil of the
mist fell between them.

And as she walked swiftly onward her hands
were locked close over her breast. Once she pressed
the gold-piece to her lips. " I have served him," she
muttered, " truly served him, and he has given me
a token. Ah, Venda, luck is good to you since you
did throw away the knife of the man by the wine-
shop — good to you. See that you are — faithful —
faithful to — the dead ! "

CHAPTER IX.

THE VOUDOU.

In the days following, events proved the truth of
the report that Monsieur Lamort was really bringing to light forgotten slave-laws and making revelations a thing of dread to more than one family.

It was sad, indeed sad, lamented more than one
member of the older families. That was always to
be expected, however, from newcomers — they so
often arrived on Orleans Island full of projects and
ambitions for the bettering of things. It takes time

to convince strangers that life in every land takes
coloring from and adapts itself to the influences of
the soil.   It was folly to expect all at once a life in
the new country like that in the old.   The laws?
Oh, yes — the laws had been made, that was quite
true, and they were well meant, no doubt; but
without doubt they had been suggested by just
such zealous enthusiasts as the good Monsieur
Lamort himself.   For had there not also been a law
passed that the slaves must at a marriageable age be
joined in wedlock, with a priest, so please you, to
officiate?   Ah, there had been many a laugh in the
colony over that law, and finally the king was convinced there would be wisdom in annulling it.

But all were convinced that there yet remained
many of those old musty laws that should be repealed.
The sudden unearthing of Article 6 of the Black Code
was an assurance of the fact to the colonists who
owned slaves, and chose to keep them.

And Chevalier Delogne in his capacity of secretary
to Monsieur Lamort grew suddenly wise regarding
the many technical points of law, and daily wondered
at the vast amount of energy and zeal displayed by
his chief for the thing he considered justice.

Well might his abode be termed the refuge of
exiles, for truly not an outcast of any race or
tribe would find himself friendless but that some
one would direct him to the house of Monsieur
Lamort.

And in the gardens where Felice and Basil had
years ago pledged their passionate love-vows there
stalked the red men of the north asking council, the

exiles of France asking friendship, and the ever-
present black with his endless grievances.

The owners of the blacks also came at times,
and discussed warmly some disputed point of right,
and outwardly at least they conceded their full
belief in the fact that the zeal of Monsieur Lamort
arose from motives most Christian.

But — well, even the zeal of the blessed apostles
could easily grow into a nuisance if directed toward
a new colony where one had to make the best one
could of those animals — the blacks ! But if any
of the planters ever thus expressed themselves,
Monsieur Lamort would only smile in his serious,
courteous way, and chide them as a priest might for
their short-sightedness.

" Your children in the days to come will approve
if you do not to-day," he contented himself with
saying. And Delogne would marvel sometimes at
his even patience.

" Ah ! monsieur, do you never lose your temper
over anything?" he asked one morning when an
unusually tiresome audience had been given to a
Dutchman of the river above. " I look at you in
wonder."

"At your age I too would have marveled at
patience," nodded Lamort, with a smile. " Believe
me, no one is born with it."

"Glad am I of that assurance, Monsieur Lamort,"
said a voice back of them, and Constante Raynel
came forward. " Were you discussing state secrets?
If so I will retire, and proceed to forget your words.
But I need patience so sadly myself, and was sent

into this world so lacking it, that it is a consolation to know it is a thing which grows by length of days, and that I am not entirely peculiar in that respect."

"What is your quarrel now against life?" asked Lamort. "Does our old earth go round too slowly to suit your fancy, or has some model failed at the moment when genius burned within you and you desired to catch all the beauty of life for some picture?"

"Oh, yes; you may laugh, and fancy Raynel is the one soul on earth exempt from care," he retorted; "but I assure you I have my troubles too — very serious ones."

"Ah! Which portrait did you commence?" asked Delogne, slyly, and laughed aloud when the artist answered, with ill-concealed irritation:

"Madame Zanalta's."

"I knew it — I was sure of it! Ah, my painter of beauty, you have made a little purgatory for yourself while you are yet alive, and heartily do I wish that the lesson may teach you something of that patience you deplore."

"Nay, Maurice," objected Monsieur Lamort. "You surely attribute Monsieur Raynel's impatience to the wrong cause; for what gallant would ask a greater happiness than to paint the likeness of his lady-love? I am loath to leave at the moment you make your call, my dear sir, but I am expected in the town — so *au revoir!*"

Constante bowed with commendable self-possession, but bit his lip as he discerned the humorous twitch of the suave Frenchman's cheek, and stamped across the room twice after his exit ere he would trust himself to speak.

"There! do you see that?" he demanded. "Did you note his meaning? What wonder that I am half distracted! By heavens! if the banns of — of that antique and myself had been read from the altar, people could not take more fully in earnest the fact that I belong to her."

"And does that disturb you, *mon ami?*" asked Delogne, trying to look serious, and sorting some papers in a little mahogany case. "Do you fear the lady will beat a retreat because of the general acceptance of the fact?"

"A retreat?" growled Constante. "Never! You don't know her. Death and devils! — to think that I have crossed the seas only to fall into such fortune!"

"Pray sit down and tell me your perplexities with more of composure," suggested Delogne. "Are those sketches you carry? I should like to be allowed to look at them when I have done with these documents."

Constante placed the portfolio on a couch of old Spanish leather, and walked the circuit of the room, drawing back curtains, pushing aside draperies, and peering into every shadowy corner, while the chevalier followed him with surprised eyes.

"On my life, but you assume strange habits in this new land," he commented. "Will you be pleased to tell me for what you are searching?"

"Assuredly; for something I am by no means anxious to find — that voudou creature with the white head. You are a braver man than I, Maurice, or you would not be living where that sphinx is one of the household. Ugh! she makes my flesh creep if she only turns round and looks at me."

"But do you not perceive it would be impossible for her to be in that old water-pitcher?" laughed his friend; for Raynel was in all seriousness peering into a silver pitcher that would hold perhaps a gallon.

"No; where she — he — or it is concerned the word 'impossible' is not to be applied," returned the searcher. "Have I not seen her suddenly arise from a corner where no human thing was seen but an instant before? Do you remember our first evening here, and how suddenly she was in our midst when some one expressed a wish for her? No; if I rest myself here for a chat I have no desire that her satanic majesty form one of the party. Pray tell me, does she ever in the world do aught but walk around and make music with her anklets?"

"She is without exception the most devoted creature to her master that I have ever seen in my life," said Delogne, emphatically. "She seems to divine by a look the thing he wants, while to the other slaves he must speak."

"If she would only speak occasionally she might seem a bit less horrible to me; but she moves about so silently, and looks at one in a way that says she could say so much if she only wished to. I tell you I'm as bad as the blacks; I would not meet that creature alone on a dark night — ugh!"

And he shivered at the mere idea of it; but having finished his survey, he seated himself and watched Delogne, who was looking at the sketches in the portfolio.

"Some of these are very interesting sketches, Constante," he acknowledged, with friendly pride; "quite the best things I have seen of yours; and you have been making these little studies in such a short space of time, too. I am glad to see you so industrious. But as I understand your present work to be of Señora Zanalta, how do you manage to accomplish favorable results from the sketches made of Madame Villette?"

"Eh? Well — you see —" Poor Raynel looked red and uncomfortable.

"Oh, yes; quite clearly — case 999. And are these sketches the reason of your discontent with your present portrait work?"

Constante groaned, and tramped about the room again.

"I really wish you would not do that," complained Delogne; "you are as bad for one's nerves as the voudou woman. Ah, Constante, you are ever a slave to the last glance shot at you — or the last hand you have kissed."

"Slave! — not a bit of it," denied the poor fellow with unnecessary vehemence. "But what is a man to do when he is in a good working mood, and there is only one thing of beauty in range of his eyes — I ask you now, what is he to do?"

"Just what you have done, I suppose," assented his friend; "but does not Señora Zanalta grow tired of posing while you make sketches of the younger lady?"

"Tired!—you evidently have not the happiness of knowing Señora Mercedes Zanalta very well. If she wears all her jewels, and her brocades, and has her hair dressed to her taste, she never grows tired—not for one instant will she leave that throne-like chair of hers, or the room."

"And Madame Villette?"

"The most provoking, bewitching, and mischievous lady it has ever been my perplexed fortune to meet. She assumes all the airs of a chaperonne in guard over a treasure I might be tempted to steal—think of it! She is gracious to me at times in a lofty manner, as though to remind me that I am after all only an artisan while she is a grand lady of rank—ah, this cursed caste! it rules here as in our own land; but then there are other times when she grows charming, and laughs like a child, and makes many a jest of both the portrait and artist, as though she knew that the work on it is not pleasant to me. She said to-day that of course she dared not hope that the portrait I am to make of her will be such a treasure as that I am doing now, and that it was easy to perceive that my heart was in the work. Ah! women were given so many modes of warfare."

"One can combat those who make war, and perhaps vanquish them," commented Delogne, with an impatient sigh; "but how much more difficult when one's fair adversary walks unconscious past you, or tells her beads when you would endeavor to meet her glance."

"So!—blows the wind with such a storm in that

direction ? Ah, well ; a novice can not prove nearly so vexatious as a widow — of that I am sure. But do you really mean that Mademoiselle Denise refuses to entertain any · regard whatever for you — and after you saving her life, too ? "

" Entertain a regard ! I have never yet dared to suggest such a thing. Indeed, she seems entirely unconscious of the fact that I am in the world. To be sure she spoke sweetly that night — that one night; but when I called to inquire about her, it was the lady abbess who received me, and bestowed gracious thanks, but with it a wall of reserve concerning the mademoiselle, and mademoiselle herself has evidently acquired a share of it. She walks no more in the evenings, and she will not give me a look."

" Willingly would I assist you if my wits would but tell me how. I might of course break an arm or two for you so that you could gain an entrance to the hospital. You know she entertains a lively interest for cripples."

" Possibly, but I will not put your friendship to such a test as maiming me ; and — ah, well — even that might fail to overcome her indifference. She simply does not think of me, and of course there is no visible reason why she should."

" How modest we are growing ! " remarked Raynel, mockingly. " But really it is a most fatal sign when one begins to fancy himself unfit even for a lackey to his lady-love. I've felt so, often, but I always realize through that feeling that I am growing serious, and when one grows serious — well, the

pain of love begins, and the laughter of it is
ended."

"You speak as a professor of the art, if art it be,"
remarked Delogne, with some displeasure apparent in
his tone. "For my part, I should not fancy the love
turned out by your academy. The lesson of love
would surely read more musically from not having
been studied at all."

"Interesting as the subject is, I fear we must defer
it," sighed Raynel, gathering up his sketches, "for
see! there come some gentlemen. Is not the one
Señor Ronando? The other is Villeneuve."

"Yes; and a most pleasant gentleman. Of all the
youth in this town I like him the best."

"And the other?"

"Ah, I have not the privilege of knowing Señor
Ronando well." And the chevalier went forward to
meet the gentlemen, while Raynel smiled and told
himself that, after all, Maurice might turn diplomat
in the school of Orleans.

"Gone out — gone out, has he?" sputtered Señor
Ronando, who was very fat and very short of breath.
"Ah — ah! that is a disappointment. It is seldom I
walk to any man's house, and now to find him out!
Well, well, I will seat myself and recover my
breath; patience may come with it. And may I
ask, my young sir, who you may be that receives
guests in the absence of Monsieur Lamort?"

"Allow me to remind you," said Villeneuve,
quickly, "that this is the Chevalier Delogne, late of
Versailles, and at present of the household of Monsieur Lamort. You met him but yesterday in the
house of my father."

" Possibly, possibly." And the old gentleman took snuff with a fine air of indifference. "One can not remember all the new faces crowding into our town since this uproar commenced in France — a most ungodly country, let them say what they will. And so you are the newcomer whom Lamort honors with his confidence, eh? Yes, I heard of it — a secretary. One would think he was the keeper of the colony that he must have so many helpers." And the caller looked sharply at Constante, who returned his stare with great serenity.

" Monsieur Lamort is certainly a very busy man," agreed Delogne, with cool courtesy, for Villeneuve's eyes mutely asked toleration for the old man ; "and I am proud to be the assistant of one so worthy."

"Aye, aye, no doubt; but say what you will, it makes trouble in a country when any one wants business so much that he turns the laws topsy-turvy for pastime."

" Monsieur Lamort lives for more than pastime," remarked Raynel, coolly. " He evidently tries to improve his time, and times."

" Hah! what's that?" And Señor Ronando whirled about, facing the speaker. " Since you have such learned ideas, I should like to know by what name you are called."

" By the same as at this time yesterday, at which hour I had the honor to be introduced to you, Señor Ronando," returned Constante, and turned away after a bow excessively humble, while the impatient old gentleman blinked his eyes in utter astonishment. For Señor Jesus Maria Pietro Ronando

was a very great personage on his own lands, and
was accustomed to much of submission to his ideas.

"Humph! More floatings from Versailles," he
murmured, audibly. "Well, Sir Secretary, can you
give me an idea at what hour Monsieur Lamort
would be pleased to return here? Gaston Villeneuve here will tell you I am not used to waiting in
an anteroom for an audience."

"Truly not," agreed the embarrassed Villeneuve.
"And may I beg to remind you, señor, that Chevalier Maurice Delogne is also unaccustomed to the
speech one offers to an ordinary clerk. His family
is noble as any in our land. Pray remember, my
dear señor."

"Assuredly — yes," returned the other, with slight
attention. "Of late all who land with us are nobles,
it seems; yet where is the advantage of noble
blood when a stranger without family, a mercenary heretic, can land here and turn laws crooked
with the power of a purse? Our family is older
than the laws of Spain over this country, yet must
I run to a newcomer if I want justice secured.
Bah! even our governor is influenced by this law-
maker who prays in no church."

Villeneuve drew him to a window and spoke to
him alone, trying to quell his impatience and ill
temper; and the other two strove for the young
man's sake to give no heed to the very awkward
comments.

"An ill-trained bear native to this wilderness, I
suppose," remarked Raynel, who was more vexed
than his friend. "My only wonder is that the colony

has allowed him to live so long. I have heard often of the beauty of Spanish courtesy. Is this the much-commended thing?"

"Do not believe it," said Delogne, decidedly. "He is a bully who scolds, who catches words from sailors, and tone from the northern English, and between them the grace of Spain is lost to him — if he ever did possess it; but he is old, he is annoyed, so be heedless of him."

"Humph! If I promise not to kill him it will be all my conscience will let me agree to," decided Raynel, with a pantomime of pitching articles of furniture at the fat old aristocrat in the window, who was viewing the grounds and property with the eyes of reminiscence.

"This too — one of the most excellent estates in the colony — it is grievous, Gaston, to think that it too is mastered by a newcomer. Oh, yes, I know he is thought much of by you, and many of the others; but I am no courtier, I thank the saints! I say what I choose when I have the reasons of a Christian. And if the dead could walk, then would Le Noyens surely come to protest against a heretic slave-law agitator dwelling under the roof built by him. Ah, he was a man for the country. Your father knew him well — a fair gentleman, who ruled the blacks to his nod, and would brook no word as to the mastering of his own household. Alas! I was like him once, but now I grow old."

"I have heard much of the tragic story of his end-ing," returned Villeneuve, glad to keep the vindic-tive mind beside him engaged. "Was there not a

song made of it?—as a child I heard one sung by
my nurse. It was interminable, for each singer
added to it as his fancy prompted him. I know I was
kept quiet many a time by our Susette chanting:

> Ohé! Bayarde the ranger
> Did the deed — the dark deed!
> Listen, children — listen, stranger!
> Never more will he be freed.
>
> Chains a-dragging
> All along the road,
> Back all broken
> Underneath the load.
> Listen, children!
>
> And take warning,
> Chained in the mine-land
> You never see the morning.
> Ohé! — children!
> All good children!"

The young man chanted the lines slowly, with
sometimes a pause in the effort at remembrance,
and the older gentleman nodded assent and beat
time with his gold-crowned walking-stick.

"You keep the swing of the old song well,"
he said. "Yes, yes; every child heard it in that day,
for the tragedy was a famous one because of the
woman in it—there is always a woman, you know, in
the troubles of every man; or maybe you do not
know it yet, but you will."

Because of their position they had not observed
Monsieur Lamort, who had entered and halted only
a few steps from them, and who now came forward
with his usual calm courtesy.

"Monsieur Delogne wished to apprise you of my

return, but I motioned for silence that I might the better hear the strange folk-song you were singing. It is something native to the soil, I imagine?"

"Yes; the rhymed history of a tragedy Señor Ronando was recalling to my mind. Among the illiterate that fashion of memorizing is quite popular here. An elopement, a murder, or even a grand wedding is made into song and sung to the children; it is their only way of handing down traditions, and is very popular among the black people."

"I have heard of their custom." And Monsieur Lamort looked like one who is striving to be interested while the mind is really in some other direction. "And this song, is it of a grand wedding — and the histories of all the children that result? One of those songs I have heard here; it told of a family for three generations."

"On the contrary, this one is of murder and exile," answered Señor Ronando. "A well-earned exile, in which I am proud to say I assisted — a foul murder of a gallant gentleman."

"Ah! You had personal knowledge of this particular tragedy? I understand, then, the interest of Monsieur Villeneuve in the song. Has it a name?"

"'Bayarde, the Ranger,' is the only one I ever heard it called by," answered the young man. "And many a doleful moment did I pass when as a child I heard that song of the chains, and the mines where the sunlight was never supposed to penetrate. It brought me the first suggestion of life-long punishment that ever came to me. Such things are landmarks in the thought of a child."

13

"Truly they are," assented Lamort, and glanced at Delogne. "It seems, Chevalier, that we are to hear much of this De Bayarde, though so little of the more respectable bearer of the name; but faults will win attention, while virtues are too often unheeded."

"Bosh!" And Señor Ronando showed in his fat face his satisfaction at possessing knowledge beyond the rest. "That may be a fact, but in this case it was not the crime he committed which made him famous in the provinces, but the fact that the daintiest señorita in all these lands had opened her lattice for his serenades — that is the thing which made him talked of; and strange stories were afloat of dawns when she had been seen stepping from his canoe and speeding through these gardens to a door left open. And there must have been some truth in it, else would she have gone mad, as they say she did?"

"The horror of the murder may have been sufficient reason for that," suggested Delogne. But the señor looked displeasure at having the truth of his theory questioned in the slightest.

"I have reasons for my suppositions, young sir," he said, tartly. "Her uncle was my friend — yes, gentlemen, my friend, and a true son of the church — the saints find him rest! So I was one who knew her only female relative in this land; and that lady, Madame Sollé (dead these several years), took charge of her, and had a grievous time of it by her own statement, for the girl Felice raved for months, shouting for 'Basil' — that was the fellow's name — until the blacks feared to sleep in the house with

her. She could not be kept in the town at all, and
so was taken miles up the river to a small plantation
of the Sollé family. Her grave is there, they say,
and I suppose that of her child."

"Child! Oh, I never heard of that," said Villeneuve; and Señor Ronando blinked with unctuous
satisfaction.

"I thought not. I thought I could tell you something of that story — something you had never heard.
Well, the family is all gone now; none is left to bear
the disgrace. But, ah! how Madame Sollé raved
over it! My wife lived then; she was her confidante
— she knew. And when they died, Felice and her
ranger's brat, Madame Sollé had them interred on
the plantation, with never a white friend near, not
even a priest. But then the poor woman was half
mad herself, and no one judged her coldly. For if
the soul of Felice was lost for lack of the sacraments
— well, it was only a fault of her own. To think of
such a fine creature turning into a light love for a
voyageur — those animals who have a wife in each
Indian tribe they visit! Was it not deplorable?"

"Such things always are," assented Monsieur
Lamort. "And yet — well, they have been, and
will be."

But he sighed as he spoke, and his face looked as
sad as his words. Delogne glancing at him thought
what a generous heart was his that had a sigh and a
tone of compassion for the actors in that long-dead
tragedy.

"Will you not be seated, monsieur?" he asked,
coming forward with a chair. "You have perhaps

walked rapidly and grown tired, for you are paler than when you went out."

Lamort wheeled about as though vexed at being supposed feeble, but recovering himself, declined the proffered courtesy with a gesture.

"Thanks, Chevalier; I am a little tired, but that is no excuse for me resting so early in the day. I only returned because I heard Señor Ronando had come this morning to make me a special business visit. So, my dear señor, I have postponed my other work for this part of the day and am at your service."

"Work, work!" grunted Ronando, with grim lips. "Has Orleans Island become such a place of turmoil that all repose is driven from it by this eagerness to work? Monsieur Lamort, when we get gray in our hair we have surely earned the right to sit in the shade and leave the work to younger hands."

"Right enough," assented the other; "and yet a slothful old age is a bad example for youth to pattern from, and some men love action better than repose. I, perhaps, am one of them. And now that I am here, tell me in what way I can serve you."

Señor Ronando blinked at him in indecision. He did not fancy much this courteous newcomer who parried his thrusts of speech and was so quietly confident of himself.

"Well, monsieur, I must tell you that I — that, in fact, Don Diego Zanalta was to have met me here. He knows my business, and knows more of law crooks than do I. Can not we await his arrival?"

"Assuredly. Meanwhile we will have a glass of wine in the court within. The air is more pleasing

there, I fancy. Will you come with us, young gentlemen, or have you other plans of entertainment?"

"I have those papers yet to arrange," said Delogne. "Our artist here is going to attempt a sketch
of Monsieur Villeneuve, and as the breakfast-room
has the best light they were about to ask for possession of it."

"At their service — all my house," nodded Lamort, and led Señor Ronando through the arched
door into the court where the palms grew, and
where blossoms hung heavy and fragrant against
the lattice-work of the verandas.

Delogne was left sorting the papers according to
the labels. Several of them, tied with black cord
and yellow and brittle with age, were to go in a case
by themselves; the rest were to go in the great
locked drawers of a mahogany cabinet standing
against the wall.

Having concluded the task, he looked in vain
for the key to the drawers; but it had been mis-
laid. He looked on the cabinet, even in the portfolio on the couch, and felt in his pockets.

Then he remembered he had changed his coat
just before Constante had entered, and the key had
no doubt been left in the other garment.

He had but left the room when Raynel reëntered.

"Where are those drawings, Maurice? Oh, here
they are, though you are not." And he bent over the
portfolio to select some certain bits of paper.

Suddenly the couch on which the drawings lay
moved. He had not touched it; he knew he had
not touched it, yet it had certainly moved, and
toward him.

He passed his hand over his hair as though to level the curls suddenly grown bristling, and his eyes grew wondrous large as he let fall the drawings and stepped backward, for not only the couch, but a bear's hide, seemed possessed by something infernal and moved on the floor.

And then, carelessly uncoiling, Venda arose before him, and stooped to pick up the scattered drawings — never speaking. She looked at him over her shoulder, and he thought she was laughing at him. Really she was not, but his earnest dread of her made everything she did significant and of much meaning to him. When she stood straight before him and offered him the bits of paper, he seized them and commenced a detour for the door, not desiring to even turn his back on her.

But on reaching the threshold his eyes wandered an instant from her white-framed face of bronze to that spot where she had lain flat on the floor beneath the skin of the black bear. He would not have been much surprised to see numberless little black imps of darkness creep forth in her wake, all with shiny, strange eyes and white hair, and form around the couch where he had been seated and expressed adverse criticism on that voudou. He had never before thought himself a coward, but a most troublesome trembling seized his knees, and the chill of horror wavered over him as he remembered his words; and he hastened back to his waiting model, with the self-query as to whether it would be possible to frustrate by either charms or prayers the potency of voudou spells.

But Venda gave little heed to his presence. She sat again on the rug near the couch, where she muttered, rocking from side to side, and nodding her head as though some feeling — it seemed anger — was too strong in her for utter silence.

If Constante could have seen her thus! Then another step sounded on the tiled floor, and she turned with eager eyes to the door.

"Master, my master!" she said, in a tone of veneration so profound as to resemble that of a pagan who bows to an idol. And as he entered she moved to him with silent haste.

"You, Venda?" he observed, with that gracious manner he always had for his bond-slaves. He was to Venda as to the others, though he watched her with more interest than the other blacks — she suggested so much more; and then she was ever so strangely near when he needed her.

"Yes, master," she answered, bending before him and holding her hands tight-clasped, as one who would put restraint upon himself. "Is Venda needed?"

"Some one is, and you are ever nearest to my hand," he replied. "We want coffee there in the court. You made it pleasant to the taste yesterday; bring us more like that. I looked in here for Chevalier Delogne. Send him to me if he is within, and then bring the coffee."

"Yes, master. Master — "

She stopped and looked at him with a gaze so concentrated, so searching, that he unconsciously stepped back from her.

"Speak, Venda! What have you to say to me?"

" What I say to you? Oam-me! The words, they
here," and she pointed to her throat. " They don't
come clear, maybe; but master — good Master
Lamort, you called just — you called right — but you
drink coffee with that " — and she pointed with
growing rage toward Señor Ronando — "you drink
friends with him? I look in your eyes, but no see.
Master, Venda see some things clear; she see pain
long ago — long ago when that man judge, when
that man help put chains on where they no have
right. She hear lady scream all the night like he
laugh, and tell of — scream for the man they put in
chains. Master, he comes to ask favor of you — much
favor. Hate is in his heart, but he asks favor.
When he says the words, when he waits you to speak,
oh, master, think in your heart of the man who
laughed at the cries of the lily-white lady. Master,
he has ever been as a tiger in a jungle; every fawn
drinking at the brook was food for him; every
fruit ripening in the sun he put out his hand to. So
he put out his hand to the sweet Ma'm'selle Felice.
So he wrongs her in his words because she did walk
ever away from him as one walks from a snake if it
comes close with its poison. So it is with the father,
so it is with the son. Oh, master! you smile kind
on him, and Venda — Venda afraid. But when he
ask favor of you — favor for his son there at the
judge place — then — then do not forget the lily
Lady Felice, and the judges who said, ' Let him
suffer.' Oh, master — "

"Cease!" commanded her master, and his voice

was low and strained. His face, pale before, was colorless under the fierceness and pleading of her words. He stood quite still looking at her, when all at once his eyes closed; he staggered slightly, reaching out his hand mechanically as though for support.

But he did not fall, only leaned on her quickly proffered shoulder, and passed his hand over his eyes — a hand cold and damp, as she found when it touched her own. Then with an effort he drew himself erect with a determined air and walked unaided to the couch.

"Some hate of yours has made you blindly mad, I fear, Venda," he said, reprovingly, "and I am not well enough for agitating discussions this morning. So if in the future you have a cause to plead, pray do so with less of violence, and remember, no more words such as you spoke just now; they are useless. I have decided what I shall do, and words from others will have no weight. You make good coffee, Venda, but when I want your advice in other things I will ask for it. Now go, my good girl; make the coffee, but I warn you if you should think of putting in poison for Señor Ronando that I am to drink it too."

He spoke lightly, but did not look at her. His head was bent on his hand in an attitude of weariness; but he could not help seeing that the strange vengeful creature knelt for one instant beside him as at an altar, and then passed out as she was bidden. Over her lips was pressed one of her hands. He felt strangely the sense of her devotion to him, but did not know it was the hand his own fingers had touched when he reached out to her for support.

———

CHAPTER X.

ECHOES FROM THE PAST.

IN the garden of the Ursulines there walked in the sweet breath of the early day two women. One, a sad-eyed, beautiful woman, whose expression was one of peaceful repose, spoke earnestly to the other, who was Denise.

"But, my child, I am not supreme here; it is to our mother superior you must go for direction in this. And if the man but only look at you —"

"Ah, Sister Andrea, his words have been spoken often — words such as are spoken by courtiers, I think, but I fear them — I fear them! All the more since that night when the blacks did seize me. I dare not accuse him lest I be wrong, yet I felt that only he could have done it; and when I met him last evening I grew ill and weak at the look in his eyes. People say he is a good Catholic, and he does give to my poor, yet do I fear he is evil."

"Your heart tells you truly," said Sister Andrea, thoughtfully. "Then why not leave the charity work to others who would be in less danger?"

"But my poor people would miss me — I would miss them," answered the girl, quickly. "That is

why I fear to go to our mother; she is so decided,
she would say, 'Well, since you are afraid, I will
give you a class to teach, and you need never go
without the gate.' But I love to pass the gate; of
course I am glad to come back to it again, but sometimes I fear it would not be so dear to me if I was
once bound to remain within it always. It is wicked
of me, perhaps, sister"—and she bowed her head
humbly—"but I do not think I could be happy
under bonds of any kind, not even of the convent.
I want to do the work of it always, but I want to
work free. That is self-pride. I know, and it is
strong in me."

"It is strong in all youth," agreed the older
woman. "The years wear it away, however, from
many hearts. It may prove so with you, so be not
vexed with your own self."

"Ah, sister, you are ever kind to my faults, ever
excusing me to myself." And Denise pressed fondly
the hand of the nun. "I never knew what a mother
was, but I used to long blindly for a mother's love
—always, always I would dream of a face I thought
my mother's. But in the year of the great sickness here, when you came from the convent across
the water, and you looked in my eyes and said, 'I
am glad you are the convent child, for I shall love
to have you near me'—well, dear Sister Andrea,
I never longed so for a mother after that; but at
times a great dread comes over me for fear that
you may leave us too at some distant call of distress,
and then—then this island would seem to me desolate as the winter-time of the north country."

A faint smile, caressive as an embrace, touched the beautiful lips of Sister Andrea.

"Fear no sorrow until it touches you, Denise," she said, gently. "But we need never be far apart in this world if we wish to be together. Have you never known that in all my eight years of life here my bonds to the order are so lax that I am allowed to follow my own desires as to my place of abode? I wished it so at first that I might be free to offer my help in sickness or battle — any place my conscience and duty led me. So you see, my child, my bonds are scarcely stronger than your own. I go where my duty calls me."

"Ah, sister! — and I never knew! Do you know I am happy at what you tell me — and also astonished? You nurse the sick, you are devoted to good, but you never go without the gates: I always thought you had taken vows to never look beyond these walls."

"No; those vows were not for me. But this morning we were to speak of you, not of myself. I am concerned because of the persecution of this Señor Zanalta. I would we had the advice of some one out in the world, some one who could not be awed by his position."

"I know of such a one — of two, but it would ill become a maid to seek them; at least our mother did speak chidingly once because he walked home with me in the dark, or rather because he called to see me the day after."

"Ah! — he?" And the eyes of Sister Andrea smiled at the shy confession. "You commenced to tell me of two, and end by speaking of only him. Have they names?"

"Monsieur Victor Lamort is the other one," explained the girl, with an appealing upward glance.

"The *other* one — and who is the one?"

"Ah, sister, it amuses you to confuse me, and in truth it is not hard to do it; but I spoke of the gentleman, a chevalier of France, who came to my rescue that night, he and his friend — the name is Delogne."

"Yes, yes; and they are at once knights of chivalry to maidenhood. You need not blush, child; only it is well to remember, Denise, that a foundling of the convent gate and a chevalier of France are widely set apart by the rules of the world he lives in — do you understand?"

"Yes, sister"— and the young face was not so rosy as she bowed her head —" I hear, and will remember. It was so that the good mother admonished me after she had spoken with him, but her words hurt more than yours, dear Sister Andrea."

"Well, well; our mother superior has many things to think of where we have only one, Denise, and we must save her care when we can. Now why not confess to Monsieur Lamort that you did suspect your assailant that night on his grounds? You say he is a powerful man, and has even asked how he could serve you."

"Yes, it is true," assented Denise. "But, sister, I heard words but yesterday that make me feel strangely about him. I admire him so much; but the world is so wicked that no one — even he can not escape suspicion."

"How so? Tell me what has occurred. Your words of that man have ever been words of reverence."

"Yes, and even now — but listen: It was down where the fever sickness is so busy; I was there. Two men of the boats talked of monsieur. I could hear their words: one said he was very kind with his gold; another said it was only a trick by which to win the love of the poor and gain votes and influence with the people against the time when it would please him to reach for position in this land. One said, 'Have you noted that he has ever a most fatherly smile for our convent child?' and another said, 'Aye; he knows there are scores among the poor who would take her word as their law, so he would win even her.'"

"Well," said Sister Andrea, as the other halted, "is that all? They were perhaps simply making talk, as idle men will, to help the time to pass."

"I know — so I thought; but even as I left there I met monsieur. He was kind; he asked after the sick, and then — then he spoke of their affection for me, of my influence for good over them, and of certain ways in which they needed to be influenced; of the rights of the poor whites and the freed blacks, who were each subject to many indignities escaped by those possessing the saving-power of gold or of caste. He talked wisely, no doubt, but I was thinking more of the words of the other men than of his; and sorry was I to think that maybe they spoke truly, and that every smile he has given me was not for Denise, but for the sake of some law of which she knows nothing."

Her face was flushed, and her lips were trembling. Sister Andrea was astonished to see tears in her eyes.

"What, Denise! You care so much? I will come to believe indeed that this wise Monsieur Lamort is a wizard who charms people. Lend not your thoughts to suspicion of those you love, child. Of all emotions of the heart it is the one most miserable. And what if this good gentleman should show you how to serve those who need help? It is not as if the cause was an unworthy one."

"No, sister — but —"

"But you are very much of a woman after all, Denise," said Sister Andrea. "You have grown so worldly during one springtime that you fancy even this gray-haired diplomat should forget his cares when you are in his vision. Fie! child; I did not fancy you so vain."

"It pleases you to tease me, and I can not set myself right," declared the girl, "because I can not tell what it is I feel when he looks at me. He kissed my hand that night at his house — see! — just here; and I press it over my cheek every night ere I sleep. Nay, do not reprove," as Sister Andrea was about to speak. "I can tell you as I can no other; but it is only that he looks in that grand house as though his heart was lonely and sad. He looks at me, and I want to put out my hands and comfort him."

"And this of a grande monsieur who lives like a prince, they say! Truly it is a strange impulse. Your hands have until now gone out only to the poor and sick. Do not be won from them to the palaces, child. But it seems to me this gentleman is most worthy; the oppressed have many blessings for him. And since you prefer not to go to the priest—"

"He drinks wine and laughs late with Don Zanalta," answered Denise, shaking her head.

"Well, then speak to this gentleman whose gray hair and kind words have won your sympathy. Tell him I—a nun here—advised you to go to him, as you are fatherless, motherless, and need advice beyond my knowledge. He knows the town and its dangers. We will rest on his judgment, Denise, for a woman shut out from the world as I am may not advise you wisely. My heart makes me fearful. I would gather you close to me, close these gates, and never let the eyes of men rest on you; but that might not be either happiness or great good to you, dear. No; we will speak to the stranger."

Peculiarly intimate were the relations of those two, considering the fact that each wore the convent garb — the robes that are recognized barriers against worldly personal loves; but Denise had explained her own attraction to the beautiful sad-eyed nun, and Sister Andrea — well, from the day when she had stepped ashore there, sent from a convent in old Madrid in the time of a great sickness eight years before, from that day when Denise had met her just inside the gate and offered her a lily flower, her heart had gone out to the lovely little one who had never known any home but the convent walls, and their liking had grown with the years until their love was that of sisters in truth.

And so it was at the suggestion of Sister Andrea that Denise took the path to the gardens of Monsieur Lamort.

She went alone, as a boy might have done, for the foundling of the convent had never a duenna to guard her; the dress of a novice had ever been respected but that one night.

And was it so strange that all unexpected she should have come face to face with Chevalier Delogne at the arbor of the very first gate? For is there not ever a certain guardian spirit of life over all? and it draws so surely youth to meetings with fair youth; and Delogne arose as one who has dreamed of some sweet thing come true, and looked in her face with eyes that said " At last !"

" I trust that I did not startle you, mademoiselle?" he asked, as the slow pink crept up to her cheek. " I sit often in this arbor with a volume for company, though my eyes and thoughts wander far beyond the parchment at times."

" Yes," remarked the girl, glancing about. " You can see the water across there on which the ships go out to the sea, and across to your own land; it is natural you should watch it with fondness."

" True, mademoiselle; but I can see two ways, and the other is across to the sacred place where your days are lived. I can often discern forms passing

14

to and fro, and test my wits to discover if one should be you."

"There are many besides myself there, monsieur, and all of more importance," she returned, walking slowly beside him to the house.

"I dare not contradict you lest you show me disfavor, Mademoiselle Denise, but will content myself with protesting that as I do not know the other excellent ladies and have been privileged to know you — a little — of course it is your face I strive to discover and not that of a stranger."

The girl could make no reply to that — she felt confused; she knew the good mother superior would not approve, and yet she could not be rude, and the conscience-troubling thought was the certainty that she did not wish to be. It was entrancing thus to walk under the whispering leaves keeping pace with the step of another who spoke with all-caressing deference to her. Her heart beat warmly, and her hand crept to her rosary.

He looked at her. They were nearing the door; a few moments and there would be no more words alone.

"Will you never speak to me when we meet by chance?" he asked, gently; and she did not raise her head.

"I have spoken to you this morning."

"Yes, this once, a few words; but, ah, mademoiselle, do you never give a kind glance to any but the invalids or the very aged? A man in a strange land can starve for kind words as surely as the poor people whom you befriend grow hungry for the taste of meats."

"But you are not alone — you have friends — they are attached to you."

"Friends — oh, yes; Monsieur Lamort and my dear Raynel. But it is ever the sympathy just beyond us for which we yearn."

"I suppose you mean gentlemen when you say 'we,'" she answered, with a delightfully prim little manner obtained from correcting at times the younger pupils of the classes. "But ingratitude is most lamentable, and surely the friendship of Monsieur Lamort is a thing to be satisfied with."

"Ungrateful! You think I make a low estimate of his kindness because I long for something more sweet? Ah, mademoiselle, if you would but be a little gracious, you would find me grateful, I promise you."

"I am not a fine lady, monsieur, from whom courtiers beg grace," she said, as they reached the doorway, and her face grew more decided as she looked up once at him. "I am only Denise of the convent, and know little of the world's ways; but this I believe, that he who is not satisfied with that which he has would not be content with that which he thinks he would like to have."

And then she passed before him and entered the hall leading to the court where the palms drooped their feathery fans; and under their shifting shadows sat the man she had come to speak of, Don Zanalta, and beside him, with a cigarette between his fingers, stood Monsieur Lamort.

She saw it all in an instant, before she was observed herself, and stepped back in the shadows out of range of their eyes. Was it for this she had chosen Monsieur Lamort instead of the convivial Father Joseph? To her eyes there must be close friendship when Monsieur Lamort smiled thus down on the dark head of Zanalta; and her resolve was taken quickly — she would not speak of the errand for which she had come.

She could not hear the words of the man standing there, or guess that he was refusing a boon the other had striven for.

"No, my dear Zanalta," he was saying, with that decided voice but easy smile, "I can not move in this matter if I would, and I have not yet met with any evidence to convince me that I should."

"But I assure you, though the letter of the law will oblige the Alcaldes to give judgment against Ronando, their sympathies will be with him."

"All the better for him; then he will have no difficulty in posing as a martyr."

"But truly, do you care not at all that the prejudice of the nobles will be turned against you?"

"Will that also result?" asked Lamort, with a curious smile. "Do they then dislike justice so earnestly? Ah, well, perhaps that creole slave, the mother of Ronando's child, may have a good word for me at the day of judgment; it may even weigh against those of the voluptuous nobles."

"But if she be content — "

"Content to be beaten like a beast by him in his drunken fits! Pray speak no more of it, my dear sir. The things I learned of that plantation are not pleasant to dwell on. And, by the way, can you tell me from whom Colonel Durande made purchase of that adjoining plantation — the one that lies between your own and Ronando's?"

"I forget the name — something like Semour. I have it on papers at my house, for we had trouble once with this same Durande over the boundary-lines, and I was always convinced that they still hold many acres which by right belong to my plantation. I would like your judgment on the question some day."

"It is at your service. Let me know any time I can befriend you."

"Have I not let you know this morning?" retorted Zanalta. "And you closed your heart against my plea, just as you did to old Señor Ronando yesterday. He is angry and astounded that he has been refused consideration."

The two men passed out by another door to the garden, and did not perceive the girl, who stood uncertain which way to turn; uncertain what to say to Delogne, to whom she had motioned for silence, and who stood silently watching her, and showing plainly that he was puzzled.

And then from among the palms Venda walked, a brighter-faced Venda than usual, and Denise, with a little gasp of relief, pointed to her.

"You will pardon me, monsieur, but it is this woman for whom I have words. I did not want to interrupt the gentlemen, but Venda will understand."

He noticed her embarrassment, but bowed and placed a seat for her, then taking himself into the court. And the slave-woman stood before her with questioning eyes.

"Venda, you will think it strange that I have nothing to say to you, only to trust you a little. I would not go forward to speak to your new master because — because your former master was there too, and I could not explain to Monsieur Delogne; but you, Venda, maybe you know without me explaining."

"Venda knows; you have wise thoughts, little mistress—Venda see that too. And your tongue has been still about the night out there by the garden; but be not afraid —Venda watch, Venda make sign to you if danger comes, sure! You trust?"

"Yes." And the girl felt a dread lifted off her heart at the words of the woman. "You know what — who I fear — I came to tell monsieur, but I will not now — perhaps I can another day; until then I trust you."

"And is there any other thing Venda may do for you?"

The girl arose, smiling, and shook her head.

"Then please, little mistress, you do something for slave Venda — little bit. To-day she like to ask how you be convent child?"

"Would you care to hear?" asked Denise, and sat again to talk. "Well, the story is not a long one, Venda. In the time of good Mother Agnace I was left at the convent gate; that was all."

"You little then?"

"Very little, only a baby."

"No one know where you come from?"

"No one, Venda. Some thought Mother Agnace knew, but she died before I could talk; she told the sisters, however, that I was to take vows when I grew old enough — when I was eighteen; that is over a year away yet. So you see I have not a long story to tell you. Why do you care to know?"

"Um! Nothing much." But the woman's eyes searched her face with so keen a scrutiny that the girl drew back, startled by the intensity of it; and then she saw Lamort and Zanalta, who stood in the door as though they had stopped to look at the picture made by the two figures.

Zanalta had his hat in his hand about to depart, and an unpleasant smile touched his lips as he looked at them, then with a bow he passed out; but once in the garden he smote one hand against another and smiled at some thought that was pleasant.

"Admirable! most admirable!" he said to himself, and nodded assent. "A foundling and utterly unknown to any one now living. I never suspected that. It will go hard with me if I do not find a claimant for her ere long, the saintly slip; she has caused me more than one unquiet moment, though. I have feared to move again in the matter so soon; but I'll have her! Would not Rochelle come handy in this enterprise? I fancy so. Once get her aboard his vessel — by heavens, it shall be done! Ah, Diego, you have not accomplished much for Ronando by this visit to-day, but you have found a trail to a soft nest for yourself."

Monsieur Lamort greeted Denise with his usual

courtesy, but his tones had a little more than his usual tenderness as he looked at her.

"I heard a portion of your discourse as we entered here," he said, as he sat beside her, "and you will pardon in an old man that which you have pardoned his slave — a little curiosity. And are you then utterly without family?"

"I was a foundling of the convent, of whom no one seems to know anything but that I was left at the gate one night," replied the girl; while Venda, withdrawn a space, watched the two — the young face with its youthful grace, the old one with the gray hair, the sad eyes, and the scar on the cheek that lent a warrior-like character to his face.

"It is desolate enough for age to be alone, but the loneliness of youth can also have its sad coloring; and is not even your nationality known?"

"Nothing — not even my name; but Sister Andrea always insists that I come of French people. Mother Agnace must also have thought it when she called me Denise; no other name was given me, for in the convent life no other is needed."

"But in the days to come, when perhaps wedding-bells are sounded for you, you must let me know, and I shall see that you do not go undowered. You have earned that, mademoiselle, by your labor among those who can not afford to repay you."

"You are gracious, Monsieur Lamort. But you do not know, then, that this dress of a novice has its own significance? There will be no marriage-bells for me. I am to be a nun when I grow older. I owe my life to the church."

"And to no one else a thought — not even to yourself?"

As she raised her eyes to answer him she noted that Delogne stood in the doorway and was observing her. The color swept over her throat and brow like a lily that the red sun tints. Lamort followed her eyes, and smiled.

"To no one, monsieur. I am nameless; but only from the church will a name be given me. I must be away on my errands now. I was speaking to your slave-woman, but did not think to stay so long."

She had arisen, when Lamort asked, kindly, "Is there anything in which I can serve you to-day? If so, you must let me know."

Her original errand occurred to her, but she had lost the courage to mention it. She only bowed and moved to the door.

"If a day comes when I need service I will remember your offer, and will remind you of it. Meanwhile I thank you; I pray blessings for you."

"Blessings," repeated the older man, turning to Delogne after she had gone. "Is it not blessing · enough for one day to receive such sweet words, or so gracious a glance from those clear eyes?"

Receiving no reply, he glanced around to find the young man staring dejectedly from the lattice.

"You are not very sympathetic, Chevalier," he remarked, drily.

"What can you expect, monsieur — that I will rejoice at the fact that the Lady Denise dispenses sweet glances, but will direct never one to me? I am not yet saint enough for that."

"What!" And the other turned and looked at him with more attention. "Something in your tone tells me you are serious."

"Serious!" And Delogne faced him, with knit brows and determined eyes. "So serious that, though she has spoken to me but twice in her life, I would give all I wish to possess if I could hope to win her from those vows to the jealous church."

"Nay, nay, Maurice," said the older man, kindly. " Be content that your rival is nothing more human. But would not your aunt, the marquise, think this sudden fancy a thing of folly?"

"Without doubt — yes. So would many a wise person, monsieur, for she will not look at me; and even if she did I am too poor to offer her the home such a lady should have — for she is a lady by birth, no matter how shrouded in mystery her parentage remains."

"Yes, she appears to be a lady; but really, Maurice, one can not always judge one's descent from the face. Have you not seen delicate lady mothers have clowns for sons, and fairest flowers of maidens grow up daintily amid brothers and sisters who were like uncouth cattle? I have. I have also seen a graceful, blue-eyed, brown-haired girl whose mother was a brown woman from Cuba. Those things have disturbed somewhat my old idea that blood always tells. It does not always, so far as outward appearance goes, though I am more than willing to believe that mademoiselle is all you would have her be."

"Do you know, monsieur, for the first time I am

anxious to hasten the investigation concerning the properties De Bayarde bought long since for the marquise? She told me it was to be mine if it was yet obtainable. It may prove of value — who knows? If I only had an estate of my own at my back I would dare move. Her friends at the convent might not be so persuasive then. I could promise more earnestly that her life should have every care. Ah! what a simple you must think me to thus plan and dream when I am not even encouraged by a glance from her. *Mon Dieu!* if I was but a prince with a diadem to offer her!"

"Yes," agreed Lamort, sadly, cynically, "there comes a time in every man's life when he longs for a kingdom to bestow on some woman."

"Ah, monsieur, it is a jest to you; but if you have ever known love —"

The older man raised his hand.

"Say no more, Maurice. I would help you if I could see the way. But the memory of love in my life is more like to give me cruel than kind thoughts; and yet — that girl —"

He leaned his head on his hands and seemed lost in reverie, from which Delogne made no attempt to arouse him, though he glanced at him curiously from time to time. He wondered what had made him feel bitter at the memory of love that had been — some woman who was false, perhaps.

Then Lamort raised his head and brushed his hand over his brow as one who strives to drive away thoughts unpleasant.

"Bring those papers from the cabinet to me,

Maurice—those in the private drawer. The
Ronando case is settled; those slaves will be confiscated. The heavy fine and the disgrace—well,
they will count; and then the rolls of gold for a
gambling debt that must be paid at once—ah! they
all count. Young Ronando's wife goes back to
Spain in anger at the disclosures, and takes all her
gold from their coffers. That will hurt the old man
most—the loss of gold or of dominion always hurt
him. That is one move. Now for Durande."

Delogne returned with the papers, and the older
man clutched them as if they contained much that
was precious.

"Yes, yes; we will see about that estate for you,
Maurice," he said, and smiled, with a peculiar look
at the young man. "The time is ripe, I think. Let
me see the letter from Hector de Bayarde to the
marquise—that is it—um! Now hand to me that
roll with the cord of crimson about it. Yes, my
memory is good for these things, though I have not
unrolled them for three years." And he smoothed
out the yellow, crackling parchment. "Now try
your eyes on that. What do you see?"

Delogne glanced at it, then at the letter to the
marquise, and half rose from his chair in sudden
surprise.

"Why!"—and he stared at Lamort as though
scarcely realizing that he had seen aright—"on my
life, it seems the same script—written by the same
hand."

"I thought you would discover the resemblance,"
remarked the older man, quietly. "But you do not
examine the meaning of the text."

Delogne bent over it, with a low cry of surprise.

"It is the paper mentioned in that letter," he exclaimed, excitedly. "'The transfer of the estate called Royal Grant from the Count Hector of the house of De Bayarde of Anjou to Madame la Marquise de Lescuré of Rouen, France.' So it is labeled, and so — ah, *mon Dieu!* monsieur, I feel as though a great wave had passed over me, leaving me breathless. My astonishment leaves me no words. Your finding of this is like witchcraft."

"I beg you will not league me with the witches," smiled Lamort. "I have had enough of maledictions lately from our ruling class here without adding the accusation of witchcraft."

"But pray tell me how you have found this — by what rare chance it has come to you."

"There is little of chance in this world, Maurice," returned the other, wearily; "and the only thing in this affair that seems strange to me is that you should have arrived at just the time you did in New Orleans."

"Perhaps; but that is by no means the strangest to me. This paper, supposed to be lost in the sea years ago, written by a man dead these thirty years — well, I confess it is wonderful that you should have found it."

"Not so wonderful when you learn that it has never been for one moment lost. That it never was sent to the marquise, because of delays that were many. The papers Hector de Bayarde promised to send were burned when the Indians fired a house where he was staying over in the Apalachee country.

This one was executed long after, and only two
months before the insurrection of '68 — the time of
his own death and the confiscation of all his own
property. It was sealed up with other papers of
import — papers containing many secrets of that
troublous autumn, many names of persons interested in the uprising, whose property would also
have been grasped by the Spanish governor if those
signatures had met his eyes. Oh, yes, that title deed
and transfer was in important company all those
years, though it is so yellow and unlovely."

"But you?" persisted Delogne. "I am yet amazed
that all this knowledge should have come to you;
that you could have gained so quickly all the past
records of De Bayarde."

"The knowledge at least came to me in all
honesty," declared Lamort; "and if a title is given
you to the estate it will be a clear one."

"Do not think for one instant that I suspect that,"
said Delogne, quickly. "It is my amazement that
speaks, not my doubts; and if it is not a secret, I
confess I am curious to hear more."

"Oh, no; it is not a secret I could not tell to you,"
answered the other after a moment's thought. "For
you of course would not send it abroad. I would
trust you for that."

"You may."

"Of course," resumed Lamort, "I do not promise
to tell absolutely all, as there may be those yet on
earth for whom it would result sadly, and against
whom I have no ill-will. But you may have gathered
from many things — report, the contents of my

house, or my own words — that I have been a traveler who loved the strange corners of the world. Well, it is true. For three years I have been quiet here on this Island of Orleans — I, who have never been so long in one place for more years than the number of fingers on both hands. Some day — pouf! — a fair wind will blow in the way of my mood, and I will doubtless stand again on the deck of a vessel, and head her, as of old, where my fancy leads. But to the story: Once off the far coast of Mexico inclination led me inland -- over the ranges where the yellow metal is found, through lands where the fine opals glow, and where the precious stones of amber, and blue, and green gleam on many an Indian breast; where I have seen a native guide kick over a stone by the path and find under it a topaz. In that land are labor exiles who are as slaves. Some have gone from these shores, some from the West Indies; some are really slaves stolen off the slave coasts and held there under the iron rule of the mines, working under the musketry of the guards, and risking worse dangers than quick death if they venture an escape through the country of the natives. Well, I reached a valley in one of those ranges — a valley where the gold was washed from the soil at the will of mercenaries, who filled their own coffers, and gave also a goodly portion to the state, for that was the law. The study of that country pleased me. I learned also somewhat of the traces gold and gems leave on the soil where they hide. You will find people here who will tell you I have made fortunes by such findings, though they but guess at that. But during my observations I of course met men who toiled, as well as the gold they washed in the streams. From one of those exiles I learned the story of wealth hidden, possibly, in these papers, and of the papers hidden in the marked nook of the waters near this island."

"De Bayarde!" exclaimed Delogne, with eager excitement; "the man the people here have told us of, Basil de Bayarde, the — exile."

Lamort nodded, and then smiled carelessly, as he said :

"I am wondering why you did not say as the others say — Bayarde the assassin."

"I can not say. I only know it does not seem natural for me to think of him like that; perhaps because the story of the fair lady and their love, and all, has made the legend more romantic than horrible to me, though of course the crime and expiation has horror enough too."

"Well, your avoidance of the word assassin or murderer recalled to my mind the very earnest protests the man made of his own guiltlessness of crime in that matter."

"Heavens! how horrible if he should be guiltless — if that most terrible sentence should be unjust!" exclaimed the younger man; "but of course it is not likely — the judges would of course sift well the evidence ere committing a life to such torture."

"One of the judges was Señor Ronando," remarked Lamort, grimly. "The accused man was thought of the low caste — a young ranger of the north who thought little of title, and in fact had no proof at the time that he came of other than peasant blood. Men of Ronando's stamp could forgive a murderer, but not a peasant who had dared reach for — and clasp — a princess from their midst; a maid who had disdained his judges, yet bent to his wooing. Think you such a man would judge with unbiased mind?"

"And you know all this — have known it while it has been discussed among us, yet made no comment?" said Delogne, looking at him wonderingly. But Lamort shrugged his shoulders.

"Ah! no; they have told many things I had not heard before — for you see it was his side of the story I had known, not theirs, and I find a wide difference; and to tell the truth, I trust his the most. But I commenced to tell you of this," and he touched the parchment. "It seems Hector feared death might come to him through the insurrection, and he made his arrangements accordingly, so that his boy should in after years carry on the work he would leave undone. He was an earnest lover of his native France — though to tell the truth he had been treated ill enough by some of its people, as you may have heard. He had papers fiery with political plots, documents of power in able hands, but useless of course in the hands of a boy of ten years. So when the final blow struck him, he bade the boy take him to a nook already marked as fiting; by his directions the papers, sealed in glass, were buried under the river-sands. The boy was made to promise never to unearth them until his twenty-fourth year, the father knowing that in the
15

hands of a boy they would be things of vast danger;
but if at that age he cared to use the knowledge
contained in them, and so rise to position, then
they were to be used according to written instructions wrapped with them. But here one puzzling
thing occurs. This paper in our hands was not meant
to be buried with the others; in a letter it is mentioned, also the surveyed outline of the estate is
told of, but it is plainly stated that the documents
themselves are sent to his friend in France, the
Marquise de Lescuré, and bids his son do service
for her if she ever call on him. Now that surveyed plan of the land is not here, neither is the
letter of instructions to the marquise, so the supposi-
tion to me is that in his haste he has sealed and sent
to the marquise those two papers, and overlooked
the legal documents, which he had enrolled among
the ones for his son. I also gather from his letter
to the son that he had requested, and hoped, that
the marquise would have a care of the boy, and had
written her to that effect."

"She never received the letter, monsieur — I am
assured of that," declared Delogne; "and since it
was lost, what a lucky chance it is that this document was forgotten in that time of his haste and
distraction."

"As I told you before, there is little that chances,
my dear Chevalier."

"And you tell me that De Bayarde at his trial did
not know of his family or their standing. How was
that so when he had those papers?"

"He was by no means twenty-four years old at

the time he was sentenced; and with the careless nature of a boy he never took thought that these musty political records could help him in his trouble, or that they could bear influence aside from plots of government. The lad had seen more than he cared to of revolts and their distresses, and had no disposition to take part in the schemes which his father held sacred. He had much rather make himself a pipe from a reed, and blow through it the songs of each bird or wild thing haunting the river. And so it fell that these things were left until this time to be looked into; for Bayarde, hopeless of returning in his own person, gave the clue to the documents into another's keeping."

"And that other was you?"

"I have them in my possession," agreed the other, quietly.

"Poor fellow!" said Delogne, sadly; "he little thought what influence his confidence would have on lives he knew not of."

"I don't know about that. He thought of a great many things, away off there in that living hell. He grew to hope — without ever having read those papers, mind you — he grew to hope steadily that their contents might have power to bring sorrow to some of the men who condemned him; and, strangely enough, it has proven so. This land to which these papers give your aunt legal right is now held by Durande, one of the judges. It will leave him less wealthy, and it will also take many acres from Don Zanalta; for it is no small garden, Maurice."

"I can scarcely realize it yet," said the young man, getting up and walking about; "a large estate, of which at least a considerable portion will come to me — or will there be doubt as to our right being allowed at this date?"

"The property was confiscated, together with other, as that of Hector de Bayarde, revolutionist; hence it belonged to the state, or the crown; afterward it came to Durande for services rendered the governor. But at the time it was confiscated it no longer belonged to De Bayarde, as these documents prove; so restitution must be made by the crown. Though before any word is said or any move made in the matter I would like much to have a copy of that original plat of the land as marked by the earliest surveyors, for from it the landmarks would be more easily distinguished; and in my belief there is but one in the hands of a private citizen, a brown parchment done in red ink, and that citizen is Don Zanalta."

"Ah! And what part did the Don play in the tragedy of Bayarde?"

"He was a most important person — the prosecutor," returned the other, quietly. "He and Durande have had legal trouble about the boundary-lines of their estates — they adjoin each other. That is how I came to learn of the surveyed plan of the old plantations which is in Zanalta's possession; though you understand that nothing is to be mentioned concerning it to any one at present."

"Not at any time except by your wish," promised Delogne, earnestly; "but I have been most anxious

to learn more of that man down there in the gold-
fields. Can you tell me any more of him, or have
you grown tired of my questioning?"

"Not at all. I will tell you all I have been able
to learn, and am only sorry that the 'all' is so brief
and cheerless. After I found those papers and had
settled here in Orleans for awhile, I sent a letter to
the commander of the mines out there asking about
the man whom these papers had been meant to
benefit. I have the answer somewhere among
these papers here. It said that the convict Bayarde
had been killed five years ago, by a fall into a
chasm, where he was dashed to death. His body
was never recovered, but his number was wiped
from the convict-list, and he was declared legally
dead. Not a bright finale, Chevalier, but the whole
story is gloomy. It makes me sad when I think of
it—and especially of the chance there was that he
might have been innocent. Come, let us walk out
where the wind blows; those papers stifle one with
the mold of the past."

CHAPTER XI.

THE WOOING OF NINON.

IN the house of Zanalta there were curious doings
and varying moods in these days, despite the long
hours of labor and discussion over the portrait of
the gracious señora. It was not yet completed, and

the lady sat day after day on the throne-like chair
and smiled complacently on the handsome artist,
seeing clearly enough through his ruse to prolong
the sittings, and receiving the raillery of Madame
Villette with great good humor.

And Don Zanalta had said to him, with sly meaning, "I acknowledge myself in your debt, Monsieur
Raynel, for more than the price of a portrait,
namely, so many days of fair weather in our household. The temper of my sister-in-law has ever been
variable, but she broods over us all like a dove of
peace since she has commenced to admire herself on
your canvas. Pray tell us, do you mingle a charm
with your pigments?"

"To be sure," spoke Madame Villette, with a
smile of saucy wisdom ; "what charm more potent
than the latest fashion from murderous Paris?
Alas for captives snared by Monsieur Cupid through
such arts!"

"Take care, Ninon," warned Don Zanalta, "else
some day a gallant may ride this way, and leave
your friends lamenting because you too are num-
bered among the captives."

"I?" And madame's pretty brows were arched,
and her jeweled hands flung upward in disdain.
"Pray give me credit for more of wisdom. There
will be time enough to think of that when my curls
turn to gray, and my heart is tired of wandering."

"Madame"—and Raynel's eyes met hers as he
bowed—"there is a proverb telling us it is best to
love to-day—to-morrow never comes."

"Ah! Señora Zanalta will be interested to hear

that "—and she met his glance with one of laughing defiance —"and it is a pretty playmate for an empty hour—this love! There are many proverbs about it, and among others one that says, 'Love makes time pass, but time makes love pass.' "

"Truly," remarked Diego Zanalta, "you each seem wise on the subject, as though you had perused volumes concerning it; but, Ninon, a lady exclaiming against love is like a child who sings in the dark because it is afraid."

"Oh!"—and she gazed after his retreating form with large combative eyes—"afraid!—I? Well, then, Juan Diego Zanalta, I could tell you it is not Ninon Villette who is afraid—not the least little bit."

And she seated herself decorously on the quaint carving of the window-shelf, scarce seeming to see the man who had quoted of love to her, and who looked on her with caressing eyes from the respectful distance at which he stood.

"And it pleases you to laugh, then, at the power before which so many worship, madame?" he asked. "Strong indeed must be your faith in self if never a fear comes to you lest Monsieur Cupid should some day visit you in search of revenge."

"Indeed no. Love only calls at doors where some voice sings him a welcome; and I—oh, well, monsieur, I have had other things to think of, serious things. Have you not heard of the lost Santa Barbara, a vessel swallowed in the storm of last month, when it carried to the ocean-bed so much of the dowry I might have brought to a husband? Well, monsieur, I speak to you with directness, knowing you to be a friend of the family, and you will understand that a dowerless widow can not expect the visits you are so gallant as to mention."

Ah, Ninon! it is a time-worn card to play — that for compassion; and yet, ancient as it is, adoration ever blinds one's eyes to the trap it hides. And Constante listened with a growing radiance overspreading his face. Her wealth swept away! Then that barrier was broken down. He felt so much closer to her when she said a portion of her riches was hers no longer.

And so it was that Madame Villette, glancing up, met his smiling eyes, his eager, pleased face, and shrugged her shoulders, with a reproachful expression.

"Indeed, monsieur, though you say nothing, your looks belie all sympathy for my ill fortune."

"Ill fortune! Ah, madame, do not treat me coldly for that. I — I — how am I to make you understand what I feel at the news that you are no longer the very wealthy Ninon Villette? I can not have regret for the loss of that which helped to wall me from you — the golden weight that would have ever beaten down my courage."

"Monsieur!"

"Yes, it is so. I adore you — adore you! You may dismiss me forever for saying so — well, it is said. I am poor in moneys — in everything but my heart's love, and that is doubtless nothing in your eyes; but — ah, Madame Ninon! — I have been hiding my thoughts like a thief who was afraid; now at least I can feel more like an honest man since I have spoken."

Madame Villette had retreated under the rapid passionate shower of words. It is true she retreated but a step, and the lucky beggar was not forced to let go the hand he had audaciously seized.

But even the step gave one little touch of unwillingness, and Constante, who dare scarce look in her face, groaned in spirit, though whispering, "I love you — I adore you."

"But, monsieur — pray rise! Some one may come, perhaps; and, ah! if it should be my aunt, it would be terrible."

Even his passion could not blind him to the fact that an arrival of the Zanalta at that precise moment would be a thing to dread, and he arose from his place at her feet, standing beside her, eager — adoring.

Madame Villette, glancing at him from the corner of her eye, decided that he had never before looked so handsome.

"Will you not even speak to me?" he entreated. "Consider, madame, to love you was my fate — not my fault. To remain near you and keep silent was no longer a possible thing. But speak to me, I pray you."

"You have been very foolish, monsieur," she said at last. "You have been so for a long time."

"I know — I know! ever since that first evening when my eyes rested on you — when my arms held you for a moment amid the palms. Ah, madame, if for a sweet instant a soul should stand within the

gate of paradise, and loiter ever after within sight
of its beauties, could you blame him for the longings
born there?"

"You are adding sacrilege to folly, for the longings for heaven should not be spoken of as the
wishes of earth."

"Madame, if you have ever loved, you would
know that our true loves of earth are heaven-born.
It is the one gleam of heaven allowed to us here.
The words of love can never be sacrilege against
aught that is holy. You shake your head — you do
not believe! Oh, if love's hand but touched you,
then you could not be so severe."

"Severe? I think not, monsieur. I but said you
showed folly."

" In daring to tell you my heart was at your feet?
Yes, it was madness to dream you might care, if
ever so little; but the madness was sweet; it is my
own; it will never leave me. Even your dismissal
can not rob me of it, for I have found more sweetness in its dreams than wisdom will ever bring
to me. So, madame, it is all said — all the folly.
But have you no word for me ere I go?"

"Go! — you are going — where?"

"Of that I have not thought, and I dare not hope
it is of concern to you."

"Oh, but it is. The portrait of Señora Zanalta is
not yet finished; my own is not yet commenced."

He looked at her angrily, and his teeth closed
tightly as if to strangle an oath.

"You are gracious to care where I am, madame,"
he said, bitterly; "but it is best the pictures should

remain ever as they are than that you should be
further annoyed by a love you can not return, and I
can make no promises to refrain from showing you
the folly of my feelings toward you."

He picked up his hat, looked at her a moment,
and turned away with a bow. The lovely drooping
face was flushed like a rose ; she dared not raise her
eyes to look at him. He was going, the madman ! —
he had said so. He had reached the door.

Then he heard her voice — so meek a voice — it
was almost a whisper, and it said :

" I — I have not asked for the promises, monsieur."

" Madame — Ninon ! "

" I would not know what to do with them, especially when you threaten to break them. But I am
very positive Señora Zanalta will grieve if you take
your departure without finishing her picture."

" Ninon — angel ! Do you mean —"

But she shook her head, and held out one hand
laughingly to ward him off.

" No, no ! not one word more for that sort of
questioning. If you care to tell me the answer you
would like to hear from me, then indeed it will be
time enough for me to confess, otherwise —"

But needless to say the alternative was not discussed. There were passionate words of devotion,
fond chidings, and some coquettings close there by
the lattice; and the love-making of the young
Frenchman had not quite the stately character
belonging to the devoted courtiers of Old Spain.
Hence the reason that Madame Ninon, blushing and
confused, looked sister to some wind-kissed rose,

and did frown and smile many times, and knit her pretty brows, murmuring against love's folly.

"Ah — but think, Ninon, sweet Ninon, how long I have starved for a kiss of your hand — a gracious whisper. It has not been easy for me to wait until now."

"Then do I heartily wish you had made your declaration at once on your meeting me if you think you would have been more rational than after these weeks of lingering wishes."

"But did you not accuse me of folly when I spoke but now? You would have dismissed me forever had I spoken at first."

And then Ninon, Madame Villette, laughed and blushed at her own words as she whispered:

"Your folly was that you feared to speak; it was that I meant."

And who so close to heaven as Constante?

"But no; my brother will not be pleased," confessed the lady when later they had escaped to an arbor where a tête-à-tête could be assured. "He has thought it amusing to connect your name with that of Donna Zanalta" (Constante shuddered), "but he will not be ready to laugh when he learns you have found favor with me before his favorites."

"Ah! if I had but the wealth of some of the men he would welcome!"

"What, sir! When their wealth can not win me? Do you prize so lightly victories won that you have heart to think of others yet beyond you?" And she affected chagrin so prettily that he was forced to

sue for pardon, and protest until she was graciously
pleased to be pleased once more.

"It is only that I might give the jewel won a
casket fit for its resting-place," he assured her, and
sighed happily; "but I fear me I should have to
ask you to wait until my hair was gray ere I could
accomplish that."

"Then I pray you will ask nothing so impossible
of me," she retorted. "Wait until you are old? — do
not hope it. If I cared to marry a man who is old I
might chance to do so without waiting so long, as
there are several in the colony; so be warned."

Monsieur Raynel looked at her with smiling scrutiny; and so quickly does love reflect thought that
Madame Ninon laughed and nodded, with upraised
finger.

"I can tell what you are thinking — yes, I am
quite sure. Now confess. You are thinking of
those who are forsaken because they are dowerless,
and of whom we spoke but now. Yes, but many
good people may yet think, as you yourself did
think me, still a lady of wealth, and so present
themselves."

"A lady of wealth, and are you not?" demanded
her lover. "Each word spoken by you is a golden
blossom of thought, each glance of your eyes a
jewel for which a man would sell himself into
slavery. What wealth so precious as that of your
own charms?"

"But what think you Diego will say when we
speak of our stock of charms with which to commence life together?" she laughed, gaily. "But

never mind; Diego need not know yet, even the
señora need not know." And she shot one wicked
glance at him. "Indeed, Diego has of late days
been most fitful, and the time does not seem a good
one to tell him our thoughts."

"Must we wait, then, the humor of Don Zanalta?"
asked Constante, with some impatience. "I heartily
wish that he himself had a lady-love — we could
count more surely on his sympathy; but our gracious Don singles out no lady for his devotion."

"I do not know," said Ninon, doubtfully. "He
seems to have a rose-bower ever over his fancies —
one never guesses who his smiles fall on; but this
I do know, he was severe with black Gourfi yesterday, and I heard Gourfi complain because a fight
for 'master's demoiselle' had left him with a lame
shoulder, and I have wondered much who 'master's
demoiselle' can be. It is a lady of course, else
Gourfi would not have said 'demoiselle.' But it
would go ill with his temper should he think me
curious. And well am I pleased that you will now
be near for me to confide in, for of late I have had
many curious fancies about Diego, and never a safe
ear in which to whisper them."

"By our troth, then, you are lending to me some
of your fancies," confessed Constante, at the thought
of "master's demoiselle" and the wounded shoulder.
"I pledge you I will be a willing listener."

"Very well; but you must not make oath of our
troth until we are trothed." And she shook her head
warningly.

"But what more is there to be said between us?"

demanded her lover, in dismay. "Have I not protested I adore you — have you not been gracious
enough to accept my love — have I —"

"Ah, there! there!" she laughed. "And pray,
monsieur, am I to plight troth to each gentleman
who is pleased to tell me he loves me? Believe
me, should I have done so, you would have a long
list of *fiancés* to pass ere reaching my hand."

"Never mind; I would fight my way through if
you threw but a smile of encouragement to me.
Tell me what I am to accomplish ere you will consider me your *fiancé*, and let me hear also those
puzzling fancies about the señor — your brother."

"We will commence first with the fancies," she
decided, "and afterward, if you are trusty — well, we
will see. But this is serious — this of Diego. I
thought of telling it to Father Joseph, but have
not yet found courage. Constante, some evil one
has woven a spell about Diego. He is possessed."

"Possessed! — and of what?"

"By evil spirits — *the* evil spirit. It keeps him
awake in the nights. He talks to it — I heard him.
He moans and groans for it to leave him — to go
back to the grave. He muttered of masses he
would have said. He complained that it was the
woman, the accursed woman, who held the knife
— not he. He had touched no one. Now that is
the way he did talk all alone in his chamber, and
when I, almost distracted, did call and ask after his
health he was impatient, and made reply that he
had slept poorly and had some troublous dream.
Now what think you?"

"That perhaps your brother may have been truthful, but forgot part of the truth," said Raynel, with a sympathetic understanding of such possibilities. "Did he say aught of the quality or quantity of wine he had drank before retiring?"

"Oh, you think it was wine, then? No, no indeed! I am sure not. It was an evening when he had no company; when he was engaged in looking over accounts, and sorting old papers and early records of life here. All his day had been quiet — not one thing to make him disturbed, and I am sure no drinking of wine; and then — well, there have been other times."

"Other dreams?"

"No; words in the daylight. He talks alone. It was never so before. I heard him in the garden, when the roses hid me. He spoke again of the accursed woman, and her eyes that haunted him. He was telling himself that something he had seen in the night was a shadow, nothing more, and then he told himself it was the fault of the woman whose eyes he hated; but the something he had seen he did not name, only said, 'It was but a shadow under the trees — a fancy of the darkness.' Now what am I to think — is it the priest I should speak to, or the physician?"

"Let us not be hasty in this matter; it is worth consideration. I will do anything you wish if I may help you. But ghosts under the trees, and the fear of a woman's eyes! Well, one can scarce tell what key will unlock the riddle. If we could but guess who the woman — the 'accursed' one — might

be — scarcely the 'demoiselle' of whom Gourfi
spoke?"

For in his mind was the fair, strong, bewildering
face of Denise as she looked that evening in the
house of Monsieur Lamort. That could never be
the face Zanalta shrank from; those eyes, clear as
the eyes of a child, could never be the eyes he called
'accursed.' There were evidently two women who
held the interest of Don Diego; and Raynel, in his
usual impulsive manner, had leaped to the conclusion
that he knew the one, and as quickly decided to check-
mate any little game his future brother-in-law might
have in that direction. Yet there was another part
of Ninon's confidences less easy to fathom.

That other woman — the woman with the eyes!

"I do not know," acknowledged the lady, regret-
fully; "indeed I fear it is no woman at all, only
a sick fancy of the brain, for he grows stranger than
of old. He stays away some nights, and money
is lost at games with some stranger. I heard of that
through the Ronandos, who have had much trouble
with such games. He only amuses himself with
curious rascals, so he says, but I would rather
he played games with good Father Joseph, who loves
well the pastime and a glass of good wine. Such
friends I am sure would not send him to dreams of
men's ghosts, or the awful eyes of women — for it
must be only fancy."

They had arisen and walked the length of the
arbor, their tones low and secretive. The bees
humming over the countless blossoms broke on the
silence almost as sharply as their words, and they

16

would have deemed it impossible that any ear could have heard their confidences.

But as they retraced their steps and came to a path crossing their own, Ninon gave a low cry of surprise as their former slave, Venda, walked into the arbor from that side-path of the roses, and halted respectfully that she might not cross before them.

Her eyes were nearer smiling than either had ever seen them. She walked as if from the house.

"Venda! how comes it you are in my garden?" asked Madame Villette, sharply. "Who has offered you entrance through the gate that is mine alone? You know this is never the walk for any but my friends."

"I know, mistress. I will kneel at your feet for pardon. Venda did wrong, but she was in haste. You were ever kind, so please forgive. You forgive" —she looked with wise meaning at the two—"and Venda make you a charm to bind the heart you lean toward. Venda know, and Venda wish you good."

"Oh — enough!" agreed Madame Ninon, with blushes and some confusion under the calm, certain gaze of the slave-woman. "Go your way; but in future use the gate of the other garden when you have an errand, and let Venda keep that which she knows to herself."

"It shall be as you say, little madame. To you and master I wish a paradise."

She made one of those profound oriental bows, touching her lips and her breast with her hand, and then passed out of sight beyond the roses.

"Venda is never Venda without some such strange barbaric action," remarked Madame Ninon. "I do believe she makes practice of such ceremony the better to impress the other slaves with fear, and even the whites with belief in her charms. It makes her more graceful than the others, but beyond that it means nothing."

"Perhaps not," agreed Raynel, dubiously; "but with all her soft words I would just as soon be prayed into paradise by other lips than by the dancer of that heathenish performance we witnessed in the house of Monsieur Lamort. I have shuddered in the night when I thought of her face — her eyes — and the hand held out to a dancer invisible. I have never seen any human thing that impressed me as that strange-eyed slave."

Ninon laughed. Venda had always been most docile with her, and it amused her to hear of the alarm she inspired in others, even in Diego Zanalta after years under the same roof.

She stopped abruptly in her laugh and walk, looking up into her lover's face with a sudden inspiration.

"Now if Diego had said in his sleep that it was a black woman whose eyes he hated I should think it was Venda."

'Venda!'"

"Just so; his avoidance of her was so marked. He never once took from her hand a cup or a bit of fruit. Often have I wondered that he did not sell a slave he could not endure near him. And now — but I am silly to have such thoughts; they came all in a moment, when you too spoke of her with distrust. It is not likely, is it, that Don Diego Zanalta, who has had black people by the dozens, should be haunted by one slave-woman whom he bought and sold?"

CHAPTER XII.

DIEGO ZANALTA LAYS PLANS AND SEÑORA ZANALTA SPEAKS HER MIND.

WHILE the lovers talked in the arbor and laid plans to discover the cause of Diego's ill rest, Diego himself was closeted with Father Joseph in the house of the priest, and listened eagerly to a story he had asked for.

"On a Christmas night, you say, and in the year 17—? Now tell me, did you learn nothing but the date — no family name, no trinkets — or did you ask?"

"I asked. To every question the answer was 'no.' Mother Agnace was thought to know something, but she is no longer living. Her directions were, however, that Denise was meant for the convent."

"Strange that so noble a woman would lend her aid to a thing that if known would be resented as an outrage by every gentleman's child who is instructed in the convent," said Zanalta, with a fine burst of indignation. "I beg you will not think me demented, Father — you look at me as if you feared so. I can not confide in you this morning. I must examine more deeply into this question before I dare put it in words; but if it proves, as I have reason to believe, a great wrong has been waiting all these years for our righting, ever since that Christmas night — it was the night, not the day?"

"It was the night — a night well remembered, because two infants were left at the gate after the darkness fell; the other an octoroon child that did not live the night through. But tell me, my son, all this inquiry means no harm to the girl — Denise?"

"No harm; it may mean a change in her life, but I do not think it will prove unpleasant; however, I can tell you no more than that. I am much in your debt for your investigation of this matter. Let me know if I can ever serve you so well."

But scarce waiting to hear the reply of the priest, he hastened out of the shadows of the dwelling and walked jubilant in the sunshine. His walking-stick was flourished jauntily as he moved. He wanted to laugh aloud in his content. If dreams ever troubled him, they were forgotten then. He seemed a different man. A beggar asked alms shrinkingly as he passed, and was astonished at the handful of coin flung to him. Diego was in a rare mood.

"That Christmas-night," he repeated to himself, "a day of all days the best; not one can come in evidence against my plan, for Venda at that time was with Felice St. Malo on the plantation of Madame Sollé. Madame is dead, Felice is dead — who is there to come in evidence that a child was not born of Venda there on that plantation, a child whose father was white and a child that was given no likeness to her mother? Such things have been; and if she con-fesses it — if?— she *must* — I will have little trouble to establish my claim to the child, when the mother belonged to me at the time of the birth. Popular opinion will be with me; the convent dare not com-bat strongly, for every white citizen will be enraged at the chance that his child has been educated arm in arm with a *négresse!* Ah, it all plays into my hands so smoothly; the plan is admirable. I pre-pare my paper for the recovery of my slave. I get Venda's mark to it. I receive the signature of an *alcalde.* I claim my pretty saint and spend a honey-moon somewhere among the islands of the gulf shore. I may have been unlucky at play of late — to Rochelle is that blame — but fortune is somewhat at my call despite the cards."

He was walking along the road by the river where boats of different sorts were drawn up with their noses against the shore, when, glancing out over the writhing water, his eyes fell on a boat cutting its way through and sending the spray flying to either side. Few of the blacks propelled a boat like that; they ever prefer a song to the dip of the oars, and the air one that moves slowly.

Zanalta halted to watch it, and as the rower's face was seen he walked down to the water's edge and beckoned to the man.

" I was sure of your face though afar off, Monsieur Robert," he said, as the man saluted, "and glad am I it is you instead of your men whom I chance on, for I would like much to transact a matter of business with the Sea Gull, and it pleases me to deal with principals."

"At your service, señor," said the man, quietly. "I trust it may be possible to meet your desires."

"An easy matter enough, if you can give me the vessel for a month, manned as it is," returned Zanalta, and smiled at the surprise in the sailor's eyes. "You are astonished at that? Surely, your commander can spare it to me so long. I well know he does not live in it steadily of late, for he is too often on shore, and I have reason to think spends time inland among the Natchez — but it matters not at all to me where he may roam, and I will not interfere with his traffic, whatever it is; all I ask is room for myself and — a companion."

The man Robert shook his head, with a deprecating smile.

"It would distress me to refuse you, señor, but I fear it will not be possible. You know Monsieur Rochelle is a gentleman of many moods, and as restless as a sea gull itself. He has never yet parted with his vessel to another lest a moment should come when he would need it, and to let it go to a stranger besides yourself — I can question him for you, but I fear not."

Zanalta hesitated a moment, and then:

"Perhaps when you tell him my companion will be a — a lady he will have more sympathy for my desires."

"Oh, a lady! Well"— and the man smiled and looked more encouraging —"it may be. When will you want to go aboard?"

"I will want all in readiness for three nights in succession, not counting to-night, and a small boat waiting at some given point to take us aboard at any minute we decide to go."

"I see." And the sailor nodded his comprehension. The love of an intrigue was dear to the heart of a seaman in the days when there was romance to touch it, and he was convinced it was an elopement Señor Zanalta was planning — well, it would be a diversion. "I can let you know after the stars shine to-night, not earlier," he decided.

"And where?"

"At your own house, or at a café where you have met Monsieur Rochelle; it is called Manette's."

"Let it be there. I will go for the answer instead of having it come to me. At what hour?"

"Nine by the clock."

"So let it be. A good-morning to you, Monsieur Robert; and remember I am counting much on the assistance of your vessel — indeed I would like much to see Rochelle himself in the matter if it be at all convenient, but he is such a will-o'-the-wisp."

"He shall hear of your desire, at all events," promised the other, "and if he is within easy distance he is likely to speak with you in person of the matter."

Then they parted, and Don Zanalta went on his way, well pleased at the meeting, for he observed that Robert was inclined to favor him, and that was well to begin with. And what plan so good as using the Sea Gull for his flight? In a month she would be tractable enough — she the "saintly slip," as he called her. Then it would be safe to land; she would be resigned. He would settle on some abode for her away from the town house; he was inclined to have her delicately lodged unless she prove unreasonable; and a month alone with him at sea, and only the faces of lawless seamen to meet her own! Then the certainty borne in upon her that she was, for all her fine learning, only a slave — the daughter of an African voudou — ah, the entire plan was admirable! He forgot the years of weariness that vexed him at times. He was young again with the youth of the early summer. Through the medium of this new emotion and prospective triumph, he felt that Fortune was turning with him into the path of his desires, and he walked confidently to meet her.

Other canoes were moving on the waters that morning — canoes with feather-trimmed occupants, who gathered in groups and watched curiously the faces of the white señors, who wondered at the simultaneous coming of the Natchez, and noted also that they were dressed in their richest, as if for some stately ceremony; but what affair of moment could bring them thus uninvited to the dwelling-place of the whites?

Don Zanalta noted them, though too much absorbed in himself to question; but as he passed the house of Lamort he observed a group of the somber-faced red men there too. They spoke to Delogne at the entrance. He was directing them to the Cabildo, but their interpreter, a French half-breed woman, was stupid.

"This no Cabildo?"

"No, no; this house of Lamort — *alcalde* — comprehend?"

"Lamort!" Two or three of the men repeated the name and nodded to each other.

"Where Lamort?" they asked; and Delogne looked despair. They were like stolid, persistent children.

"Who sent you here?" he demanded, in return. The woman consulted with the others, and then spoke:

"The man, Rochelle and his Natchez man, Nicholas. He say come down and hear in the Cabildo the Natchez who are slaves ask to be free. The great king over the water made them free many years ago, yet they are held. Now over the water, it is said, there is much freedom. The people sing songs and dance dances over the bodies of the dead nobles. There are nobles here in this land; they hold the people of the Natchez captive. The time has come to ask for the thing the great king sent to them."

Zanalta heard the name Rochelle, and retraced his steps.

"Can I be of any assistance to you, Chevalier?" he inquired, carelessly; and Delogne hesitated, though apparently needing assistance.

"If you could persuade these red gentlemen that no amount of waiting about the door will bring the Cabildo here, then I do not doubt you would be doing Monsieur Lamort a favor," he confessed. "They appear to have a settled idea that it is here justice is dealt."

"Did Monsieur Rochelle send you here?" Zanalta asked the woman; and she questioned the others. They shook their heads and muttered negatives.

"Cabildo," they repeated, and then —"but red men all say white Lamort."

"I see how it is," concluded Zanalta; "they are like wild animals still — these Indians — animals that have seen traps. Lamort has a fancy for interesting himself in these natives. They have learned his amiable weakness, and come no doubt for his sanction ere they will take the advice of any other. They are just so doltish — these savages. If you will allow me to call one of Lamort's blacks."

"Certainly; here, Nappo!"

Nappo appeared, with curiosity and some alarm visible in his big black eyes. Tales of massacres had made the red man the terror of the African.

"This boy will walk with you the path to the Cabildo," spoke Zanalta in a tone of authority to the natives; "do you comprehend? You go there; there you will hear the things of the law. That is all. Go!"

Nappo nodded to them, motioning the direction in which they were to be guided. The half-breed woman repeated the message, and the red men glanced from one to the other; then, with a significant grunt behind closed lips and a glance of utter disdain at poor Nappo, they turned as with one accord from the door and passed across the grounds to a different street to the one pointed out for them. The interpeter followed without a word at their heels.

" You perceive," remarked Zanalta, with amusement, "they know quite well where to go, but stubbornly waited here that they might see Monsieur Lamort, whether he wished it or not. They are doubtless little kings in their own tribes, and resented a black messenger. Is it so, then, that the red slaves have thus suddenly prepared demands for their freedom? for if so, of course Monsieur Lamort has acquaintance with the fact."

"Yes, señor. It is discussed in the Cabildo this morning. The revolution of France is sending echoes to every land; this movement of the red men is only one expression of it."

"And a useless one," commented the other. "The planters will simply see that the law for their liberation be repealed — a senseless law, made years ago in a court across the water, and by people who had no practical knowledge of this land's requirements. Who could have advised the savages that the old law was yet in existence?"

"I know not," returned Delogne, briefly. "The red men spoke of but two people, that Monsieur Rochelle whom they name the 'night-hawk,' because he is never seen among them when the sun shines, and then another who is evidently his officer, but partly of the Natchez blood. Beyond that they told me nothing."

"And Monsieur Lamort," persisted Zanalta, "is he also at the Cabildo in their interest? If so, they surely have widely different advocates — Monsieur Lamort and a lawless ranger of the waters."

"Monsieur Lamort is not here at present. When

you see him he will without doubt give you any required information on the matter, and as I have duties I must bid you good-day."

"A most assuming fellow," murmured the Span- iard, looking after him with little love, "and evi- dently cultivating as close a mouth as his master. Well, little care I for the doings of the island if I but secure the vessel and the maid. Curious that Rochelle and his men should also have a finger in this pudding of Indian slavery — one from which there is never a plum to be plucked. Um! it would go hard with Durande if the savages should get their demands — there are many of them on his plantation; though I need not waste pity on him, for I have not yet forgotten the trouble he made me once over the boundary-line. That reminds me to convey the diagram of the old estate to Monsieur Lamort. I will need his aid in claiming my slave, and it is well to pave the way by offering a favor. Strange that he cares so little about incurring the hate of the ruling class here. Within a month he has made enemies of the Ronandos and all their connection. Now it will be Durande. Well, he has been a power here for two years. It is well he is digging a pitfall for his feet, else his sway might have grown as wide as the land — yes, would have, had he been careful enough to conciliate the right people; and yet, a man may grow tired of statecraft and the ambitions of it, for all of this spring-time I have cared nothing who ruled. The eyes of Denise have been more often in my memory than all the machinery of the Cabildo; but Victor Lamort — pah!

he is too cold and correct of pulse to appreciate aught but musty documents and archive laws. Strange — he is not so old."

He had reached his own grounds, though his feet had found the way by instinct; his thoughts were elsewhere than on the path.

And on the threshold he met Señora Zanalta.

An excited, irate, and furious señora, whose bridal-veil was twisted into a rope by her restless fingers, and all the curls and brocades adjusted for the portrait were sadly disturbed.

"Ah — gr-r-r! We are disgraced, our house is no more, the name of Zanalta (thanks to the saints, I was not born of their blood) will be shrouded in shame! Diego Zanalta, have you no feeling in your breast? Is it nothing to you that your half-sister stoops to intrigue with an artisan hired by me to do service — a clever trickster whom she fancies cares for herself instead of her moneys? Oh, it is fine! We are to be made the laughter of the town, and he — he, the ingrate! Are you dumb that you say nothing? Well, then, I will not be silent. I, Mercedes Sofie Zanalta, to be thus tricked and schemed against day by day. Not that I would so much as use his coat for a carpet, or his head for a footstool. May the saints deform him! Not that I care who has him, with his brushes and his smirks. Ah — h! if he had not run so fast!"

And the beringed fingers of the lady opened and closed with a combative, destructive movement suggesting scratches and loosened tresses.

Her brother-in-law dropped on a divan, with a

sigh of resignation. And it had been so lately he praised her improved temper!

"Well, my dear señora, continue your scoldings, if they are not completed. When you have expressed all your annoyance I will be pleased to hear the reason. Who has tricked or robbed you?"

"Robbed me! Holy St. Francis! Did I want him? Do I care who he prances around? I tell you, Diego Zanalta, I have disdained courtiers in Madrid whose shoes this lackey would not be allowed to lace! Think not that because I wed with your brother it was for lack of more illustrious offers. Do you heed me?"

"I hear you, most certainly," he agreed, with weariness. "I fully understand that our family should feel honored by an alliance with your illustrious self; you can have no argument with me on that score, though my brother was at times less gallant than I, and even wished aloud that the ship had gone to the bottom of the sea ere he set sail for the port where he first met you; but for such men beauty was never intended, my honored señora. Now by me you were always held at your true worth, and if any cavalier has spurned your addresses, I promise you he shall hear from me."

"*Sacre!* — are you all demented? I care nothing for the fellow, however much he may have fancied so — and she too — the fools! Not longer shall I remain here, Diego Zanalta. Take heed, for I swear it, when the next ship leaves for Spain I depart forever from these shores, where the most illustrious names must associate with the rabble to be in the fashion of the times. Let your Ninon wed her dirty painter, as it pleases her. Oh, holy saints! that I should have found them, he at her feet, her fingers dabbling in his curls, and never a blush on her brazen cheek. But I assure you they ran finely when they saw me — a brave lover for Madame Ninon Villette, one who flies before the eyes of a lady insulted!"

"Do you mean to tell me you surprised a love-scene between my sister and this painter, Raynel?" demanded her kinsman, arousing himself to interest. "Do you not think your fancy has been warped by your fears? I have noted nothing of the kind."

"No, thanks to their duplicity — ah! did I not hear them laugh that they had cheated us so? Even my name was spoken by them, and well it was for them both that they fled."

"Raynel!" And Zanalta's brow had a deep wrinkle of thought drawn across it. The señora welcomed it as a sign of his anger, and poured out various grievances in the matter, while the ethereal bridal-veil steadily lost all semblance to anything so poetical, and with each shred of it plucked by her hands she repeated her unchangeable resolve to betake herself from the shores of the *sauvage* people, that her remaining days might be lived among surroundings more to her taste.

But the ears of Zanalta were closed to her. He was deliberating over this story she had brought him. If it should all be true, if Ninon should even want to marry the fellow! And as he had in truth not a vestige of power over her beyond what she chose to allow him — well, there were reasons why he should not be displeased, and the chief reason was that he thought Constante a fool.

"If Ninon had chosen a gallant of the town, who knew every gold-piece left to her by Villette — some one with an investigating mind, like Victor Lamort — well, it might have proven awkward for me. He would have induced her to a reckoning of every copper bit, and then — but this stranger, a fool in finances — these artists and poets and such ever are; and since she will wed where she likes when the time comes, it is best to keep in her favor and that of the man she smiles on. I may then be able to manage them both if I should ever need their offices. Others will say it is a mesalliance, no doubt; but I will know how to make it serve my turn."

"What will you do with them?" asked the señora as he arose. "You can put her in retreat with the nuns, can you not? When one shames her family —"

"Enough! I am weary of the subject. Had you, señora, chosen to smile on the gentleman whose brushes enhanced your beauty for us, think you I would have shut you in a convent? Not at all. I have too much sympathy for the dreams of love."

And leaving the señora dumb with astonishment and chagrin, he repaired to his own apartment, but not without being followed by light-footed Ninon, who slipped from behind a friendly curtain where she had been a witness to the entire scene. To say that she was joyous over Diego's reception of the damning proofs of her folly expressed feebly her

17

sensations. She had never been over-fond of her half-brother; but now for once she entered his door with a rush, and caught his shoulders with her little hands as though to hug him for his acknowledged sympathy.

"There, there!" he protested. "Has she told the truth, and does it make you act so like a child?"

But she was not to be chidden. She saw he was not angry, and her laugh was care-free.

"It is the truth, but oh, how much we were frightened!" And her eyes were big with memories. "She burst through the arbor like the tornadoes that blow on the coast. I have been hidden ever since."

"And your gallant inamorato — where is he? Did you discard him in your fright?"

Madame Villette gave him one appealing glance. In vain she strove to control the curves of her laughing mouth. The humor of the situation proved too much for her, and her complex emotions were expressed by unrestrained laughter, though the tears shone on her lashes.

"He never waited for dismissal," she confessed. "He ran one way and I ran the other. Ah, *merci!* how frightened I was lest she should catch us!"

"And you are in love, then, with a man who could desert you in the face of danger?" queried Zanalta. But she smiled at him flippantly, and a little pitifully.

"As if that made any difference," she retorted, disdainfully. "*Any* man would have run if Señora Zanalta had appeared to him with such anger. But it is not either for what he does or leaves undone

that I care for him; I care just because he is—
himself."

"And who is to tell you that he does not address
you because of the report that the Widow Villette
has a handsome store of wealth laid by for her?"

But she only laughed.

"It is not the money, Diego. How ungallant of
you to suppose a man would only look at me if I was
well-dowered!"

Zanalta seemed to scarcely hear her. He was looking with some attention and perplexity at a compart-
ment in his desk where some papers were visible,
and he tossed them about impatiently as though in
search of something.

"And, Diego, there is the Virgin Constante was
to paint for the chapel, and Donna Zanalta swears
it shall not be now; that she has influence and will
have the order for it withdrawn; that she—"

"Peace!" he commanded, sharply. "I scarce can
think for your chattering. Something has gone
from this room since I left here an hour or so ago.
Who has entered here?"

"No one—not a soul."

"No one of whom you know, perhaps," he agreed;
"but, nevertheless, there has been some pilfering
here. A parchment is gone, one with lettering in
red ink on the outside; the contents of it one of the
most ancient plans of land made on these shores—
the outline of a royal grant made in the year 1714,
surveyed by an order of Anthony Crozat. It may
be that the names or dates tell you nothing; you
are heedless of your own land boundaries as the

birds that fly; but this document is a curiosity. I held it in my hand this morning; it was left there, I could swear to it, and now it is gone."

"Is it valuable — would it be of money's worth to any one?" asked Ninon, searching diligently in every portion of the room for a parchment with lettering of red.

"Money's worth? No; not unless I should some day choose to reopen that contest of the boundary with Durande; and — but, yes, it is of worth in money, too, for I have promised a sight of it to a gentleman curious in such things, and a person from whom I will want a favor in return. It is like witchcraft that it should go just at this time. Go question all the house-servants; learn if any of them were seen to enter here. It must be found. A roll the size of this, but marked with red letters."

"Yes, Diego." But Ninon eyed him with attention as she neared the door. Was this loss perhaps only an imaginary thing, she was asking herself — of kindred to the phantoms with which he talked in the night-time? "I will make search, Diego; but I am just the least afraid of Donna Zanalta. She is still furious; and Constante —"

"Oh, may the devil seize Constante! Get you gone!"

And then Madame Villette withdrew in haste, and was fully convinced that the loss was an imaginary one. For how could any well-balanced mind fling execrations at the devoted head of Constante Raynel?

And straightway the lady concluded to search for

that wisely cautious knight, and confer with him on the subject, instead of wasting precious time in search for an old parchment, red-lettered and ancient though Diego thought it.

CHAPTER XIII.

MONSIEUR LAMORT PAYS A VISIT.

AND so when Victor Lamort himself chanced to drop in for a chat the paper was not yet found, though Señor Zanalta quickly smoothed his disturbed countenance, and came forward to greet his rare guest.

"I am weary of the jangling across there at the Cabildo," he confessed, "and your gardens looked so inviting with their shade that I yielded to the temptation of them and have arrived at your door."

"My house is honored by your visit, Monsieur Lamort," returned Zanalta. "It is an honor few houses of Orleans can boast of, for you ever seem too busy a man for rest under any man's roof but your own. And are the affairs of the Cabildo ended for the day? And what of the red slaves?"

"They will be slaves but for a little longer, señor," affirmed the other with confident tone. "It has been many years since O'Reilly, acting for the king of Spain, prohibited further traffic in Indian slaves, and yet after more than twenty years they toil on the plantations. They are bought and sold again to the highest bidder. But now that they have wakened to a sense of their rights, and now that chiefs from every tribe are coming to the judgment, the question can no longer be dismissed as an indifferent one; even Corondalet perceives that, though he objects to an immediate sweeping aside of the present state of things, and recommends compromise. But that of itself would be a link weakened in the chain the red slave wears."

"Of course you are aware that the planters will fight the case," hazarded Zanalta, "and that every owner of slaves, no matter what their color may be, will range themselves against you and your protégés?"

Lamort smiled indifferent assent.

"Yes, they tried to make me understand that; but it will not matter. Every reform must combat prejudice."

"You are courageous, monsieur, to face the prospect of social ostracism for the sake of some stupid savages who can never comprehend your sacrifice for them."

"Scarcely that," returned Lamort, still with the little smile about his lips. "You see, notwithstanding the fact that I have remained three years on your shores, I am likely to leave them in three hours if I no longer find pleasure here, or work to interest me."

"And the work to interest you must mean reform of some sort," said Zanalta, with assumed brightness. "To me it ever appears a matter for pity that you direct your endeavors only to the more wealthy and intelligent class. One grows sorry to see forever some of his friends being led to the Cabildo for judgment, as though they were the most insignificant of artisans, while in fact more than one who has been brought to defeat at your word served as a law-giver himself at some time. You have a scent like an Indian for game that has stepped from the straight path into the shadows for an instant."

Lamort rubbed his palms together in a pleased way, accepting the words as a compliment.

"While one is in the world one must do something," he observed; "and what better than to set wrong right? The ruling class should, in justice, pay a heavier price for faults committed than the masses of humanity, for their superior intelligence should be weighed with the fault."

Zanalta glanced at him, with a little shiver. He could see a certain narrow groove after all in the man they all thought so calm, so evenly balanced. He seemed for one instant to perceive in him one idea embodied, and that idea the meting out of justice according to his conception of the word. It is the one-idea man who develops into the fanatic — later into the madman. And Zanalta arose, with a strange foreboding of evil as the revelation of the man's character came to him. He only crossed the room for some water and wine; but the mere sense of movement was a relief after that fancy, and he shook his shoulders as though flinging off a weight, and told himself, as Rochelle had told him, that he was to be congratulated since this justice-hunter had never shown signs of suspicion toward him — not even a hint of smuggling, a thing for which many gentlemen had been made to pay fines and receive a black mark across an otherwise faultless record. Assuredly he had been rarely lucky.

And thinking so, he offered of his choicest wine to the fanatic who fought for justice in high places — wine brought ashore not long since from Rochelle's vessel, and presumably liable to confiscation ; and Monsieur Lamort sipped it with innocent enjoyment, and observed that he must not tarry, for Delogne had met him a little way down the street and given him tidings that a stranger guest awaited his attention, an old priest brought by some of the Indians from the far north country. He had grown ill on the journey, and they, after their fashion, had brought him to the " house of the exiles " instead of to the dwellings of his order.

" That is one of the undesirable things about popularity with the natives and lower classes," remarked Zanalta. " They would turn your house into a café with never a thought of your inconvenience."

" True ; but then, again, they might be just as willing to transform their poor wigwams into a hostelry for me should I require it," said Lamort, tranquilly ; "and if they never bring me a less welcome guest than one of those faithful pioneer priests, of whom I have heard much — well, I will have no quarrel with them on that score. By the way, señor, do you remember speaking of an old parchment in your possession of which I was promised a sight — a survey of a certain royal grant given by Crozet ?

I may need it in evidence within a few days, so take the liberty to remind you of it."

"And it shall be yours," declared Zanalta. "I am a little curious to know how it can be of use to you, yet am willing that it should be. Is it a question of Durande's land ?"

"Well, yes; it may be," agreed Lamort, as though studying whether to give or keep a secret. "A portion of that estate was illegally confiscated to the Spanish crown ; the evidence is clear, and another heir is in the field. Without that ancient survey it can be proven, but with it, all can be arranged rapidly, and with no long expensive trial as to just the position of landmarks and so on."

"And it will deprive Durande of his plantation?" asked Zanalta, with utter amazement showing in his face and voice. But Monsieur Lamort smiled in a deprecating way as he answered :

"Of part of that plantation on which he resides I think I can say — yes; but of course the crown can easily grant him another tract, and thus make amends for the fault of its officials after the insurrection of '68. Those in command of the colony at that time confiscated all properties of the revolutionists, and it has been discovered at this late day that they also, through excess of zeal, confiscated lands to which the rebels had no claim, and afterward distributed the same wherever their policy prompted them. So it was with a portion of the tract sold later to Monsieur Durande. It is to the crown to which that gentleman must look for another land grant, and it will doubtless be given. The kings of a country should take heed that honest dealing should be enacted there. Justice should be ever held in honor."

Zanalta noticed, as before, that firm setting of the mouth at the mention of justice. For an instant it made the speaker's face look harder and older.

"But the plantation — *sacre!* It is the pride of his life — that place. Even Charles of Spain could not select in all his lands an estate to recompense Durande for 'Royal Grant.' Not that I need vex my mind with it, for he reached over our boundary-line many a furlong. Yet, his Indian slaves to go, and now his homestead! Well, it will lower his high head."

There was a spice of satisfaction in his tone, though he shook his head over the evil prospect for his neighbor, and Monsieur Lamort, watching closely, took advantage of it.

"So you see I take you into my confidence concerning this legal discussion that is to be, that you may know the paper you possess is to be used only in the cause of justice. When it pleases you to let me see it, I will be in your debt, in behalf of the new heir, and I only ask an opportunity to return so gracious a favor."

"Good!" thought Zanalta; "it is worth some planning to hear him say that." But aloud he said: "The paper is for you, monsieur; this day I will look for it; and it may indeed be that when I take it to you I also may ask a document at your hands for the settlement of a provoking affair. You, as *alcalde*, might save me distraction concerning it. Nothing

more serious than the claiming of a slave whose
mother, belonging to me, tricked me into thinking
dead that the young one might be reared out of
slavery. You understand? Oh, it was well thought
out, and succeeded for a long time ; and even now
I want it settled without the woman being punished,
as she would be punished if the case should go before
the Cabildo. I feel certain you will be of one mind
with me in that."

"Indeed, yes ; but you Spanish grandees seldom
evade the spirit of the law in that way." And the
gaze of Monsieur Lamort was sharp and a little
doubtful. "Are your sympathies turning to the
side of the unwilling blacks who are brought yearly
to our shores? "

"I think not," returned Zanalta, with assumed
indifference. He knew it would never do to pretend
any such sudden change of opinion. "No, I think,
as always, that the condition of the African in our
land, surrounded by civilization and the example of
the whites, is decidedly preferable to the wild, useless, savage life they have hitherto known. But of
late you are aware they, together with the red slaves,
clamor for privileges unknown of old. The revolution over the seas breeds discontent even here, and
more than one master has of late found his black
people hard to manage. The whipping of a slave
by the authorities generates sullen antagonism
toward the master who sent him there ; and if the
slave is a strong-willed fellow — well, he will breed
discontent over an entire plantation, and the brutes
won't work so well. I've noted it often. Now I do

not want to have that sort of feeling in my fields.
I have too much work to do. And it is bad for a
plantation when people say females are flogged
there. So you comprehend my several reasons for
not going before the *regidors* with my claim.
They would be just and grant it, but they would
also be unbending, and the slave-woman would be
cut in stripes for her duplicity. Now, knowing the
case, can you without annoyance to yourself assist
in it?"

"I think so," said Victor Lamort, slowly. He
understood now why the survey had not been given
to him at once — Zanalta wished to purchase a favor
with it. Well, as Zanalta stated his own case, it
sounded reasonable enough. It would be but little
to do — that, a stroke of a pen to a document calling
for the subservience of a slave to his master, and in
exchange —

"You have proofs, of course, of your claim?" he
asked. "Are they satisfactory?"

"Entirely. The confession of the mother — but
we will speak of that when the paper is prepared, and
that may be to-night, for I dislike much to carry the
weight of a disagreeable duty undone. At what
hour could I call on you in the matter?"

"This or to-morrow evening, after the darkness
falls. All the day hours of this week I will have
little leisure."

"This or to-morrow evening? I am most grateful, monsieur. You will surely see me, and with me
the ancient survey we spoke of. In fact I think of
voyaging for a few weeks along the coast to the

east if weather promises fair; any fine wind might tempt me, and it would be well to have these land cares off my hands."

"A voyage along the coast?" remarked Monsieur Lamort, with polite interest. "Yes, the sea is attractive to many at this fair season. May good weather attend you, Señor Zanalta."

And then the gentlemen separated, each well satisfied with the meeting, and at once on the departure of his guest the Señor Zanalta commenced again the troublous search for that survey; but in no corner was it found. All the threats launched at the household — and they were many and lurid — failed to discover any vestige of it or any one who had disturbed it.

But the afternoon was slipping away. Much was to be done. When once he made a move toward the recovery of that slave he meant to act as a falcon swoops with unerring swiftness on its victim. Not time for cry or protest must be allowed, no hesitation to give others time to counter-plan; every portion of arrangement must be made ere a word was uttered of his real meaning. Meanwhile — that survey!

And then Don Diego Zanalta busied himself with various parchments, and finally selecting one, called for red ink. His memory of the main landmarks was good enough to make a rough draft of the domain. At a casual glance it might be accepted as the original; the duplicity would not be discovered until after he was aboard ship, and even on his return, how simple to protest that the original had been purloined without his knowledge, that he had acted in good faith, and the spurious copy was a mystery to him.

So he worked, completing even the red lettering on the roll, and giving it much the appearance of the one missing. Then he called for black Gourfi, who listened to some orders, departed with quickness as he was bidden, and returned ere long, but shook his head when his master glanced past him into the corridor.

"She did not come; she was not even to be seen," he announced. And his master flung the pen down, with angry words.

"Give me the reason — where has she gone?"

"No farther than an inner room, master; but a sick man is there — a priest — they name him Father Luis. He came down the river with the red men. He is old — he needs care; and the Master Lamort bade Venda not to leave his side this day and this night. So the people in the cook-house told me, and it is true. That is all."

"And enough. It will change my plans for twenty-four hours. But you, Gourfi, with a still tongue in your head, prepare for me wearing apparel for a month. Have it ready to go in a small boat any instant it is needed; and — be silent."

CHAPTER XIV.

DIEGO SEES A GHOST.

MONS. CONSTANTE RAYNEL learned that even the path of an accepted lover may have thorns amidst the roses of happiness. The thorns in his case were, first, Señora Zanalta, whose presence he dreaded to such an extent that he walked ever in the shadows when waiting in the gardens for his beloved, and even planned a rendezvous at the house of Monsieur Lamort, where they might dare speak aloud once more; and the other thing vexatious to his spirit was Diego Zanalta himself, who had disturbed Madame Villette so greatly with his fancies that she insisted her lover must haunt his steps, learn where he wandered to when the darkness fell, and what were the associations to which he must owe his unquiet hours of the night, for Ninon never guessed that the cause of those unquiet hours might have been dark memories of his own past.

And because of her wishes had her favorite knight undertaken a duty by no means safe or pleasant — that of shadowing a gentleman who was reputed to use a dagger skillfully. If he could have taken Maurice into his confidence the task would have troubled him less; but his little governor-general said "no."

"And I may be given a slit with a knife in the darkness, and never one would know what became of me," he lamented; for in his own mind he had an idea that Señor Diego was simply a smuggler, and his absence at night a most simple affair to those in his confidence.

But as the dusk fell he was at a station where the domain of Zanalta could be viewed, and as the last bar of yellow light died over the western levels he saw a sailor pass, a swarthy half-breed, with glinting tinsel showing here and there in his apparel—an expression of semi-barbaric taste. He halted opposite the house Constante was watching, and then as Zanalta himself appeared at a window he sped across to him, with one hand upheld to attract attention.

Then there followed questions and answers, and the seaman said, " Yes, the vessel will be at your control from this evening, but our commander can not speak to you of it unless it should please you to go now to the café of Manette. Later he is engaged; to-morrow he is engaged."

Zanalta smiled as he answered, " Your master will no longer bear the title of the ' night-hawk ' if he receives company so early. We may soon hope to greet him at noonday if this continues. But return to him with my compliments; say I will be with him ere long."

Constante was too far away to hear their words, only their nods and gestures were visible; and he strolled deeper into the shadows as the messenger repassed the spot where he had stood. His steps carried him so far that he found himself near a lattice where a light shone, and where the voice of Señora Zanalta made the air heavy with ire. She was venting her earnest wrath on some slave, and calling the saints to witness her own patience under the trials laid on her by that household.

The listener slipped away by a more roundabout path, lest she should look from the lattice and discover his unforgiven self. In doing so more time was consumed than he had reckoned on, and when he again came in sight of the house entrance, Don Diego was just turning the opposite corner with all possible speed; the watcher took his track, keeping as small a space as he dare between them, but he found the distance long enough, for Zanalta had a most troublesome way of looking behind him often —of stopping and peering into shadowy paths if any crossed his own — all the nervous actions of a man who is afraid of something near him but unseen.

Constante had heard rumors of his skill with hilted steel — of duels in Old Spain, and of men who had fallen victims to his excellence in that fine art. Did he carry the memory of them with him when the night fell? His follower mentally decided yes.

Much more certain was he when close by the thick willows near the river Zanalta halted, with a cry that was neither scream nor moan, but a mingling of each, a strangling, strained note of horror sounding through the darkness. It was scarcely a cry for help, yet Constante, who could move lightly and in silence because of the skin shoes he wore, sped over the path to his side; or rather behind him, where he too paused abruptly, for close in front of them a man stood in the

18

shadows — a man with a strange, pale face and stern eyes; his mouth was hidden by a mustache and the fur cap of a *voyageur* covered his head. His dress was also that of the ranger — the fringed leggings and hunting-coat, the knotted scarf of scarlet at the throat. Constante noted it all with the trained eye of an artist. Strangest of all, the loose gown of a priest was thrown over the shoulders of the figure, while the eyes were bent significantly on the face of Zanalta, and one hand was held aloft, pointing heavenward, as if in judgment.

And to this figure Diego Zanalta was muttering in supplicating tones.

"Again! Oh, cross of the Christ! Can you not rest? It is done — it is all over — masses can be — that is all. I did not do it — I never touched your knife — you know. If you would speak. O God! anything would be better than this silence, and your face everywhere! Speak, though it kill me! You poison life with your cursed eyes. Speak, De Bayarde, or I —"

He leaped forward, convulsed by a sort of furious fear, and as the figure seemed to recede before him, he fell in a fainting-fit where it had stood.

The fall broke the spell of utter wonder which had bound Raynel, and he bent over the man to see if he had indeed died in that terror. When he raised his eyes again toward that silent accuser nothing was there but the dusky shadows and the faint lights yet lingering on the willow-stems.

It was all so strange to him. His head was in a

whirl; his hair seemed to lift his hat when the form
was no longer to be seen. And then the thought
that he was there in the willows with a dead man!

But Zanalta was not dead; he soon breathed, and
even spoke, begging to be taken home, out of the
shadows.

"And it is you?" he said, finally. "How — but you
will tell me later. Well, it is you. I am ill. I will
go to-morrow — not later — you tell Rochelle; but
you do not know him. My head swims; I can't
think; but I'll go to-morrow."

And that night, despite the orders of Madame
Ninon, Constante betook himself to Maurice, and
recounted the wonderful events of the evening with
more exactness than he had ventured to tell his
betrothed, fearing she should think he also needed
a guardian if he was beginning to see forms in each
shadowy place.

And Maurice, with his mind yet filled with that late-
learned history of De Bayarde sat long after the
departure of Constante trying to fathom the mystery
of this strange appearance. He understood more
clearly now the words of Zanalta that first evening
at Monsieur Lamort's — his earnest desire to hear
what the others thought of spirit returns. Had this
wraith of the past been haunting his steps so long?
Was it a wraith, or a reality? and if the latter, who
was trading on a resemblance to that exiled man for
the purpose of giving fright to Zanalta? Was
Rochelle interested, that Zanalta had spoken of him
at once on regaining consciousness — Rochelle, the
peculiar man who was never seen on Orleans Island

when the sun shone, but whose night visits had led
people to attribute evil character to the mystery
about him?

Maurice Delogne had, however, been able to
discover no single evil thing against him in the
official annals of the island, or on the books of the
regidors. No complaints, no charges of smuggling
or other tamperings with law. After that evening when Don Zanalta had disclaimed knowledge of
the Sea Gull's commander Maurice had, out of his
instinctive dislike of the man, distrusted him. He
had learned that the sailors of Monsieur Rochelle
were all credited with being half-breeds; no man
entirely white had ever been seen with him as companion. Generally he was alone, and his wagers
and winnings at the card-table were things noto-
rious among the limited circle with whom he
played; and Delogne had learned that Zanalta was
one of the aristocratic few. Never a plebeian in
Rochelle's game, only with the best blood of Orleans would he take part in play, and the best
blood was invariably worsted by the gamester whom
they in return called a smuggler and buccaneer.
But Delogne himself decided that he was simply a
clever adventurer, who assumed a mysterious manner of life the better to awe the credulous and
impose on them with his tricky games.

And in spite of himself he could not but connect
the night-hawk — the man of whom the people loved
to romance — with the apparition seen there on the
river-walk; some wager of the gamester, perhaps.
But the motive and the manner of the phantom was

not to be fathomed by any of his conjectures, though
all his mind was alert because of those late confidences of Monsieur Lamort, whom he wished with all
his heart he could acquaint with the story ere he slept
—an impossibility, however, as Monsieur Lamort
once retired to his own rooms for the day or night
never allowed himself to be intruded upon.

But one member of the household heard the story
as Monsieur Raynel told it, one who knelt outside
the door and listened with pleased eyes and nodding
head. When the horror and fright of Don Zanalta
was described she hugged herself and rocked to and
fro as if in silent laughter, but not a sound did she
utter; and the ailing priest whom she tended scarcely
missed her brown face and gentle hand about him,
her departure and return were so swift and silent.

CHAPTER XV.

VENDA.

BUT in the waning sun of the next day it was no
laughing Venda who faced her former master and
listened to his commands with frowning brows.

"So! this why Gourfi come there and say, 'Master
lost something; he want Venda the voudou to find it
for him, quick.' I see now Gourfi lie. It is not a loss
you have met. And why should I tell lie too, eh?
No good to do it. Venda never had child; all old

négresse know that. No, Venda not want Cabildo men to put irons on her for that."

Zanalta stared at her gloomily. His own dislike to a conversation with her was made more difficult by her stupid objections.

"You are not to decide. Your master is to judge; and no matter whose gold pays for you, Diego Zanalta is ever your master — do you hear? The judges will never hear that you had no child born. I, Zanalta, say you had. You also say so, else the judges will of a certainty hear strange things of you — things worse than the irons that frighten you. Well do you know what I mean."

And her eyes showed that she did know. One dark glance of beseeching and of hatred was turned on him, but she said no word. He smiled a little at the satisfaction of his power over her.

"As for the child," he continued, "it is a child no longer. It is of mixed blood, but looks white, and is wrongfully received among ladies who are white. It is only right that it should be changed. Once, years ago, you were with your mistress, Felice, the winter she died at the plantation Sollé. A child could have been born there, and no one lives who could contradict it."

"Yes," and she looked at him with wide frightened eyes — "yes, a child might have been born there; no one would know." And then she looked relieved at some new thought. "But, master, I, Venda, could not have a white child — it could not be; not I, a dark woman."

"Such things have been — will be often, when the father is white."

"White father — oh!" And she gazed at him with questioning eyes, waiting for more she saw he was about to tell her. From his desk he took a long piece of paper and unfolded it.

"You promise?" he demanded. She hesitated. The paper looked so like one she had heard read by the Cabildo man years ago when the brand of hot iron had fallen on her. The thought of that time made her tremble in her heart. Ah, those judges!

"You promise, or I, Diego Zanalta, will say to the rulers things that will send you to death ere two suns pass. Speak! Will you claim the girl as I tell you?"

"Yes, Venda will do it," she assented, lowly.

"Tell her what she is to do. Where is the child?"

He smiled that he had vanquished her so easily, and knew well she would never willingly serve him; but after that punishment long ago her fear of the law was great.

He opened the paper, reading extracts from it that she might grasp the meaning.

"I, Diego Zanalta, affirm, etc., and hold that the slave-woman Venda, now the property of Victor Lamort, purchased by me from the estate of Gaston le Noyens, was, while my property, delivered of a child on the plantation of Madame Marie Sollé, which child, being of white skin, she concealed from her owner, and did wrongfully and in secret convey to the foundling basket of the Ursuline convent on the night of Christmas, 177–, hoping it would be reared apart from the people of color, where it belonged. At last her guilt has been discovered, and

Don Zanalta, because of her full and penitent confession, desires that no punishment be visited upon
her, and only asks the return of the girl, who is his
legal property, as her mother was owned by him at
the time of the birth. More, that he begs, for the
sake of the good nuns and their worthy work, that
the mulatto girl be given up by them without protest, and thus avert the scandal that would ensue if
it goes abroad that the daughters of the planters
and ladies of noble blood have been trained side
by side with a slave, and that she has been treated
in all ways as their peer.

"The woman Venda further confesses that the girl
is the daughter of her late master, Gaston le Noyens,
and Don Zanalta is desirous of giving the girl due
consideration because of that fact, and because of
her superior refinements, but most earnestly demands the righting of this wrong, that he may
remove this present cause of insult to every lady
who is a pupil of the convent. The girl has been
given the name of Denise by the nuns, and by that
name I do request her. Beseeching the gracious
clemency, etc.

"You see," he continued, putting aside the paper,
"you have nothing to do when the Alcalde reads
this paper but to say it is all true and that you were
the black woman who was seen bearing a child to
the convent gate. You comprehend? Say just that
and no more."

She looked at him with a face that shone ashen in
the bright light, and her lips seemed stiff when she
tried to speak.

"Oh, you need not stare like that because Le Noyens' name is mentioned," and he spoke impatiently; "that is the only safe way, and is reasonable enough. Remember if they ask you, you must say the child was born at the plantation of Madame Sollé when you were allowed by my permission to wait on Mademoiselle Felice during her last illness, and that you yourself carried the child into the town and left it at the convent gate on that Christmas night."

"On — the — Christmas — night," she repeated, as if trying to beat the meaning of it in on her own mind. "But, master — oh, the good God! — master —"

"Enough of that!" he commanded; "no protests, and no begging off. You have promised, and you must do it, just as I have told you. Must! — do you hear?"

"But — oh, listen! Yes, I promise — oh, God! Venda do all you want if you only tell her clear about that child. It died — that child at the convent basket — it died. I know — I heard."

"No doubt; you hear everything, and I am glad you remember the time. Yes, a child died there, but it was the other child died. Two were left there that night — one with a white skin and one that looked like an Indian, or colored child. The dark one was dead in the morning, but the white one is the girl Denise."

"They said it died — they said it died," she repeated, with her hands at her own throat, as one looks when strangling.

He looked at her sharply, but her wild, despairing face told him nothing but her own personal fear of the judges and the risk of the lie she was to tell.

"But I tell you it did not — it is alive, and is the child of Venda, once called Zizi, and of Gaston le Noyens, her master. That is all you are to remember; and it is to be settled at the house of your new master, Monsieur Lamort."

"At his house!" she muttered; "his house!" She was turning to walk away when Zanalta stepped in front of her.

"Mind, no trickery in this," he said, and warned her with an upraised finger. "You had better be dead than prove false in this — you know."

"I know," she assented, and her head drooped. "I have promised. I will be there; I will say I left the white child with the nuns. Speak when the time comes."

And her voice sounded dead and heavy; her step was as the step of a very old woman as she passed out through the halls where her home had once been. In the garden of roses she stopped and touched a drooping branch of white fragrance. "Venda love to touch you, little white rose," she muttered, as though speaking to a living thing. "Venda like just so the white Denise all these times and never did know why. Now maybe she never see either one of you again. Good-by, little white rose."

She walked straight to the gates of the convent. Once there she knew not what she had come to say. She felt dulled and stupid, and sat for a little on

the crisp dry grass without the gate; sat there
while people passed and crossed themselves at sight
of the black witch woman who sat as if weaving
spells at the very gate of the sacred retreat. But
she was blind for once to their shrinking and awe of
her. All her thought was, " Will they listen — will
the voudou be believed when she tells at last the
truth?"

Then she arose and walked straight to the guarded
gate, where she made request for the grand mother
superior, who seemed quite a royal person in the
colony. But no audience was possible so late in the
day, so the chatelaine of the gate replied; and, anyway, no slave would be admitted without announcing
for what her master or mistress had sent her.

And Venda was barred out by that, for she had
no message from a master; but she looked pleadingly in the gentle face of the aged nun, and bowed
her head with that barbaric obeisance of respect.

"Might the slave who has no master's orders ask
one question when it is for good and not evil?"

"Surely," assented the kindly soul, much impressed by the strange brown woman whose hair
was so white above her youthful face.

"The things that are spoken within these gates
are never whispered to the people there?" and
Venda pointed to the town.

" We keep many secrets," confessed the nun ; and
Venda's face brightened as she saw she was understood.

"So! it is good. This is secret. Listen! One
Christmas a child, Denise, was left here — is it so?

Yes? If you have love for her ask the ruler of this house to have ready any clothes or writings that came with her into the foundling basket — any of the smallest things even that would help to show what people she came of. Do not look so! I am not touched with the head sickness — I tell you earnest truth. Soon, I know not what day, a grand señor will come here and call her his. Bid them have each thing ready, that no wrong may be done. The slave-woman may tell you no more than that; but your convent child may fall in danger if you pay no heed to the word I bring. I come for good, not for evil. Good-by."

On the way to her master's house she met many Indians of the Natchez. They chattered more than usual. They talked in groups, and seemed glad; sometimes they shook hands as the white men do, and their eyes smiled even when their tongues were silent. And one man who was past middle age was embraced by a group in which was one very old Indian woman. He was her son, and had been held in slavery thirty years. Others of the group were his brothers, who had come with her to greet him when his freedom came.

Absolute freedom was not yet given, but the governor had been pleased to grant many concessions, for in the face of the law when it was held up before him he could do no less; and the half-freed slaves were joyous that even the thin edge of the wedge had been forced through the wall of the white man's wishes.

And Venda reading their faces saw they were

glad of heart — they were almost free; and she
held her hands tight over her bosom — she, who
would only know freedom through the gate of death.
Like all of her race, she feared the dark oblivion of
the grave. Yet one dies so many times while one
breathes and walks the earth; would the final death
be harder than the things she had lived through?
It seemed to her not, as she sought the master
whom she reverenced — sought him that she might
confess a long-lived evil she had lived through;
and when she had told him all, she knew he would
hate her — he would banish her forever from his
sight.

Well, it was only one more death!

But seek where she would, he was not to be found.
The sun was sinking, and she grew feverish over
her anxiety lest time enough would not be granted
her. She went away from his house and from
the Cabildo, and walked along the river-side, watching ever the forms and faces about. She was restless as the ever-moving waves on the shore.

Then she caught sight of a shapely boat fastened
to the beach, while the only occupant lounged there
lazily and smoked a cigarette. She knew the craft,
as she knew most faces that came to the town. She
went down close to the man before she spoke.

"Do you wait here for your master?" she asked;
and the sailor, Nicholas, looked up at her and
scowled sulkily.

"No such luck. I wait here for one of the noble
gallants such as you love to serve in the town
here. You are the witch, they say; so you should

know both the lord and the lady for whose pleasure-
trip this craft waits from sundown until dawn of
three nights."

"Three nights? and this is the last?"

"To-morrow is the last."

"And they elope?"

"Who knows? Who she is has not been told; but
the boat waits."

She looked out over the water. The setting sun
was just tinging it into lances of flame where the
ripples moved. She drew a long breath of relief;
she feared the truth, but was glad at the thought
that another day's time might be given, would
likely be given, for it was growing late. He could
not have meant to-night.

"Tell me — can I see your master?" she asked,
suddenly; but he only sneered at her.

"Perhaps, if you know where to look for him; I do
not."

"I think you lie," she said, carelessly; "but you
mean to keep faith, and that is good. Will you tell
me, then, if in the many people who pass you have
seen the face of Master Victor Lamort?"

"I think not," he growled, and looked at her sus-
piciously; "but you need not ask me about your
grand señors of the town there. I care little to
remember their faces or names."

"You are an ill beast for a woman to waste words
with," she remarked, and turned away. Then, noting the clear, warm sky and placid waters, added,
"Well, if Señor Zanalta makes choice of to-night for
his flitting he is like to have fine weather, eh?"

The straight, contemptuous mouth of Nicholas curved ever so little at her clever guess.

"So you do know? They tell me you are a voudou witch and know most things. Now down in San Domingo I knew a voudou woman; she —"

But Venda walked away, as if careless of his words. She had learned more than she came for, and with her added fund of knowledge sought again her master.

And Nicholas watched her go, and muttered sullenly to himself:

"Master Captain told me once to do good turn for that white-head nigger if she ever came my way. Um! Master is queer in the head with his kindness. What she want with captain — her? I always did hate niggers."

And he smoothed his hair where the black blood showed in the ebon curls, and stared with somber envy at the men of the Natchez moving along the banquette in their gay woven blankets, and that proud, unconquered look in their eyes — they, the red men, could walk out from their shackles and be hailed by their kindred as warriors once more, but the African! And Nicholas muttered curses on the curse set in the blood of the black people -- a curse so heavy that it was ground into their hearts and brains; and their courage and hope dwindled under the weight of it until they did never dare in the presence of white men to bear themselves dauntless as those red men whom he envied.

And so he lay there and sulked, thinking of the black blood in his own veins — the blood he hated;

and not realizing that the greatest general the
world had seen for a century past, or would see in
the next century to come, was a black man, even
then growing into power on that same island of San
Domingo — the man who freed his brother slaves
despite the allied forces of England and Spain, whose
strongholds and ships he destroyed, and drove them
from the Southern waters despite the trained endeavors of France, who sent an army against him ;
and fifty thousand French graves are left on that
island as testimony to his prowess. The man whose
name and deeds would be sung as the world sings of
heroes, had not the most powerful nations of that
time been smarting under the hurts he had given
them. Their poets had no songs of praise for the
"accursed black" who left but fragments of their
defeated armies.

But Nicholas swaying idly there in his boat knew
nothing of that great heart of slave-born Toussaint
L'Ouverture, the heart aching even then over the
woes of the dark people ; and looking across at the
Natchez, who called him the "curled head," Nicholas
wished himself all of Natchez blood, because he
fancied in his ignorance that the black blood came
from the heart of cowards.

CHAPTER XVI.

A RENDEZVOUS.

ALL that day Maurice Delogne had been restless as the very spirit of the wind. The prospect held out to him by Monsieur Lamort, the recovery of the estate he had hoped so little for, opened up a new vista — and then, perhaps, he would dare kneel for the favors of the Lady Denise.

The Lady Denise! It was the title dearest of all dear things to him, and he was even foolishly glad that she had no added name. She was not as other maidens; she was a fair white mystery, a strong, gentle spirit, such as old legends tell of. All the soft warm winds of the south brought him whispers of Denise — Denise; every rustle of the leaves, every ripple along the edge of the water where it made music kissing the shore; and the silent influence of her seldom-seen face, her name, her voice wrought wondrous changes in the young man's mind. The Lady Denise — it was a name to conjure with, and under the witchery of it Maurice grew more tolerant of even the love affairs of Constante, and listened with more sympathy to his course of latest true love and the disturbing influence of Señora Zanalta.

And ere the dusk fell he was amused to see the approach of Madame Ninon Villette from one direction and the ardent Constante from another, each

19

bending uncertain steps toward the dwelling of
Monsieur Lamort — a rendezvous without a doubt,
and a pretty sure sign that the irate lady from
Madrid was yet formidable.

"Their infatuation is most surely blinding them
to the conventional in conduct," he thought as he
observed them. "They defy comment and slip here
like two guilty people to confer in secret — here
where no lady's presence gives countenance to their
meeting. Ah, well, I too would lack wisdom after
the same fashion if the lady of my love would give
me smiles as are lavished on Constante. Yet — yet
her eyes surely fell kindly on me, though her words
were chill and chiding. Oh! that I dared hope she
was chiding her own heart when she spoke to me."

He entered with eager interest into the gossip of
the lovers over the strange state of mind into which
Diego Zanalta had fallen of late, and calmed somewhat the fears of Madame Villette on the question.
The times were troublous ones in state affairs —
revolt among the French people and among the
slaves of the Spanish islands. Many a master of
of plantations was nervous and watchful these days,
and slept none too soundly of nights. So he
assured her, and she was rather glad to be convinced that his unrest had a substantial cause
instead of an imaginary one; it seemed less un-
canny.

Monsieur Lamort was not visible, but Delogne
explained that much of his time had been spent with
the aged priest brought by the red men from the far
north lakes, and now a guest in the house, and one

requiring many attentions because of fatigue and the infirmities of age.

Madame Villette would willingly have added her share to the attentions paid the long-exiled holy man, but that he was not yet thought strong enough; and the fetters of Constante were riveted even more tightly by the tender interest she evinced in the unknown one.

" He shall be at our house if he will so far honor us," she declared. " It is a blessed privilege to entertain warriors so dauntless as those who travel with but a staff and the love of heaven wherewith to conquer the souls of the savage men. He shall be of our household at his own pleasure."

Delogne had withdrawn for a short space, and her words were to Constante, for whom her smile was sweetly inquiring, as of one who would mutely ask commendation. It is so sweet in the earlier stages of love's fever to defer thus to the ideas of one other.

" To be sure," assented Raynel, airily. " The sooner the better, madame. Perhaps with a priest ever at your elbow you would be sooner impelled to change vows with me at his bidding."

" To plight my troth to you, as the English say."

" More, oh star of love in my night-time! To vow yourself my bride."

" How impetuous. Surely, the troth comes first. Have you then considered in seriousness our idle chat by the lattice ? "

" Madame, you are pleased to jest this evening, and your own eyes deny the tone of your speech. I

pray you, give over making light of emotions so
earnest. Wit is brilliant, but cruel; it kills feeling."

"Oh, monsieur, how fortunate your own is insured
so long a life!"

"Do you want me to destroy myself?" he demanded, with a ferocious expression, and tramped
back and forward past her in the most successful
melodramatic fashion, while Madame Ninon, not ill
pleased, watched him from the corners of her charming eyes.

"Of a truth, monsieur, I wish no harm to you;
yet I have indeed envied those beauties whom men
loved well enough to die for." And madame glanced
up to mark the effect of her words, for he had halted
directly before her. "But for myself — oh, no; I
never hope to be loved so well."

"Ah! but I entreat you to believe that it is so,"
he declared. "Love like that awaits your pleasure.
But why should I die unless cause comes? Then,
if it were to serve you, I would live no more."

"You say so," hesitated the coquette. "But after
all you are a gay cavalier — oh, I have heard so,
monsieur. You dare not say I am the first of your
loves; and what assurance have I that I am to be
your best?"

Constante's face actually paled at her words.
Angels of heaven! what stories had come to
her? With all his heart he wished he could present
a record like that of a stolid vegetable gardener
of the German coast up the river. But, alas! the
fancies of days long forgotten came trooping into

his memory like jovial ghosts, every one of them laughing at him.

"In fact," continued his tormentor, "remarks have not been lacking in our household to the effect that you would not have wooed so eagerly the poor Ninon Villette had the poor Ninon not owned a gilded name — nay, monsieur, look not so angry; I only make this mention that you may understand how I have been assailed, and how I have been brought to consider your haste. I protest I find you a most gentle cavalier, but to speak of troth so hastily — well, even yet I fancy you do not understand what it will mean to wed on these shores a lady who is poor. You have not seen the poor but gently born people who live here, many of them in the most humble way; and until you understand that my husband's will was peculiar, and that even the portion of his wealth that is mine during widowhood will be —"

But Constante checked her revelations with the impetuosity of a lover, and again his arms were about her as he knelt at her feet.

"Give over, I pray you, all this wise chatter of gold and its weight," he protested; "all words from your lips sound sweetly to me, but why waste our chance happy moments with such conjectures? In every land an able man can win a home for the woman he loves, and with your love as a goal — ah, heavens! — I feel I could conquer half this wilderness. You shake your head — you yet think of the gold of which I think no more? Believe me, if by ending your widowhood you lose your fortune, I vow to make a cottage love so joyous to you that you will never regret the mansion you leave behind."

Now Madame Ninon adored such love-making. It was much more to her liking than the more ceremonious proposals addressed to her by various dignified and important gentlemen of the colony. But content as she was with her wooer, she was not wise enough to let well alone, but said, with archness and provoking glances at his rapturous face:

"You speak of the gold for which you think no more; do you acknowledge, then, that you did once care for it?"

And Constante, in the idiocy of love, and with the conviction that he must not aspire to the sanctity of her heart with any shadow of a lie on his own soul, did then most foolishly reveal former fancies and visions of wealth that now paled into insignificance beside the day-star of his passion.

"Then you once did have mercenary dreams?"

Constante thought her soft tones filled with incredulity and sympathy, and blundered on.

"Most certainly. Ask Maurice — he knows. You see I was foolish; I had dreamed of finding a rich wife on these shores."

"Oh, you did?"

"Indeed, yes. How far away that folly looks! So when I heard — yes, beloved, I will confess all the sin of it — when I heard of the beautiful widow of Villette — charming, and rich —"

"Oh, monster! He will kill me, this French barbarian! Was the end of your scheme, monsieur, to

lock me in a convent or strangle me in the waters of
the great river? Oh, I shall die! Do not seek to
argue with me. I am sure I shall die !"

And as a recompense for his sincere rendering up
of the truth to her, Constante found himself on his
knees before an empty chair and the departing
vision of his lady-love as she impetuously made a
stormy retreat into the court.

"Shall I follow her? Will she forever refuse to
look on me again? Must my life then end in some
monk's cell — alone and desolate?" were a few of the
questions he asked of himself in despair. "Oh, fool
that I am! Why did I tell her? Fool — angel that
she is! Why did she not hear the rest of the story?
I'll go mad !"

But in the going he almost fell over Maurice, who
entered at that moment, and who gazed on Constante
with astonished eyes.

"Did you see her? Is she angry beyond pardon?
Oh, I beg you to tell me, when my soul's happiness
depends on it."

"You mean Madame Villette? Yes, I passed her
in the room beyond. Pray what has chanced to
separate you so soon ?"

"Oh, my accursed tongue — my lack of wit. She
spoke truly when she said I lacked wit sadly. Tell
me, I beg of you, how did she look — what did she
say? Was she weeping? Oh, Ninon, Ninon !"

Delogne managed at last to learn the reason of his
despair, but avoided making any statement as to
the lady's expression or possible state of mind, for,
amused as he was, he dare not tell the frantic lover

that he had come upon Madame Ninon laughing most heartily under the palm-trees.

"She asked only to be admitted to the aged priest of whom we spoke, so you had best not follow her there with your stumbling speech. It is only right that you do penance in solitude for awhile. You, upon my word, the last man I should think so simple as to tell such truths to a woman."

"I vow if she forgives me this time never to tell her the truth again," declared the troubled wooer with great earnestness; "and if you will permit me I will at least remain here until she needs an escort home. May the saints move her to pardon me!"

"Stay, and welcome. Have you been at the Cabildo to-day, or heard more of the red men and their cause? What say the planters?"

"Much that is not complimentary to our friend Lamort," confessed the other. "I assure you there is a divided idea abroad as to whether he is an angel of light for the help of the lower classes or a demon of darkness for the overthrow of the rulers, and for the stripping away all the cloaks from their luxurious, careless sins. It is well he is brave, else he could not hope to weather the storm he has raised."

"Is Durande so bitter about the red slaves?"

"Furious. And Señor Ronando is ever at his elbow to exclaim over the injustice of setting them free; in fact more than one planter sees in it perhaps a future uprising of the black slaves as well, and of course it would ruin the colony to set them free. But Monsieur Lamort is a comparative stranger and does not think for the future here. They say he only follows wild whims, and Satan seems to aid him in his schemes. I tell you, Maurice, I esteem him highly, but strange things are said of him, even witchcraft is whispered, for he brings forward laws and testaments that the judges dare not disdain — legal documents of the early Spanish rule, things singular for a stranger to own; and by them he has forced unwilling judgment in his favor there at the Cabildo; and even the officials who grant his claims disapprove them. So you see our friend is stirring up days of storm for himself."

"Perhaps; I doubt if he cares. But tell me, has there come to you any further word of Don Diego and the specter?"

"Not a whisper. I did but show my face there this noon, and the voice of Señora Zanalta sounded so dangerously near that I made most hasty retreat. However, I met him on the banquette later, and he appeared strong and composed."

"The banquette at noon-time is not a favorite promenade with most noble gentlemen here."

"True; but Zanalta is often a busy man, and goes where his interests call him. A half-Indian boatman was his object to-day. *Sacre!* there he is now."

"The Indian boatman?"

"Oh, confusion — no. It is Zanalta, and he will not fail to discover Ninon here, and he will think it a fine piece of folly that we sally forth to meet in another house than his. Hide me, can you not? If he finds her alone with the old priest he will think her what she is, an angel; but if I also am discovered he will think her a fool."

Delogne pointed to an adjoining room, and Raynel quickly took the hint and disappeared there, and, settling himself behind some curtains, listened, expecting each instant to hear the soft tones of the Spanish gentleman; but not a sound came to him, not even the step of Maurice, who must still be standing there by the window facing the street.

With the idea that Don Zanalta had perhaps halted at the portal for a chat with some one, and would directly enter, Constante remained in his nook until the sunlight was all gone from the sky. An early star had slipped from its blue draperies and shone gleaming and silvery through the lattice at him. The half of an hour must have passed, and not a sound. He arose impatiently and crossed the threshold of the reception-room.

Delogne yet stood at the lattice, his eyes gazing earnestly out, and his hands clasped tightly behind him. His face was pale from some effort of self-control.

"Would you have left me there all of the night, Maurice?" complained his friend. "Each instant I expected to hear him speak, yet he evidently passed on, and you never called me."

The complaint fell on deaf ears, and looking at Delogne in wonder for a moment, he crossed over beside him, taking him affectionately by the arm. "Maurice, you are ill — what is it? Come, rest here. By my faith, you stood there as though made of wood or stone. What ails you, man?"

" He went there — to the convent." And Delogne, despite the detaining hand of his friend, returned again to his point of lookout.

" Who do you mean — Zanalta? "

" He."

" But what of that! Saints in heaven, what a fright you gave me! Your hand is cold, your face looks like the dead, and all because a gentleman of the town takes the air near the convent gate of an evening."

" Be wary! Though you are my friend, I will ever check your jesting on this one subject. I tell you his visit there this night bodes ill."

" How could that be — whence comes your fancy? "

" I can not tell, but I dare swear I am right. All this day a heavy cloud has weighed upon me. All my endeavors could not set it aside — a dark unformed shadow of foreboding. Here at this lattice that shadow took form as I saw Diego Zanalta pass onward to the convent. He goes not there in the cause of any charity at this hour; I am possessed by the fear that he is there for harm to the Lady Denise."

" Pooh! you are affrighted at shadows. What substance have you to found those fancies upon? "

"Only the manner of the man when at any time she has come in range of his eyes; and she herself dreads him — I know it, for she ever avoids his speech or his glance. Oh, I tell you —"

He stopped abruptly, with a look on his face as if some long-delayed comprehension had been granted him.

"Constante, tell me, where is the knife we picked up on the sward that night when the lady was assaulted — is it here, or did you keep it? Some chance there is to find substance instead of shadow for my theory. Where did you put the knife?"

"In your own chest brought over from France; if you have not removed it you will doubtless find it there in all safety."

"Come, then, we will see."

A minute later they were bending over the chest, and Constante drew the knife out from the place where he had put it — a slender, wicked blade with a handle of ivory wreathed about with twisted silver, a thing too handsome for a poor negro to own unless perchance by theft. It recalled his own silent suspicion as to the owner.

Then Delogne sent a slave with a message to Madame Ninon Villette, and a moment later the patter, patter of her little heels was heard on the tiled floor. She assumed an expression of great dignity at sight of humble Constante, but smiled in a maddening way at the chevalier.

"Madame, I asked but to be received for an instant, and did not presume to ask that you come to me," said Maurice, bowing low.

"What matters it, monsieur? And really I was reading aloud to the missionary of the red men's country, and fancied the interruption of my absence for a moment would not so much disturb him as to hear converse in his presence on other topics."

"Ever thinking of others in that kindly heart of yours," smiled the chevalier; "and I promise not to detain you long from so laudable a duty. To settle a vexed question I only wish to ask if you have ever before seen this?"

She drew back, looking with startled inquiry into his face.

"What has happened — why do you ask, and look so exceedingly earnest? I entreat you to tell me if he has done himself aught of injury."

"If who has done himself injury?" asked Delogne. But she turned to the other.

"You, Constante, you know who I mean — tell me!"

"No, madame; no injury has been done by the knife, if that is what you mean." And Raynel dared move a step or two nearer her in the joy of hearing her address him once more. "The weapon has been found, and we were not sure as to the owner — that is all."

"Oh!" And she gave a great sigh of relief. "How silly you will think me, my dear Chevalier! But really I have had many disturbing fancies of late because of my half-brother's ill health, or sleeplessness, for he is not ill, by his own confession, but only nervous; and to be asked so strangely about his knife — well, I feared some harm had come to him."

"I am disconsolate at having disturbed you." And Delogne's face was full of kindly regret. "But you have decided our ideas as to the ownership; and may I now conduct you back to your post of mercy?"

She bowed and rested her fingers on his arm, bequeathing to the wistful eyes of Raynel only a cool little nod. But he felt sure he was no longer beyond hope. Had she not turned to him in her wonder and fear?

"Now do you see the substance for that fancy of mine?" demanded Delogne as he returned.

"You mean that this belonged to Zanalta?"

"More than that. The blacks who tried to kidnap her were hirelings of Zanalta. He armed them, or else one of them armed himself from his master's store of cutlery. I felt it was so ere I put it in words, just as I felt the approach of evil all this day; and it is evil to her again, and from that man. Come! I myself will guard the convent gate to-night, lest some plot of his should draw her out into the darkness. Will you be with me?"

"Wait! Is that not the voice of Zanalta now in the court?" whispered Constante.

A moment's listening proved it true. He was asking questions impatiently of a slave at the door, a slave who was so stupid as not to know when his master would be in.

But even while they listened a step sounded behind them, and Monsieur Lamort entered, serene and calm as ever. He bowed to the two gentlemen, and passed through to the reception-room, where he could easily distinguish the voice of Zanalta, and also a most impatient tramping as he paced the floor.

And at the instant Lamort disappeared through the one door the slave-woman Venda appeared at the other as though following him. Not the tranquil Venda of old, but a woman who breathed hard, as one who has moved swiftly. Her eyes were bloodshot and strained; she lifted her feet heavily, as one who is old. She seemed hastening to reach her master, but stopped as that other voice was heard greeting him.

Then she turned her face toward the young men, gazed on them in strange, troubled fashion, and raised one hand as though waving them back, or beseeching them not to follow.

And with only that mute sign to express her prayer, she moved on toward the reception-room — alone.

CHAPTER XVII.

DENISE AND SISTER ANDREA.

IN the early dusk two figures stood together at the western casement of the convent, two with but little of heaven's peace in their eyes. The bonds of earth are strong in the flesh, and the beautiful serene Sister Andrea was the most despairing of the two.

She dropped on her knees sobbingly, and strove to draw Denise with her, but the young girl stood white and cold and would not bend.

" If it is true — if they give me up to him, I will never pray again," she said, with hard decision.

"Oh, my child, prayer helps women to bear their burdens. You will learn as you grow older how it lightens the sorrows that are sent to us. Women are weak, Denise, and— "

" I am not weak," and she stretched out her arms, and clasped and unclasped her white hands. "See, do they look like weak hands? You know they do not. And if they let him touch me, he will need the prayers, not I. I would never pray again."

" Denise, my poor child, it is terrible to hear one so young speak like that ; it is wicked, wicked ! And you poor dove, what would all your strength do against that man's will? Many a strong man has been caught helpless in his traps, so what can you, a mere child, do? Kneel down and pray — pray for this cross to be lifted aside."

" No; what use is it? Did not our mother confess that if the signature of the governor or of Monsieur Lamort was set to that paper she would be obliged to give me up, and that I must at least be removed to-morrow, for the reputation of the school, lest it be known that one who has shared their advantages is after all only a slave ? "

"Oh, Denise, speak not with so much of bitterness. The good mother is in great distress of mind. She must do the thing she sees to be her duty to the convent. All her acts must be answerable to the church ; and she knows well this man spoke wisely when he said her refusal could be made to ruin utterly the school she has tended with so much of care. And can you not see she longs to favor you, else he would have won his argument even without the signature, as he evidently hoped to do. Oh, Denise, grow not cruel in your heart against all people just because of one man whose heart is bad."

" I could never be cruel in thought to you," and

the cold hand of Denise pressed the head of the kneeling nun against her; "and though I should find strength to kill him, I know your lips would ever utter pitiful prayers for me."

"Oh, Denise, Denise! It must not be! All saints help us! What shall we do?"

The girl gazed out with somber eyes at the sky where the stars shone. Each instant she listened for the sound of the bell and the opening of the convent gate to the man who called himself her master.

"We can only wait until he comes, I think," she said, in that cold, unchildlike way. "When I begged the mother superior to let me go to the house of Monsieur Lamort she said, 'No, there must be no scandal; we must wait for the law to judge; and that monsieur would not sign it unless it was right;' so that leaves us nothing to do but wait. And when he does come, with all the power of the law, she will expect me to bow my head to my master and walk out of that gate at his bidding. I! Do they not guess that I would sooner cast myself from the roof to that stone paving?"

The older woman only moaned and knelt, still praying beside the girl who stood as though carved of stone. And thus they waited the dread tidings.

Then a hurried step approached in the corridor; not the step of a man, nor had the bell at the gate sounded. It halted at the door, and without tapping the abbess entered the room.

Her strong, wise face was much agitated. She held a flat packet and her hands were trembling.

"Child, be in haste," she said, and reached out the

20

little package. " I give my consent that you go at once to the house of the good Monsieur Lamort. Take with you this, and tell him I said he must read it ere making decision. Its contents I know not, and no time is to be lost by reading it here. Our blessed Mother Agnace left it. You were but a baby when I saw it last, done up just as it is now. It is of you, perhaps of your parents, it tells. See, there is your name —' The child called Denise.' Ah! the saints be praised that I did chance on it among those old parchments! But go — go quickly. Take with you old Marie of the gate."

But Sister Andrea, yet on her knees, spoke:

" I pray you no, good mother. If this girl is to go thus for judgment, I ask that I may be the one to guard her."

" You, Sister Andrea, who never go without the gate?"

" It is my first request, mother, and we lose time."

" True. I consent, and may the blessing of God go with you. Until you return I shall never cease to pray that these papers may prove Señor Zanalta's claim a great mistake by which he has been blinded. Denise — my child!"

She raised her hands in benediction; but Denise, who had ever before bent humble knee to that gesture, only bent her head to the blessing, and raised it a little higher as she passed out by the lady. The thing she felt was a wrong had for the first time made her haughty and cold instead of humble. And the mother superior smiled sadly as she watched her go.

"It is said that Gaston le Noyens was a proud man," she mused, "and his price will live as long as she lives if she indeed prove to be his daughter. A very proud slave, Don Zanalta, and I fear me some one will suffer besides Denise if she should be proven the child of a slave-woman."

CHAPTER XVIII.

ONCE MORE ZIZI.

IN the house of Monsieur Lamort the master stood facing Diego Zanalta and hesitating over the paper before him.

"But this is so astonishing! The convent child is then the daughter of Gaston le Noyens and his slave-girl Zizi?"

"Exactly. Since that time the brown woman has called herself Venda, but the change of name has not changed the woman. She is your slave now, but she was mine when that child was born. She confessed all to-day and made her mark there. You know the evil wrought in this land by white-skinned slaves sharing the associations of their superiors, hence my anxiety to remove her at once from among these daughters of gentlemen at the convent. The abbess prays it may be done to-night, though she needs legal papers ere the girl is transferred to me."

He was trying, with what show of indifference he could, to assume that it was to serve the abbess more than himself that he came at so unseemly an hour, but his eyes were alight with eagerness as he watched Lamort.

"And my slave Venda was once Zizi of the house of Le Noyens?" remarked that gentleman, dreamily. "Strange it never occurred to me. That explains —"

"Explains what, monsieur?"

Lamort aroused himself from his reveries and smiled.

"When one commences to think aloud it is a sure sign that he is growing old, is it not, señor? But I was thinking that her identity with Zizi would explain her strange knowledge from the very first of every corner of my house, for of course she had lived here."

"Yes, yes — but this paper, it waits your signing." And Zanalta dipped a quill in the ink-well and reached it to Monsieur Lamort.

"I strangely dislike the task you bring me," he confessed. "She is a fair maiden for such a curse to have been her portion. Tell me, when once she is in your possession would you sell her to me at your own price, that I may be sure she never will meet the black hands as one they dare claim? Whatever her mother's blood, she is too white a soul for the life fair slaves drift into on these shores. Pardon my blunt speech, señor, but I would save her for higher uses and a life somewhere away from her mother's race."

Zanalta smiled and nodded.

"You think about the girl as I think, monsieur; and though she is the daughter of my slave, by that slave's confession, yet I remember also she is the child of the one friend I had in my youth here — Gaston le Noyens. My sister-in-law sails for Madrid in the next ship. The girl shall go with her and live her life in fair Spain. So you see I too think of her welfare."

And his gaze was so open, so kindly, that Victor Lamort believed him. He looked at the space where his name was to be written — he, one of the dispensers of justice! And his purpose wavered as the thought of Maurice came to him — Maurice, whose heart would be broken by the knowledge of that paper; Maurice, who idolized her, whose every hope was toward winning her; and yet, an illegitimate child, and one of the slave blood, to be selected as a wife for one of the Delogne family! No, it would not be wise to allow it.

"You are sensible to give so much of thought ere you act for justice, monsieur," remarked Zanalta, easily. "But it grows late, and I have brought you that ancient plan of the lands you desired so much to see. We might find time to examine it after we have this other business disposed of. I heard it said only to-day in a discussion of a land question that no such accurate survey had ever been made of Royal Grant and the surrounding estates, and I was at once reminded to look it up and bring it over."

He held in his hand the roll of yellow parchment,

with the dull-red lettering on the outer scroll and the seal of the crown showing on its gilt cord.

Lamort's eyes narrowed and shone with a different light. His hobby, whatever it was, suddenly recurred at the sight of that legal-looking document from which he could glean power. This other paper before him, with the fate of a life in it — with the broken heart of Maurice in it — what was all their tinsel joys or sorrows beside the work to which he had devoted his soul and strength — the dream of his manhood, the realization that was now coming to him in his older years?

"Nothing," he decided, and himself dipped the quill again in the ink and signed the paper.

Denise by those strokes of the pen was legally declared a slave, and the possession of her person was granted to Don Diego Zanalta.

Zanalta drew a long breath, and laid the survey of the Royal Grant on the desk where the ink rested.

It had been a close battle of wits, and he had won. He reached out his hand for the paper Lamort had signed, but ere Zanalta's fingers touched it he was dashed aside, the paper was snatched from Lamort's extended hand, and the slave-woman stood between them tearing the document into bits.

With a guttural cry like a mad beast Zanalta sprung toward her, with the gleam of steel showing in his hand; but quick as light she avoided him and sped to the other side of her master, clutching his arm.

"I ask your help for one hour — because of this," she said; and drawing forth a chain from her neck she held up a piece of coin attached to it, a gold-piece with a hole in it — a hole through the king's head on it. "You have not forgotten," she said; but his hand only came down heavily on her shoulder as she knelt; with the other he touched his sword.

"We do not knife slaves in our parlors, Don Zanalta, even for so great an impertinence as this has been. To me she will give account of her action. Speak, Venda." •

"No!" And she glanced at Zanalta, who was watching her with threatening eyes.

"Venda!"

"No, master, not Venda." And she crouched at her master's feet. "Vendiant — Venda, that is name of betrayal. Oh, master! just now, this once more, I am Zizi again — I am faithful. The false is there — the man who betrayed you, who would betray you again, who brings you there a paper of the lands that is a lie — for see!" And she moved to the heavy old desk and from some receptacle at the back of it brought the original paper that Zanalta had sought in vain. "But that is little — is nothing," she said, as she laid it in her master's hand. "He is most false of all when he says Mademoiselle Denise is of slave blood. She — never!"

Steps were heard behind them. Their exclamations had been heard even beyond the court, and Madame Ninon stood there in wonder beside the old priest to whom she had been reading. Constante crossed to her intending to quiet any alarm she might feel; but Maurice stood in the doorway as

one paralyzed at the fragment heard: "Made·
moiselle Denise of slave blood."

"You slave, beware!" And Zanalta took a step
toward the woman, by his tone forcing her to look
up and meet the intense significance of his gaze.
She felt the meaning of it, and for one instant
shivered. "You are mad," he went on. "Did you
not acknowledge that the child was taken to the
convent by you?"

Just then Maurice saw two figures move hand in
hand through the palms. He went to meet them;
one the beautiful distressed face of the nun the
other was Denise, who looked at him with eyes of
anguish.

"Yes," said Venda, reluctantly, to Zanalta's
question.

"So! yours; the child of a white father. Mine,
for you were my property at its birth. You see,
monsieur, the word of a slave —"

Victor Lamort's eyes were on the face of Venda.
What did she mean? Was she indeed that Zizi who
had been favorite in the last days of Le Noyens?
And what else was she that she knew so much, and
dared assert her knowledge — she who had known
all the life and loves in this house years ago! He
touched her on the head.

"Whose is the child?" he asked. "Whatever
your blood, I can trust your word, Zizi."

"Who spoke then?" asked Sister Andrea of Mau·
rice; and he smiled reassuringly in her troubled
eyes.

"That is Monsieur Victor Lamort," he said; "and

you may trust safely to his justice. If you will allow me, I will present those papers for his notice, and you may rest here under the palms for a moment until he comes to you; and in God's name — in love's name, Denise, look not so coldly hopeless."

The girl only looked at him with all that blind pain in her eyes. The mere thought that she was a slave by birth!

But the nun leaned back in the shadows of the palm-leaves.

"Monsieur Victor Lamort," she whispered to herself. "Victor Lamort — *the victor of death!* What does it mean? And Zizi!"

The lips of Zizi were pressed on her master's hand in a sort of adoration at the sound of the tender Old World name uttered by him.

"To-morrow, master," and her eyes were turned on Zanalta, defiantly, "when we are alone, I will tell you."

"To-morrow — devils! That will be too late —"

"Too late? Oh, yes," and Lamort smiled carelessly; "you had planned a little sailing trip, had you not, and waiting will interfere? Well, the weather promises fair, and a day sooner or later should not matter."

"What do you know of my plans?" he demanded, angrily, though he was striving hard to keep his temper.

"Only that the former commander of the Sea Gull has sold her to me, and will be seen no more on these shores," remarked the other; "and in the transfer it was mentioned that the vessel had been promised you for a few weeks. It was a matter of indifference then, but not quite so much so now, señor. This false paper has changed much in my eyes, and I am suddenly reminded that a companion — a lady — was to go with you." His voice grew more and more stern as he continued, and in the wake of his own words came the realization that it must have been Denise who was to go with him. "I shall trouble you now, Don Zanalta, to inform me who that lady is."

"It was to have been Señora Zanalta," declared the Spaniard, impatiently. "But you do me injustice, monsieur; and my holiday has nothing to do with to-night's business. Listen, monsieur. You saw that woman's confession, which she now denies. The girl is my slave, but refuses to own her bond to me. She has won the poorer classes to her by her charity and youth, and if there is time to warn those plebeians who think her a saint, there may be a rising of that mob, and perhaps the blacks as well. You know what that would mean. They would blindly burn the house of every aristocrat. I only ask that which is legally mine. I swear she has bewitched those papers of the survey. I know nothing of it. You signed the claim once, monsieur; sign another. I ask only my slave."

His feverish eagerness told against him; and more, Maurice Delogne came forward at that moment with the packet given him by Sister Andrea.

"Monsieur, this is from the good abbess at the convent. You are asked by her to read the contents ere deciding the claim of Señor Zanalta."

· "Facts pertaining to the child called Denise,"
Monsieur Lamort read from the enveloping scroll.
"Chevalier Delogne, will you do me the favor to
open and read us the main points contained in
this?"

He looked weary, and seated himself on the couch,
leaving Venda kneeling there alone in the middle
of the floor. He had not yet turned his head to see
who it was had entered the room of the palms as
messenger.

Señor Zanalta picked up his hat, with a fine air of
indifference. "I see some plot has been set afoot
since my visit to the convent," he said, meaningly;
"for less than an hour ago the abbess pretended to
no knowledge of such a document. I will leave
you, monsieur, to the perusal of these forgeries."

"I think you will find this genuine enough,"
declared Delogne; "it is in the main a letter
from the mother of the child. She writes to the
abbess on the last days she expects to live. She
confesses herself utterly friendless but for a slave-
girl, Zizi, who may be taken from her any hour by
her relatives, who consider she has disgraced them.
She has no means of proving her marriage, but de-
clares that she is a wife. And here is a note signed
by Mother Agnace, saying, 'This letter is from
the mother of the child Denise, whom she in this
testament wishes to be reared in the convent, and
later take the veil, as her life in the world, a
woman child and nameless, would be one of sorrow
and of shame.'"

The pale, beautiful nun had involuntarily arisen,

with a low cry, as those lines were quoted. Denise caught her hand, and found her trembling so she could scarcely stand.

"Oh, continue — continue!" she muttered. Her agitation was much greater than that of Denise.

"More," went on Delogne. "The abbess of that day, Mother Agnace, affirms that she knew the writer of this letter from her childhood, and firmly believes in the statement that she was at some time married, though circumstances were such that she was forced to live and die under the name of Mademoiselle Felice Henriette St. Malo."

"*Master!*" cried the slave-woman, warningly, but too late.

He arose, looking at them with a deathlike face.

"Felice — my wife! Our child, then — our own child, that I signed away for this hunger of vengeance. Oh, my God!"

They thought him mad. Denise arose and stood beside the nun.

"What does it mean?" she asked. "Oh, tell me, some one! I am not a slave, then — I am not a slave?"

But Delogne, looking from the strange face of Venda to that of her master, doubted his madness. He remembered too well a story told him by Lamort — that story of the exile.

"Your child? Be careful what you say, for there are listeners. Your child, Monsieur Lamort?"

"Not that name," he said, shaking his head; "the quest I borrowed it for is dead from this hour. The vengeance I have followed for years has turned a weapon against my own heart. Zizi, you were faithful. Bring to me my daughter; bring to me also the priest from the country of the red men. He knows if Felice St. Malo was a wife or not. He must tell these people, every one must know, and then my child and I will sail far out to lands like paradise. Oh, my child, my child!"

"Ah!"—a field of unrivaled expanse spread before Zanalta as he realized who Lamort must be to have been married to Felice St. Malo—"monsieur, if I am on the right track at last, you and I were rivals once, and you have played me some ghostly pranks since. All at once a veil has dropped from my eyes, and I see I was blind never to suspect until now, for your voice was often a puzzle to me; but we can not afford to be enemies, you and I, and if Denise is your daughter I present myself as a suitor."

Monsieur Lamort seemed not to hear. Delogne touched his shoulder, and when he turned Denise was standing beside him with her hands held out and all her face aglow.

He dropped his head on her shoulder with a sob. He had withstood all the cruel blows of years and made no outcry, but at the sweet lingering of his child's hands about his face his heart seemed to break.

"And you forgive me! Oh, child! I never dreamed there was aught in this world left to me but to harden my heart and crush the people who had hurt your adored mother and me. It is over now. We will go away from here — you and I and faithful Zizi. I am bewildered with my joy. Speak to me, Denise; tell me you are glad."

"I would not know how to find words enough," she said, with smiles and hands caressing him. "I have scarce heard how it is that you have announced yourself my father, but I accept it without question, and am happy."

Then she held out her hand to Delogne. "It was you who said to me, 'Your father wants you,' and you will always be my friend because of those words."

Lamort smiled into Delogne's eyes. "Is that not better than a plantation?" he asked; "but perhaps the plantation will come to you too — but not that one," and he nodded to the survey of the Royal Grant. "I am done warring. Take back your scrolls, Diego Zanalta. It was your land I would have stripped you of by that survey; but it is all over. I have found Denise; and you, Maurice, shall not be the loser. Come now, my child: we will see good Father Luis and let you learn how I came to be your father."

The slave-woman had but entered the room of palms on her errand to the aged priest when she saw him in a group gathered about the form of Sister Andrea, who had suddenly swooned. Madame Ninon held her head on her knees, while the priest fanned her and whispered prayers over the form that looked so lifeless. Monsieur Raynel had been dispatched for water.

"May I help?" asked the slave. "Pardon, little madame, but all that cloth is too much about her face and throat — if you could loosen it —"

But Ninon drew back. It seemed to her a sacrilege to disturb the garb of a devotee.

Venda herself pushed back the bands from about
the face, and as she did so the light for the first
time fell clearly across the closed eyes, and with a
loud cry the slave fell on her knees.

"Oh-a-me! oh-a-me! little mistress! my little
mistress!" She rocked herself in a very ecstasy of
excitement. "Oh, master — Master Basil! May your
God strike Zizi dead if she knew. They at the convent said child died, and I took the word back to little
mistress, and she went crazy. Oh, master! that not
fault of Zizi. Then Mistress Marie Sollé sent me back
to town house, for reason that I love little Mistress
Felice too well. Then by and by word come that
my Mistress Felice dead and buried way out there
on the plantation. Oam-me! that make my heart
ache! Nothing left for Zizi to love then, and Zizi
seem to die, and the white wool come on her head.
No one was left alive and kind but you, my master,
far away — away from Zizi, where she never can
kneel to you; and each time she think of you in
all the years, the wool get more and more white,
like when the old, old years come on heads. And
all the time I never was told little mistress was alive
in the world."

She was groveling at the feet of Monsieur Lamort
while she uttered all the passionate disjointed sentences. All looked at her in affright, for they could
see no cause for her cries. She was between her
master and the figure on the floor, and he could not
see the face of the woman there, only the garb of
a nun.

"Be silent," he said, and dropped his hand on her shoulder. "You shall tell me some other time how it was you took my daughter to the convent gate. You have served me well. I will not forget."

She drew aside at his bidding, and sat there crouched against the wall, watching him with a strange yearning in her eyes.

"Zizi has served you well, has she?" she muttered to herself. "Zizi served you well — oh, my master!"

Lamort released Denise when she perceived Sister Andrea there on the cushions, and she was watching anxiously for the bits of color coming back to the lips.

"Dear Sister Andrea," she said, with great tenderness, as the eyes of the nun opened and gazed at her dreamily, as if scarce awake, "you have made yourself ill over my sorrows and joys; but the joys are so sweet now, you need only rejoice with me."

"Yes," said the nun, with her eyes still on the happy face of the girl. "Do not mention his name, but only kiss me for him."

"She is not yet conscious of where she is," whispered Denise to the priest; but he, with a long look at the two, arose tremblingly, a frail, weather-beaten old man, but with the light of a strong soul shining through his eyes.

He walked over to Lamort, who had just ceased speech to Zizi, and who reached his hand eagerly to the priest.

"Pardon me, father, if I have scarce heeded your presence or that of the nun who was companion to my child; but you, to whom all my life is known,

will understand what finding my child — the child
of Felice — means to me. In truth, I feel like
one in a dream. And I was just about to visit
you, that you might tell our daughter how it
chanced we were wed in secret, and how—"

"Yes — yes, we will tell her in good time,"
assented Father Luis; "but just now there is one
other thing of which I would speak, my son. Your
wedding was secret in that year long past; but the
man who was *you* long ago is legally dead by the
records, so you tell me. Why, if Felice yet lived,
could you not claim her now, with all your world for
witness?"

"Why? Father, do you know how a man can
suffer if asked that question when the object of his
love has passed up above life's claims? To claim
her before the world! Yes, if she yet lived — yes, a
thousand times. Oh, you know — you know! Why
do you speak like this to-night?" And he dropped
his head on the high-carved cabinet, hiding his face
as though to conceal tears.

"Come!" said the priest, and took his hand as
though leading a child; with a gesture he waved
back Madame Ninon and the two young gentlemen
from the couch where the nun lay. "Sit you still,
my child," he said to Denise; "they may want you
as a witness this time."

"They?" Lamort had walked where he was led,
not seeing, because of bitter, longing tears that
could not be cleared from his eyes in an instant;
then he was conscious that Denise was kneeling
beside the couch.

21

And on the couch!

He stepped back, with a cry akin to horror, it was so piercing, and stared at the face there as though frozen and mute.

And then the sweet-faced nun reached out her hand.

"Basil," she whispered, "I am not dead, though I thought all else was dead for me."

Silently he gathered her in his arms, great tears falling on her face as he kissed her; but he spoke no word, and she seemed to expect none; they were together with content.

"It is your mother," said the priest to the wondering Denise; and the woman she had called "sister" reached a hand to her.

"Could we have loved each other better had we known?" she asked; and the fond kiss of Denise said "no."

And over against the wall still sat the slave-woman, rocking, and watching like a figure of fate first Lamort and then Zanalta, waiting for something she felt was coming.

And the eyes of Zanalta saw that embrace, and he heard again "Basil"— and "Basil" whispered in utter fondness.

"Who is it — what does it all mean?" asked Madame Ninon, in half-fear of the wild emotions surging around her. She was clinging to the arm of Constante, in all forgetfulness of her late pique.

The priest heard her question, and spoke from the head of the couch where he stood with hands stretched out over the group there as though in blessing — a great joy shining in his aged eyes:

"Eighteen years ago the hands of this man and this woman were joined by me in marriage. They were but a youth and maiden then, and each dear to my heart. We have drifted wide apart since those days, and whispers arose against her fair fame in this town of Orleans. But here, with their child as witness, I, Brother Luis, declare that Felice St. Malo was made the honest wife of this man. Let no breath of shame ever again touch the air about her."

But Zanalta, followed by the watchful eyes of the black woman, stepped nearer the man known so long as Victor Lamort, and touched him on the shoulder.

"Monsieur Basil de Bayarde, you do not reply. I make offer of my hand and name for your daughter."

"My daughter shall make her own choice of a husband," said the other without raising his head.

"Have you forgotten that you may yet need a friend on this island of Orleans? Where will you find so able a one as myself to fight the things you must fight when word gets abroad that you are here? Come, we need each other — you and I; what bond so strong as your daughter?"

But the other waved him away by a gesture of disdain, and Madame Villette laid a persuasive hand on the arm of Zanalta.

"Come, Diego, it is best for you to be in your own house, is it not? From what I have heard here you do not seem to play a pretty part in the affairs of our neighbors; and as you wished but to-day that I make purchase of your estate here and leave you free to roam for a season, I think it well now to give assent to your wish; and I fancy also that the farther you sail the happier will be those who do not sail with you."

But he broke loose from her fingers, with an oath.

"I do not sail until I have stripped that galley-slave of a part of his wealth," he declared, with a cruel laugh. "Wife, daughter, and landed estates, eh? Well, my man, I will put you back in your chains again or die trying; for you are Basil de Bayarde, an outlaw, whose life is forfeit to the crown. You are the man who in these gardens did eighteen years ago murder Gaston le Noyens."

"No!"

In his fury he had forgotten the slave-woman coiled there like a crouching animal, and so strange a light in her eyes as she arose to her feet.

"He did not," she said, in a strange level tone. All the color and excitement was gone from it now; but as Zanalta made a step to her she smiled quietly and showed in her hand the slim, wicked-looking dagger Madame Ninon had identified but awhile before. "You will keep away, Master Diego, until I speak — I, Venda, once called Zizi in this house long ago. That man," and she pointed to her master, "has felt pain enough in his heart — no more. For years he has ached under a load a coward woman let him bear because the blackness of death made her afraid, and she loved to live in the warm sunshine. But I will tell you, old master, whom the people

call Father Luis—open your ears and hear, for you
are the church witness. To the land where my people ruled came one of your race when I was a girl,
young as that," and she pointed to Denise. "Slaves
were bought from us and decoyed to the decks of
their boat, but one went bound only by the love of
her lover. She was not of the slave caste. She trusted
when he said that on his shores she should rule as on
her own. She dreamed the dreams he taught her, for
she was a child — not more. On his own shores he
was called Le Noyens, and he was false. He placed
her like the slaves in his house, and when she was
hurt in her pride and cried out against it, then what
did he? The arms he had caressed were bound
with chains. The shoulder he had kissed was
burned deep with an iron, as they brand slaves for
evil deeds — you see?" And she bared her shoulder
that they might see the cruel stamp of the *fleur-de-
lis.* "It was burned so with that sign of a king who
lived across the water, and she took her vengeance
when it came to her, and he died from a knife in her
hand. That man, Diego Zanalta, saw it. He has
known the truth all these years — the years when I
was a coward. That is over. Oh, my master, my
master! I can see you suffer no more. You shall
never more stand before the judges. Nor will Zizi
ever wear their chains again, though I confess. I
ask you all to hear. I killed Gaston le Noyens — *so!*
— in pay for — the gift he — he gave me —for this
flower of — France."

The slender dagger was driven to the ivory
handle in her own bosom ere any of them guessed

her design; and her eyes — devoted, appealing —
turned to the man who had borne her guilt, but for
whom she now was dying.

"Zizi! Zizi! our poor Zizi!" he moaned, and
raised her head, while Felice sped to her side, weeping and caressing her brown hands.

The dying slave gazed at her mistress and at
Denise. "Good-by, little white one," she said, and
then rested her white-crowned head fondly against
the arm of Basil de Bayarde and looked up at him
with all the unspeakable devotion that had oppressed
and ennobled her.

"My master!" she whispered, and then all was
still; and Basil de Bayarde raised in his arms a
dead woman — a dead woman who had at last lifted
the cloud from his life and the lives of his loved
ones.

And in all the sunshine and honor of the years
that followed he never forgot her.

FINALE.

Is it needful to say that Ninon recovered from
her pique and shared her whims and her poverty
with Constante for many a year? She also succeeded
in persuading Diego that departure from Louisiana
was the one bit of wisdom left to him, and he,
together with Señora Mercedes Sofie Zanalta, took
ship together for Spain.

Denise did indeed sail in the Sea Gull, much as
Don Zanalta had arranged, except that he was not
of the party. But Ninon was there with her fiancé,
and Chevalier Delogne was ever within whispering

distance, and even Father Luis was with them in
their holidays; while those two older hearts, separated long ago by a tragedy, and beside a tragedy
united, paced the deck of their pleasure-ship many
a starlight night, and took up again the thread of
their love-story — a love never forgotten by the nun
Sister Andrea or the exiled ranger De Bayarde.

And over the water would sound sometimes the
tones of a violin, and the young people would listen
in wonder to the wild sweet notes flung out over the
sea, and would slip away in a group to whisper of
the eerie spell it wove around them. They could
seldom laugh or dance when Monsieur De Bayarde
played thus in the dark. It was the only remnant of
expression he retained of those long years of sorrow.
But Felice understood, and her gentle caressing
hands would lead him away from the dark thoughts
of the past; though she never heard of that
other wild musician and gamester who had once
walked the same deck, for though the sailors of the
vessel were the same men, they were faithful, and
cared little by what title it pleased their captain to
be known.

So Rochelle was heard of no more, and only to
Zizi's love had his secret been known — Zizi, who lay
in the tomb with that pierced coin on her breast,
and above her a marble put there by Basil and his
wife Felice.

And on it was cut the name " Zizi," and below
that the sculptured graceful lines of the *fleur-de-lis*.

THE END.

www.ingramcontent.com/pod-product-compliance
Lightning Source LLC
Chambersburg PA
CBHW060523030726
47498CB00004B/1061